SUBTEXT

A NERVOUS NOVEL

FRANK ANGELETTI

Published by Firebrand Publishing Atlanta, GA USA

ISBN: 978-1-941907-51-1 Paperback

ISBN: 978-1-941907-52-8 eBook

Printed in the United States of America

For my father, who taught me I could be anything I wanted to be as long as I wanted it badly enough.

And for Craig, who never once stopped believing in me.

Only Heaven knows how glory goes,
what each of us was meant to be.
In the starlight, that is what we are.
I can see so far.

ADAM GUETTEL, FLOYD COLLINS

ONE

I CAN HEAR her voice still—piercing the milky sunlight with her nasal Chicago accent, perforating every amber-colored, late September daydream within miles that possesses the preposterous fortitude to stand up to her. And I feel the tiny hairs at the scruff of my neck stand tall with mock-petulance as I stall for time in my second-floor bedroom, all knotty pine and avocado shag rug. I can hear the urgency of her beckoning above the hum of my stoned, racing adolescent mind and the buzz of Billy Joel delivered from the aluminum speakers of a portable eight-track player. I stub out what's left of a joint between my fingers and tuck it away between the mattress and bed frame as Long Island's favorite son is having a heart attack-ack-ack-ack-ack-ack. Even as I avoid the window and fresh air, I can see her standing there screaming at the world, exasperated because nobody is listening. With one hand on her hip and the other brandishing a rake at my retreat above the garage, and further onward toward the heavens, her gaze incinerates.

So, do you know what I do? I roll off of the bed tactical

combat style, drop to my knees, and shimmy my plump, pubescent body across the floorboards to dodge the window and the sunlight altogether. I travel in a world beneath John Travolta posters hung with shiny brass tacks, beside Village People albums housed in an orange plastic milk crate, and on top of Torso Magazines strategically hidden in mine bomb fashion and concealed with masking tape to the underside of the shag carpeting. It's time for liberation alright. Oh, how I yearn. Yet all too soon I will stand beside her, my mother, stuffing a rusted-out iron drum with dead leaves, gathering damp twigs with twine, and at all costs avoiding the crack-ack-ack-ack-ack-ack of the rake handle across my shoulders and back.

But, for just one moment, if I scrunch my eyes closed as tightly as I am able...

"Dominic! Dominic!"

And so the story goes. I pull on jeans around my fat fourteen-year-old body. I tie my sneakers in double-knots and purposefully avoid the windbreaker hanging in my closet. I refuse to wear it; it's ugly and it identifies me too directly with her, and them, and it's hideous and it stinks of charred, dead leaves. Maybe if I'm cold or appear cold she'll let me off easy this one time. Or maybe I'll grow cold and miserable just like her.

I shut the door on everything I care about and make my way down the back stairwell hurriedly, without time to trace the pattern of the sage green, velveteen chevron wallpaper with my fingertips. Not even time enough to count stair steps as I move to take my place. And I've found my pace by the time I pass my sister Anna in the kitchen, who flips me the bird and never once lifts her eyes from her Modern Bride Magazine or her astringent, spaghetti gravy bubbling on the stovetop.

"Dominic! Dominic!

DAAHHHHHMMIIIIINNAAAAAHHHHHCCKK!!"

My tummy is turning cartwheels by this point. I've twisted my fingers into treasonous weapons inside the pockets of my jeans. I deliberately gouge my fingernails into my own palms to punish myself because maybe I've stalled for too long this time and maybe I've mistakenly pissed her off forever. And I'm really moving as the screen door clack-ack-ack-ack-ack-acks closed and I feel my mother's hot breath on my face.

"You didn't hear me calling you, Dominic?" Instantly she is menacing.

"Yes, Mom—umm, I didn't. I didn't."

"Either you did. Or you didn't? Which one? Otherwise, you're a liar. I hate a gaddammed liar. Don't you lie to me! I'll never trust you if you lie to me, Dominic! I'll never trust you again. Now I don't trust you."

"I didn't—"

"Liar."

"I didn't hear you calling me—is what I'm saying. I didn't hear you call me."

"Nah. You're a liar. I'll never believe you again."

"But I didn't—"

"Help me burn these leaves. Do it!"

Inside her head she's been arguing with me since before I arrived, for fourteen years now.

"How do I—"

"You know how. You know how. You gather the leaves from the piles that I raked. No, not that one! Here! This one!" Either choice would have been the wrong choice.

"The fire is out—"

"*The fire is out!*" She mocks me. "You just gather the leaves. I'll worry about the gaddammed fire."

"I hate this."

"*I hate this!*" She's invented and finessed her own impersonation of me, replete with a sing-song Pollyanna tone and wet spaghetti limbs.

"It's gross."

"*It's gross! It's so gross!*" In her eyes, evidently I look like a floppy, balloon creature at a car lot, except my right shoulder is hunched. And my head is permanently cocked alongside it.

"Well, it is gross!"

"You think I like it? This? You think I like it out here in the cold? You think I like raking leaves in this gaddammed backyard in this lousy city with a little fairy that's all the company I can keep? You think your father likes it? Well, do you? And what good is he to me? All alone—that's who I am. Left out in the cold. Like garbage. Yeah, he threw me away just like garbage. Oh, one day we'll get our own place, Dominic. I'll take you with me. Just you and me. An apartment. With no leaves. Because that's who I am! And you wanna know what life is, Dominic? Ya wanna know? Life is you take whatever you can get. Life is you make the most of whatever you can take. Now, I said move your ass. Bend. At the waist. Bend, Dominic! Put some effort in. Maybe you'll lose some gaddammed weight."

"What about Anna?"

"*What about Anna??*" Again with the wildly deformed posture and the flailing balloon arms.

"Why can't she help is all I'm asking?"

"She's making gravy. That's what girls do. Hurry up! It's getting dark."

"Why can't we hire someone?"

"Because we have you. And you gotta do something. Move your ass."

"I'm trying as fast as I can." I am, too.

"Well, try faster!"

"What if we hire someone and I could—"

"You could do what? What could you do? You're not good for shit. Who are we gonna hire, Dominic? Who are we gonna hire?"

"I dunno."

"You dunno? You don't know!"

"I hate this. My hands are getting dirty."

"Boys don't care."

"I care."

"Just do it! Sissy! You sissy, you!"

I catch sideways glances of her as I gather the colorless, dead leaves. Her eyes are gray and tired, and her mouth is sealed in a permanent frown like some malevolent god dropped it right there crooked and broken. Just as carelessly as it dropped her right here in this gaddammed backyard in this lousy city. Her auburn hair is shocking against the soot gray horizon and its windblown locks dance in furious, frightening time with the squalls of an impending autumn storm. Her hands are bony and twisted with arthritis as she performs her role, proceeds as she threatened, and sets fire to nature.

"Come on, Dominic! Faster. This wind! There's a storm coming." Even the fire succumbs and leaps to attention, the product of her incantation.

She is equal parts Aunt Em and the Wicked Witch of the West, standing tall with the help of her rake, the temperamental midwestern horizon at once silhouetting her debilitating osteoporosis and framing the life she was handed, made the most of, and grew to loathe.

"STOP DAYDREAMING!"

Whack goes the rake! As I raise my arm to shield my face, its handle bears down furiously against my forearm.

"OUCH!!"

"Don't you hit me, Dominic! Don't you ever try to gaddammed hit me—"

"But I didn't—"

"—because I'll put you in a home. I'll put you in a gaddammed home you ever lay a hand on me."

"I won't ever, Mama! I won't ever hit you! I promise!"

"I'll put you in a home and nobody will ever see you again."

"Noooo! I'll be good!"

"Don't you ever try to gaddammed hit me. I'll make your head spin. I'll plant you in a home so fast I'll make your gaddammed head turn circles."

"I promise! I'll be good!" But it's too late.

Whack goes the rake!

My mother wages a battle against the Sun for setting before she's completed her yard work and swings her weapons of war with disregard, unaware how the blows land, so blinded by resentment and fury is her anger. The wind spirals around her and the rusted-out iron drum erupts with belches of orange cinder with every strike.

Whack goes the rake! Whack goes the rake! Whack goes the rake!

"You wanna stay in this house? You'll help with the gaddammed work."

"I'll help! I'll help you, Mama!"

"The fresh. Air. Is good. For you." Whack! Whack! Whack! Whack!

With each lunge of her body, a primeval growl from inside her twists itself into the sorrowful moan of a wounded animal—snared in a trap that's not even merciful enough to kill, simply immobilize. And that enrages her, this cruel existence that was constructed to cause her a lifetime of suffering. She grew up poor. Whack! And without love. Whack! That's who she is! Whack!

As the flames howl ferociously and snap indiscriminately at the sky, her rake collides violently with her cauldron, and the back of a leg, and a wrist, and a temple. When she aims her rage to roar at the impending storm, she willfully breathes life into it, as all the while I'm squirming on hands and knees to find shelter from my mother.

"Oh no you don't!" Whack goes the rake across the small of my back.

When she retreats to find breath, she steadies herself on the rake and with a bony hand on her knee. I gather myself trembling in a pile of dead, brown leaves at her feet. She gasps to bring the air back inside her, exhales, in and then out, and with a tremendous clap of thunder the skies open wide, and sheets of rain pelt the battleground and its whimpering, beaten-down infantry.

Curled up protectively inside my pathetic teenage self I sob, even as I am millions of lifetimes away from a paneled bedroom with Tony Manero posters, dirty magazines, and my abusive mother. And as I gaze directly through all of the years into her outraged, resent-fueled eyes, I swear to myself that I will never be mean, or miserable, or cold.

"You shoulda wore your gaddammed jacket," she spits, and she casts the rake to the sorrowful, wet earth and makes her way inside.

One moment I'm listening to my mother berate me and the next I'm the final ember born to escape her cauldron of burning leaves; a tiny, red-yellow spark that flies fearlessly and higher into the stormy Chicago skyline toward freedom. A leaf that evades the garbage pile and dances in the breeze—sometimes soaring, sometimes dipping, tripping over itself and landing as a bartender at a notorious leather bar in New York City's Meatpacking District.

I'm in the tiny stall next to the urinal in the john with the sick-green, fluorescent lighting at The Meat Market, rolling a twenty with one hand and balancing a quarter gram of blow cut into four fat lines on the palm of the other hand, when I hear Guasparre Gagliardi *"va fongooling"* in his Staten Island Italian accent.

"Maddon' mi! Meengya!"

That's when I drop the coke all down the front of my bare chest and watch with indifferent eyes as the twenty-dollar bill cascades in slow motion directly into the sick-green, toilet water. Deliberate and unhurried, it turns circles like a colorless autumn leaf failing and then falling from a tree.

"What'd you say?"

"I tink I might happen tuh be in a little bit of trouble ovuh here. *Mi Meengya, Stonato!* Ya dig?"

The blow, a tip from a new customer, arrived in familiar fashion—a shiny white seal wrapped in a Hamilton and delivered under the guise of a handshake. I wouldn't have dropped it if I wasn't so fucking nervous all the time. But there's always more where that came from, and it tasted mostly like baking soda anyway. I lick the back of my palm, wipe my nose with my index finger and thumb, then suck my fingertips and swallow hard as the bitter cocaine numbs my throat.

"What's wrong?" I ask nonchalantly as I think to myself, "*Do I fish for the twenty dollar bill or leave it for the next guy?*"

"I could really use some help ovuh here. I can't believe I fuckin' did dis same fuckin' ting all ovuh again. What a *stronzo* I am. Are yuh wit' me?"

I leave the twenty for the next guy and step out of the tiny stall to find Guasparre standing frozen, afraid to move for the pain, in the center of the tiny john with the sick-green, checkered floor tile.

"'Sparre, what in the world is the—"

"Aye! Aye! Aye! *Vaffanculo!* It hurts me so much tuh even tawhk about, but I really am not able tuh move at dis particular moment in time."

"Okay, what's the matter?"

"If yuh could just come a little closuh and take a look at dis wit' which I need some attenshun."

I look. "Oh, for fucks'sake. Again? 'Sparre, again?"

So now, I'm on my knees in front of Guasparre Gagliardi in the tiny john with the sick-green fluorescent lighting and the sick-green checkered floor tile at The Meat Market, the leather bar where I work. But it isn't what it seems. If there's one thing Aunty Em forgot to tell Dorothy Gale, it's that lessons are rarely learned when the situation is solely viewed in black-and-white and that an enlightened understanding of the technicolor broad view depends on travel to foreign countrysides and an innate ability to swallow other folk's peculiarities. Also, to always pack a second pair of sensible shoes—like combat boots. Because it's *never* what it seems.

"Is it my fault I was bawhn into dis wawhld wit' such an

admirable *cazzo. Un pene così bello!* Do yuh know what I mean, Brudduh?"

For a brief moment, his pain disappears as he puffs out his enormous chest and exaggerated cleft chin and positively preens at the picture of his perfect, prevalent prick, all bravado and charisma like Marky Mark—the sexy rapper turned Calvin Klein underwear model, immortalized and groping himself on a billboard in Times Square.

"Uh-huh," I say as I'm understanding the technicolor broad view.

"Would yuh mind doin' a guy a good ovuh here, *mio amico Nicolo?*"

"Uh-huh," as I'm traveling foreign countrysides. "It's Dominic, okay?"

"*Perchè no!* You're a *ginzbawl* just like de rest of us and everybody stabs deir meatball de same way. Wit' a fawhk, yuh fuwhk. Okay? Are ya wit' me?"

"Yes, I'm Italian. But I don't have three yards of foreskin that gets tangled up in my zipper every other evening," as I'm swallowing other folk's peculiarities. "See, this is why you uncut guys should always wear button-fly jeans."

Again he puffs up. Even harder this time. Then he shuffles with his jeans around his ankles, poses on the sick-green, checkered floor tile, and turns to take a self-adoring inventory of his uncircumcised member in the sick-green, graffitied mirror beneath the sick-green, fluorescent lighting.

"Yuh look very nice down dere right here in front of me, *Googootz!*"

"Now, this may hurt a little bit."

"Go ahead. Just give me a little smoocharoo first. Okay? I ain't gonna tell nobody nuttin' I swear it tuh yuh. Not even your boyfriend de doawhman of dis fine establishment. On my mudder —may she rest in peace, of cawhse. Yuh wit' me?"

I yank the zipper hard on Guasparre Gagliardi and his chest deflates as he thrusts involuntarily. He spews a hot stream of Italian curses guaranteed to rouse his dead mother: "*Va fongool! Vai a fare in culo! Facia-brota skifosa. Mi Meengya, Stonato!*"

"Everybody okay in here?" asks the doorman as he pokes his head through the toilet door.

"Wha? Huh?"

"You okay?" he mouths in an over-exaggerated manner.

"We're fine. I mean, I'm fine. I'm fine."

"You sure?" he mouths with just the lips this time, not a sound from his kisser.

"Huh?"

"Shit, baby, where are you tonight?"

"I'm right here." On my knees in front of 'Sparre Gagliardi with his pants around his ankles in the tiny john with the sick-green, fluorescent lighting and the sick-green, checkered floor tile.

"Well, we need you behind the bar. It's getting kinda busy, baby."

"I know, Doorman. Be right there."

"They'll be plenty of time for extracurricular later, baby."

"Uh-huh."

It is never what it seems, Dorothy Gale, and things are seldom the way they appear. In truth, I'm somewhere beyond the hand-painted technicolor filmstrip of casual sex: miles away from growing up in Chicago and thousands of lightyears removed from eyes that connect with urgent reciprocation and bodies that instinctively crash and retreat, crash and retreat.

"Do your best to hurry huh, baby?" And the kindness of his smile lights up the entire john.

"I'll be right out, Doorman."

"And you, Gagliardi—pull your damn pants up or go someplace where that kinda shit is allowed! *Capisce?*"

He winks at me playfully, and with a silent, over-exaggerated "Who me?" the toilet door swings closed.

"Well, do yuh see dat? Now I getcha permission tuh kiss me. Yuh got me so fahr? Maybe yuh suck me and I feel all bettuh? And den yuh feel all bettuh, too."

"I gotta go!"

The doorman is waiting for me outside the john, stalling for time by pretending to check the batteries in his flashlight. "Go for a beer with me tonight after work, baby?" as he brushes cocaine residue from the hair on my chest and all down the trail to my navel.

"Sorry, Doorman. Not tonight, okay?"

"Wha? Okay then. You do have extracurricular on your mind," he says, teasing.

Why do I say no when I want to answer yes? No, I'm not thinking about strange dick. *Yes, I'd love to have a beer with you, Doorman.*

"Well...I, er, better get back behind the bar."

"Sure thing, baby." He pulls a pretend punch on me and kisses me sweetly on the cheek instead. I study his gray buzzcut glinting in the disco lights, his chiseled torso and tattoo sleeves, and his perfect, cantaloupe ass as he disappears into the crowd.

I take my place behind the bar. The first thing I do is reach for the pack of Reds that I keep to the right of the cash register. I light a smoke with a branded The Meat Market book of matches that reads *A Butcher Bar*, and I look into the enormous gilt mirror behind the shelves of booze, taking desperate care to not stare too deeply into the reflection of my own eyes—I can't afford to travel that path right now, right here—and size up the formidable line of leathermen gathering at my station.

I stack the cardboard Meat Market coasters, secure a flashlight for the cooler, and tuck a clean bar towel into the back of my jeans at the small of my back.

I inhale hard and take in cigarette smoke, the sexually charged arena, and the men in their leather gear who assemble here at one of the last remaining public spaces for cruising and exploration of backroom sex. History. Our history. It fascinates me. So many of our unexpected predilections reveal something deeper about us that we don't wish to catch in our own reflection and stare down.

I exhale a cloud of smoke into the night, the blue-black lights, the throbbing primal rites, and turn to face a collection of leathermen who all look the same—same haircut, same harness, same probing eyes, and off we go.

Wipe the bar, Meat Market coaster, smile handsome for tips to pay my electric bill.

"Hey! Hey, buddy. Over here!"

"Heya. What can I get ya?"

"Can I get a drink or are you gonna spend the night counting your tips and staring at your reflection in the mirror?"

"Believe me, I don't wanna look too closely at either one. What can I get ya?"

"Yeah-huh. I should have your problems. Lite beer in a bottle."

Unapologetic fetishist. Likes to just lie there during sex. Into feet. Digs getting trampled.

"I got Bud Lite, Coors Lite, Keystone Lite, Miller Lite, Michelob Ultra, Amstel Light, Corona Light Mexican Lager, and Wachusett Light IPA."

"Which one is the cheapest?"

"Bud Lite. Three fifty."

"For a fuckin' lite beer? How much for a Coors?"

"Regular Coors is on special tonight. Three bucks in a can. Coors Lite is three fifty. The can is extra."

"Har dee har. Now you're a comedian?"

"I was just making a little joke. Three fifty. The can is on me."

"Yeah, yeah, Paula Poundstone. Coors Lite. Three fifty."

Grab the flashlight, Bud Lite from the cooler on the left.

I make his change and he slides one quarter in my direction and stomps off, girth spilling from the exposed sections of his harness and bootstraps jangling, to make someone else's life miserable. It amazes me that these same men who can't afford a lite beer somehow show up at the most extravagant shares on Fire Island every summer.

Wipe the bar, Meat Market coaster, smile handsome for tips to pay my gas bill.

"*Hola, Papi! Como tu ta?* Ju got shotsss?"

"*Hermosa! Hola!* What can I get ya?"

"Leeesssin! I neet sometheeen to make me dance like Cheeeta RRRiberrra ant fuck like RRReeecky Marrrteeen."

"Hmmm. That's pretty ambitious. I think...maybe Tequila?"

"Jayyys! The cheeep sheeet, pleeessse. I won't be rrrich until I meeet my husbant, ju know."

Always goes home with the first man at the bar who hits on him. Pretty dick. Extra *grande*.

"I hear ya. Coming right up."

Rocks glass with my left hand, house Tequila from the speed

rack, three-count pour—one one-thousand, two one-thousand, three one-thousand.

"*Juan dólares,* two *dólares, tRRRes dólares, quatro dólares.*"

"This should make you shake your bon-bon, *mijo.*"

"Thank you, Neeecky!" He poses himself at the bar all Chita Rivera from *Kiss of The Spider Woman*—black sequins, Diamanté brooches, and a smokey blue spotlight—to offer up a dramatic reading in the form of a toast: "*Dios te salve, Maria,* full of Garcia. Blessed are thy wooomb y Jesus Christo with the fine-ass clone bearttt. Am I riiight? Bleeese forgibbb us our seeensss and slap a big juan eeen my face tonight. Haaaymen."

"Amen!"

"Dunt yoke. Leeesssin, Heee is alwaysss watcheeen." And after a beat: "*No hay noche como esta noche. Weeeeeeeepaaaaaaaaaa!*"

And he dances off. Smokey blue spotlight fade black.

I gave up on Puerto Ricans years ago. So handsome with their latte-colored skin and those sensuous lips you just wanna chew on for days. Always hung, every single time. But, man, can they bring the drama! Always looking to marry their mother. Every single time. And always still single.

Wipe the bar, Meat Market coaster, smile handsome for tips to pay my rent which is due in a week.

"Heya. What can I get ya?"

"Hey, I'm Garrett. Nice to meet you."

"Hi Garrett. I've met you like eleven times."

Works at Macy's, positions himself as a fashionista. Everyone knows he's only in it for the Calvin Klein underwear employee discount. Boxer briefs. The expensive kind.

"Sorry. I have to pee. Can you point me to the bathroom?"

"Wha? Huh? You're at this bar more than I am. You've been to the john like a million times—and that's just tonight. Okaaayyy. It's just beyond...wait a minute. You stood in a line of men for twenty minutes to ask me where the john is, Garrett?"

"It's like I said...I have to pee."

"You didn't think to ask someone around you for directions to the bathroom?"

"How are they supposed to know directions to the bathroom?"

"Wha? Huh? It's past the pool table and just beyond the cigarette machine. Two doors. Right is for tops. Bottoms is left. There's probably a line. After that the dark room with the red light is...well, don't pee in there. Unless you're into that."

"Okay. Well thanks, Tommy."

Tommy? Tommy who? Hilfiger? Christ, is it too soon for another smoke?

Wipe the bar, Meat Market coaster, smile handsome for tips toward a decent share on Fire Island this year.

"Heya. What can I get ya?"

"Hi. Can I get a Lite Beer?"

"I got Bud Lite, Coors Lite, Keystone Lite, Miller Lite, Michelob Ultra, Amstel Light, and Corona Light Mexican Lager, and Wachusett Light IPA."

"No Heineken Lite?"

"They don't make Heineken in a lite beer, pal."

"They make Beck's Lite. I had it at Splooge just last week!"

Particularly receptive to discourse. Likes to give directions during sex. Bossy bottom.

"I got Bud Lite, Coors Lite, Keystone Lite, Miller Lite, Michelob Ultra, Amstel Light, and Corona Light Mexican Lager, and Wachusett Light IPA."

"I'll take Grand Marnier in a rocks glass instead. Neat."

Rocks glass with my left hand, Grand Marnier from the shelf behind me, third up from the counter, without even turning my torso, three-count pour—one one-thousand, two one-thousand, three one-thousand.

"Here ya go."

And he lays out a sick-green, sopping-wet twenty dollar bill, which immediately flattens itself and adheres to the bar. I don't wanna touch it. But, for just one moment, if I scrunch my eyes closed as tightly as I am able...

"Thank you very much. Keep the change."

No, thank you. For the Hepatitis B. Yuccckk! Ick! Ewww! as I peel Mr. Jackson from the countertop.

For ten years I've tended bar at The Meat Market. When I was twenty-two, I dropped out of Loyola University of Chicago and left behind a pointless career as an accountant. I ran fast and furiously away from rusted-out iron drums filled with dead leaves belching orange cinder into the soot gray skyline and damp twigs ensnared with twine.

I kissed my childhood goodbye, got on a Greyhound, and didn't know where I'd stop until I landed in New York City. Eighteen hours on a bus that sliced a path from boy to man, and I was relieved to never travel the back roads of adolescence again. I walked from the Port Authority Bus Terminal to a stale, semen-stained room at the 14th Street Y and almost thought I found God there surrounded by all the men performing unchristian-like sex acts on each other. Unfortunately, my tenure with divinity only lasted three days until I was no longer the new guy anymore and, therefore, instantly less hallowed. And I used the biggest portion of a paltry wad of cash that I shrouded in my front pocket to secure an illegal basement sublet in the West Village.

I paced Christopher Street from the West Street Pier to Sixth Avenue, connecting the dots between slice joints until I was bored with bumming cigarettes, chafed raw from sex with strangers, and nearly strapped broke. There was a short stint as a hustler, and three shifts as a tuxedoed busboy at a French bistro in Times Square, but The Meat Market intoxicated me with its easy money making opportunities, salacious neon surroundings, and blatant sexuality.

I joined the bar staff in the mid-eighties when the nightclub was enjoying its initial success. I filled out an application, citing limited service industry experience, and was behind the bar shirtless and serving up cocktails to mustached men in leather thirty minutes later. In between, there was an interview cum physical examination that I barely remember—administered by a sweaty, business owner that took place in a sick-green, windowless basement office.

"Ya on the horse?"

"Wha? Huh?"

"The horse. Are ya on the horse? The heroin."

"Wha? No!"

"Here. Lemme see your hands. In between the fingers. Ya on the take?"

"I don't unders—"

"The take. The take! Are ya gonna steal from me?"

"Wha? No."

"Of course you're gonna steal from me. You're a bartender, right? They all steal from me. They think I don't know it, but I know it. The question is *how much* are you gonna steal from me?"

"Look, I could really use the job."

"Any physical abnormalities?"

"Huh?"

"Here. Take your t-shirt off. Do ya got any physical deformities?" He takes uninterested, obligatory inventory of shirtless me from brow to balls.

"No."

"Scabies?"

"No."

"AIDS?"

"No!"

"I got three nights a week behind the bar. You can have 'em if you start today. If you're fast enough, and if these dumbfuck drunks like the looks of you, I'll throw you on Saturday nights, too. Don't steal from me! And keep your shirt off. Always keep your shirt off. Keeps 'em coming back for more. Dumbfuck drunks! And no horse, ya hear?"

In an effort to establish The Meat Market as the preeminent leather bar to integrate New York City's Meatpacking District, and to discourage late-night denizen dockworkers as well as unsuspecting straight people, a strict dress code was established that prohibited patrons from wearing polo shirts, cologne, and designer jeans and encouraged them to don muscle shirts, leather vests, chaps, and engineer boots. A doorman was put in place to enforce uniform standards and also intimidate local neighborhood dwellers, prostitutes, and misplaced tourists from stumbling into an ill-famed backroom sex club.

To me, the experience of landing a job at a gay bar was watershed. Working in an environment entirely staffed by homosexuals for the sole enjoyment of other homosexuals and taking part as a community unfurled, blossomed even, offered up the sensation of belonging someplace. At twenty-two, for the first time in my life, I discovered an identity, comrades, and social circumstances of which I could be proud.

Identifying yourself is a situation that presents itself seemingly by accident—a transition that occurs gradually, and a state of being that happens gracefully and with unseen eyes. If you spend a moment listening to sniggering drag queens, lusting after good-looking leathermen, and creating surroundings with your flannel-shirted brothers, the change has happened. Growth sneaks up on people right before their eyes. They deny it, try to prevent it, even swear it isn't so until it becomes them. One day you look around and think, *"Okay, this is who I am now."*

"I interrupted three different, almost-consummated sex acts in the john tonight. You'd think we didn't have a backroom just one door over, eh?"

I'm distracted by the doorman's hands as he speaks to me, the massive veins, the muscles that dance on his forearms when he gestures.

"You'd think we didn't have a backroom just one door over, huh, Doorman?"

"Wha? Oh, yeah. Or something like that, baby." He playfully cuffs my ear.

The doorman's hands are enormous. Lumbering lion's paws he uses to communicate with, to pull people into him and speak intimately with his thick mustache bristling against their eardrums, and to signal drunks with a gentle touch to the shoulder that, perhaps, they've consumed their share of drink.

"Caught some weirdo fishing a twenty-dollar bill outta the toilet in the stall of the john!"

"Ewww. That's so gross."

My eyes travel his tattooed sleeves to his expansive shoulders, and I can picture the two of us spiraling through the years, safeguarded in one another's embrace. I look too long. He smiles too big, fully aware. And instantly I am revealed.

"Did you notice the way that kid's eyes were eating you up over the bar earlier?"

"Wha? Huh?"

"Jeez, baby, you *are* out of it lately. The dark-eyed boy wearing the leather harness? He was *cruising* you!"

I noticed no boy. "See him? Fuhgeddaboudit. If looks were blowjobs I'd have spilled my seed all over the bar."

He turns to leave, satisfied and guffawing, but not before pretending to land a fake punch on my chin as gentle as a breeze off the Hudson and slipping in to playfully tug on my nipple ring. His smile and all over-exaggerated "Who me?" could light up fucking Times Square. I've known him for years, but it's the last three months that have fostered a desire in me to find rest and seek shelter in his benevolent arms. More and more, there are nights when I lose myself inside our silly banter, envisioning this man pulling me close with the mass of his arms and lifting me up inside his muscle-ripped embrace to a safer place.

"So, I should probably—"

"Wha? Oh, yeah, yeah, I know, baby. Get back to work. I know, I know." He smiles his mischievous, 42nd Street marquee grin at me and winks—and I swear it's as if he's alternating between fragments of raunchy sentences in my ear and tiny kisses on my neck.

Wipe the bar, Meat Market coaster, smile handsome for tips to pay my electric bill.

"So, spill it! Spill the beans, Sis!"

"Bruiser!"

"I'll take a Screwdriver, dear. Heavy on the screw. I don't particularly care who's driving."

Highball glass with my left hand, house Vodka from the speed rack, five-count pour—one one-thousand, two one-thousand, three one-thousand—I'm always counting—four one-thousand, five one-thousand, splash of stale OJ diluted with water.

"Are you gonna tell me or do I have to fuck it outta you?"

"What?"

"What she says! How much do I owe ya?"

"This one is on me, Bruiser."

"Oh, you're not getting off that easy. Spill it! What's going on with you and the doorman, Little Sister?"

"Nothing is *going on*. We're friends."

"Riiight." They could hear him slurp his cocktail in Yonkers.

"No, really. I've known the man for ten years. Maybe more."

"Then it's about time you saw his *schmekel*."

"His *schmekel*?"

"His peter. His putz. His pecker. His impressively large, veined phallus." Shhhlurrrppp.

"Bruiser, when you've known somebody that long—"

"Are you gonna try to tell me it would be easier to suck a perfect stranger's schlong through a glory hole than to make love with somebody you know?"

"That's not what I—"

"She prefers a plywood husband. Would you believe it? Not in it for the love. She's in it for the loads."

"That isn't what I—"

"I'm just saying." Shhhhhhlurrrrrrppppppp.

"Now I need a drink."

"You better make it a stiff one, Dominic. You look a little wobbly."

"Very funny."

"Ya get it?"

"I got it."

"Not yet ya ain't."

Bruiser has been a community personality dating back to the days just after Stonewall. In the seventies, he all but led the stampede of mustached men in plaid lumberjack shirts and tight-fitting jeans, some of them shirtless in the cool Northeastern evenings, who stood on line for an hour or more to gobble Black Beauties and boogie to live performances by The Ritchie Family and Vickie Sue Robinson. Today, he's practically an institution at any of the gay bars that dot the landscape on either side of the Village, East or West.

"You thought the Wicked Witch of the East was evil? Well, you haven't met her sister from the Westside!"

He's an attractive man with a close-cropped blond buzzcut, a thick red-blond mustache, and tiny round glasses that exploit his intellect.

Shhhhhhlurrrrrrppppppp. "I'll have another, dearie."

Highball glass with my left hand, house Vodka from the speed rack, five-count pour, splash of stale OJ diluted with water.

"Coming right up, Bruce."

"Bruiser! Now, what did I tell you? It's Bruiser. Bruiser. Never Bruce. Bruce might be somebody's husband."

Bruiser has three dime-sized Kaposi sarcoma lesions that trail his jawline, all in a perfect row, that he's named Un, Deux, and Trois, and another beside his ear that he calls Lola.

"I'd name the new girl in accordance with the others, Dominic, but you know what happened to the four cats in the boat, dontcha?"

"What's that?"

"*Un Deux Trois Cat Sank!*"

Oh, how he makes me laugh. Really laugh. There are nights when I'm so happy to see him. He'll sit down at my bar with his stories of New York City in the seventies and his elaborate escapades as a hair-burner or a flight attendant or a florist. I know him well enough to understand the stories are fiction, but one day somebody has gotta write it down...record all the intimate observations before they're gone and nobody remembers it right. Add to that, in my life I've never met such a raconteur. Judy Garland had Noël Coward. I've got Bruce.

"Did I ever tell you about the time I was a Maître D at this really fancy-schmancy Italian joint on the Upper East Side?"

"Uh-huh, go on."

"A real majordomo I was. Well, majorette domo—if there is such a thing. Now, where was I?"

"On the Upper East Side."

"Right. So, I'm this high-powered *Domo Majorette* at this ultra-pretentious, ostentatious, over-priced eatery on the Upper East Side. And it's filled to the brim with overdressed Park Avenue matriarchs and their just-a-little-bit too too escorts wearing their just-a-little-bit too too expensive suits and flamboyant ties with matching pocket squares. You get the picture. All of the old ladies are pretending they can read the menu without their reading glasses, and all of the fine gentlemen are craning their necks to flirt with the just-a-little-bit too too tooty fruity fine gentleman at the table next door."

"Keep going."

Shhhhhhlurrrrrrppppppp. "I'll have another, dear."

"I'm on it."

Highball glass with my left hand, house Vodka from the speed rack, five-count pour, splash of stale OJ diluted with water.

Out of the corner of my eye, I notice zipper-adjusting leathermen amassing—slapping one another on the ass, mopping their brows, and heading toward the bar as if a perfunctory scrimmage played out successfully and a field goal was landed in the backroom, and now the players need sustenance. Go team!

"Now, where was I again? Sometimes I get so confused."

"Still on the Upper East Side."

"Exactly. You *are* paying attention. Well now, I'm manning the podium and doing all I can to make the plebes without rezzos feel insignificant because management encourages that sort of behavior. I mean, it is New York City, after all. The customers deserve punishment. When in walks none other than Miss Meryl Streep. True story. It's Meryl alright. All dressed up in some chichi gold lamé number. She looks like a...like a...great, big, drapery. She's very tall, you know? Giant-like, ya know? And she's wearing someone's curtains!"

"I guess I never thought of her as tall."

"Oh, it's for real. She's practically a behemoth. I heard Dusty Hoffman had to stand on a box in their scenes together. Oh, but that's another story, Mrs. Kramer. And I don't want to lose my place in *this* story. Sooo. There's Miss Meryl taking her entrance and she's appointed exactly like Karl Lagerfeld's Gramercy Park penthouse, and I tell you, all of the old broads are primping and preening and digging through their Gucci Marmont Matelassé bags to locate their opera glasses for a little looksee. And all of the old broads' too too queer escorts are craning their necks to garner a glimpse of this great, big, drapery." Shhhhhhlurrrrrrppppp. "Now, Dominic, be a sweetheart and make your big sister another cocktail, wontcha? Maybe a teensy-weensy triple this time? That way you won't have to keep interrupting my stories, Dreamboat."

"I gotcha covered, Bruiser."

Highball glass with my left hand, house Vodka from the speed rack, five-count pour, splash of stale OJ diluted with water.

By this time, the thirsty leathermen have completely filed out of the backroom and formed a line for drinks. And it's aimed directly at me. But what kind of a friend would I be if I didn't at least let Bruiser have his punch line?

"Thank you, Little Sister. Ummm...preening matriarchs, craning queers—oh, that's right! Now Miss Meryl turns to me, stares at my forehead, and she announces she'll be needing a table for five. And didn't her assistant call earlier to request something quiet and out of the way? And could I please be an angel and make it someplace inconspicuous where she's not going to cause any commotion? Huh? As if the entirety of the Upper East Side didn't notice the seven-foot-tall Goliath lady departing her over-sized limousine and schlepping down Park Avenue dressed in Karl Lagerfeld's Gramercy Park penthouse! Well, I'll tell you what. I informed Miss Meryl that at the moment we haven't any tables available even if she did star in *She-Devil* with Roseanne Barr—"

Leathermen are anxious for their refreshments before the next darkroom scrimmage kicks off and I'm ignoring them. I mean, it is New York City, after all. The customers deserve punishment. Even so, I can feel their impatient eyes.

"—and she looks down that nose of hers, all the while staring directly at my forehead. You do know she's had her nose done at least a half a dozen times. True story. And that was just during *Silkwood*. Every new character, she gets a new nose."

Parched leathermen are shifting their weight, bootstraps jangling, hands on their hips, drumming their fingers on the bar and preparing to eat me alive. But, for just one moment, if I scrunch my eyes closed as tightly as I am able...

Shhhhhhlurrrrrrpppppp. "Now, Miss Meryl Streep looks down that disjointed nose of hers that Doctor Josef Mengele mangled himself especially for her star turn in *Sophie's Choice*—because somebody in that flick had to look handsomer than Kevin Kline. She looks directly at my forehead and asks me if I know who she might be? And I stand on my tiptoes, and I say to her—I say to her...if you don't know who you are, Madam, how do you expect me to know who you are? But, in the spirit of good hospitality, I'll have a go at your little game. I'm happy to give it a guess. Now, let me see...hmmm? How about Goldie Hawn? No, that's not right—too tall. Kate Hepburn. No, that can't be right—too dead. Aha! I've got it. Susan Lucci! That's the ticket. You're Susan Lucci!"

"Very clever, Bruiser."

"But I haven't finished my story yet!"

"I'll be right back."

Wipe the bar, Meat Market coaster, smile handsome for tips to pay my gas bill.

"Heya. What can I get ya?"

"Brandy and Coke."

"So, that's gonna be four bucks even-steven, please."

Clean-cut. Dapper even. Crazy as fuck kinky in the sack. I'd bet tonight's tips he was at the bottom of the backroom scrimmage pile.

Highball glass with my left hand, house brandy from the speed rack, cola from the soda gun, three-count pour—one one-thousand, two one-thousand, three one-thousand.

"Can you break a fifty?"

"This ain't Côte Basque, pal, but I'll see what we can do."

Change delivered from a crisp, fifty-dollar bill. Even his money is clean-cut. He's the first wrinkle-free, wide-receiver I've ever met.

"Thank you, Mister."

"You are quite welcome. Enjoy the night."

Wipe the bar, Meat Market coaster, smile handsome for tips to pay my rent which is due in a week.

"Heya. What can I get ya?"

"That backroom smells like some old queen exploded her fuckin' Depends in there."

"I'll mention it to someone."

"S'nasty. Stale chocolate mousse and lilac water everywhere. Stinks like the inside of my grandmother's pocketbook."

"Sorry. What'll it be?"

"Dewar's. Neat."

Masculine for masculine. Only dates men who are a carbon copy—same haircut, same harness, same probing eyes.

Rocks glass with my left hand, Dewar's from the shelf behind me, second up from the counter, without even turning my torso, three-count pour—one one-thousand, two one-thousand, three one-thousand.

"Five, please."

"Shit, man. All I have is a five-dollar bill in my wallet. Can I hit you up with a gratuity next time?"

"Sure thing."

"There's also three Ken Dolls butt-fucking in the toilet. Just so ya know."

"Yup. Thanks for the tip, pal."

I watch as the doorman escorts three glassy-eyed, button-fly securing muscle clones from the bathroom. If I were to guess, somebody's ecstasy kicked in and opportunity knocked on the tiny, sick-green stall door. The doorman sets the muscle boys free with a gentle, chiding finger to find their place in the crowd. He turns toward me with a confident, toothy grin that lights up the room as he curls a bicep and mouths the words, "Hi Baby." Then he pretends to be overtaken by a whiff of his own armpit and pantomimes faltering on his feet and fainting and laughs and laughs and laughs and never once loses hold of my eyes. Whew! When did it get so warm in here anyway?

Wipe the bar, Meat Market coaster, smile handsome for tips toward a decent share on Fire Island this year.

"Heya. What can I get ya?"

"Lite beer. Cans only."

"I got Bud Lite, Coors Lite, Miller Lite and Wachusett Light IPA."

"Whattchasaid? I pee ale?"

"Wha? Huh?"

"Never mind. Dumb joke. I'll have a Wachusett, please."

Has gym memberships at Chelsea Gym, Nautilus, East Bank Club, West Side Club, and Gold's. You'd never guess it to look at him.

"Three fifty, Robin Williams."

"Ha! The Mork from Ork. Here's a ten. Keep the change, Handsome."

"Thank you. Thank you very much."

"Nanoo Nanoo."

I break for a smoke and this time I catch myself in the enormous gilt mirror behind the shelves of booze. Despite the circles of sleeplessness beneath my eyes, I am a handsome man. Masculine facial features with a smile that forms gratuitously. Even underneath the sick-green, bar lighting I am easy to look at with a close-cropped, blue-black buzzcut and a space between my two front teeth big enough to pass a dime. My arms and chest are well-developed. That's ten years' worth of lugging cases of liquor to stock the bar upstairs from the sick-green, windowless basement office. My pecs and tummy are covered by clipped black hair accented with one shiny, steel horseshoe-shaped piercing in my nipple.

For a long moment, I search my hesitant, brown eyes and follow the lines of my thick mustache that extends well beyond the corners of my mouth and trails past smile lines to touch my chin, until I'm looking directly into my tangible future. This is the path my thoughts follow lately. Ideas clumsily progress, stumbling forward, falling back upon themselves, and here and there the ability to consider in a calm, well-grounded manner is precluded by the overwhelming perception that some disastrous nightmare is about to consume my life.

All alone—that's who I am. Left out in the cold. Everything is shrouded in an enveloping darkness, and if I stand as tall as I'm able on tiptoes, light slashes like a razor blade across my outstretched fingertips. One day you look around and think, "Okay, this is who I am now."

And for just one moment, I scrunch my eyes closed as tightly as I am able and I'm counting again. Eight Reds left in the pack. Two dumbfuck drunks standing on line. Counting anything. Any means for distraction. Three hours until the end of my shift. Two pre-rolled joints in the tip jar.

"Have a short snort with me, Little Sister?"

"Huh? Yeah," I say as I turn on my heels. "I don't see how a little Scotch could hurt."

"Thatta girl."

"Bruiser, how many times do I gotta remind you that I'm not a girl. In various circles, I'm very butch, ya know?" I pour myself a long slug from the Twenty Year Scotch, purposefully not counting this time.

"Honey, you make Lee Majors look like Kathy Lee Gifford."

"Awww. You always say the kindest things!"

Highball glass with my left hand, house Vodka from the speed rack, five-count pour, splash of stale OJ diluted with water.

I'm throwing back a belt of Twenty Year Scotch and surveying my surroundings: the men coupling in threes and fours and laughing at their own folly, and the couples uniting without words and finding shelter in the darkest corners to explore each other's mouths and bodies and crotches; the pulsating purple and blue strobes, and the animalistic beats of the DJ throbbing, throbbing, throbbing.

This sinuous lifestyle is spiraling toward another evening's zenith, and the entire barroom is inching toward a cumulative climax as I turn to notice the doorman's amorous gaze from twenty feet away. And his smile lights up the entire night. My face feels on fire and my gaze drops to my drink. I add to it one ice cube, two ice cubes, three ice cubes, and when I look up again our eyes reunite.

Instantly, every motion in the barroom screeches to an abrupt halt, all the tiny movements in this lifetime momentarily cease, and even the throbbing, throbbing, throbbing of the DJ's beats fade blackout-style with an eerie, grinding growl.

Like a tableau painting depicting action frozen in time, something by Manet, or Renoir, or Degas that you could stare at for hours in a museum, you can look right through the characters in this barroom stumbling forward, falling backward upon themselves, in midair, and suspended in time—until you yourself are no longer a spectator but one of those characters, stumbling forward, falling backward, and suspended in time.

Detached from my surroundings. Disconnected from the reality of The Meat Market until the ordinary objects, cardboard coasters, flashlight for the cooler, clean bar towel tucked into the back of my jeans at the small of my back, become unreal and distorted. And the people grow cartoon-like and grotesque, floppy balloon creatures, with sing-song Pollyanna tones and wet spaghetti limbs. Terrifying stuff this—being detached from my body, no longer inhabiting my physical person and observing it from a distance.

It's clear I'm losing touch with reality. The very reason I take desperate care to not stare too deeply into the reflection of my own eyes is because I can't afford to lose control—I can't afford to travel that path right now, right here—and because I know one day, I will look for too long, stare too deep, and no longer recognize the person on display in front of me.

Shadows drip from street signs and walk-ups until suddenly you survey your strange surroundings and ask, "When did the transition come?" "When did the change happen?" "Where did the time go?" One day, I'll simply disappear. Forever.

For singular moments, I create the world; a lonely, frightened painter armed with a box of paints for protection. I brushstroke the soot gray horizon and the furious, frightening squalls of an impending storm. And with a tremendous clap of thunder, the skies open wide and sheets of rain pelt the battleground and its whimpering, beaten-down infantry.

With a resounding whirr, the animalistic beats of the DJ's throbbing, throbbing, throbbing recommences, the pulsating purple and blue strobes reignite, every interrupted motion in the barroom comes to life, and all the tiny movements in this lifetime resume.

Shhhlurrrppp. "Why don't you just fuck him?"

"Wha? Huh?"

"I said fuck him. Fuck him! Why don't you finally fuck the guy?"

"That's enough, Bruiser."

"Alrighty. If you won't fuck the doorman, then how about you fuck me? I could use a rub and tug. Tell him what he wins, Bob!"

"A rub and tug, eh? Seriously—"

"I couldn't be more goddamn serious."

"Listen. Bruiser, we've been through all of this before. I don't date customers. As a rule, I don't date clientele."

Wipe the bar, Meat Market coaster, smile handsome for tips to pay my electric bill.

"Heya, Chico. What can I get ya?"

"Hennessy. How did you dig the stuff?"

Drug dealer from earlier, with the shiny white seal wrapped in a Hamilton and delivered under the guise of a handshake.

"I'm ripped to the tits, man!"

Rocks glass with my left hand, Hennessy from the shelf behind me, third up from the counter, without even turning my torso, five-count pour—one onc-thousand, two one-thousand, three one-thousand, four one-thousand, five one-thousand.

"Excellent!"

"This one is on the house, brother."

"Right on! And there's more where that came from. If ya get my *sniffft*."

"Perfect."

Wipe the bar, Meat Market coaster, smile handsome for tips to pay my gas bill.

"Heya. What can I get ya?"

"I would like a Gin Rickey, please."

Addicted to hair-removal depilatories. Even shaves his arms and legs. Ewww. That's so gross.

Now, usually when a customer orders a drink I don't know how to prepare, I shake my head "no" and serve him a beer in a can. I've said it before, this ain't Côte Basque. But I'm trying to avoid Bruiser because I know precisely where tonight is headed, and I'm just plain eager to get through the evening without any drama. So, do you know what I do? I search the drawer beneath the register for the dilapidated, sick-green dictionary of cocktail recipes and find out a Gin Rickey is basically a Margarita made with Gin.

Highball glass with my left hand, house Gin from the speed rack, sour mix from the soda gun, three-count pour—one one-thousand, two one-thousand, three one-thousand.

"That'll be eight bucks, please."

"Wait one minute! Eight dollars for a Gin Rickey?"

"Sorry, man. That's the damage. And I gotta keep the line moving if you wouldn't mind."

If there's one thing I've learned working at The Meat Market, it's to always upcharge for research.

Wipe the bar, Meat Market coaster, smile handsome for tips to pay my rent which is due in a week.

Shhhlurrrppp. "It's because I'm sick, right?"

"What?"

"It's because I'm sick. That's the reason you won't fuck me."

"Bruiser! That's not fair."

"Be that as it may, it's completely true. And I am accepting your unwillingness to answer in a straight-forward manner as confirmation."

"No, it is not true! And I find it personally insulting that you would even imply such a thing."

"Then you explain it to me."

"I have nothing to explain. I said no."

"We're both men. Both unbetrothed as far as I can see."

"No. Now, drop it."

"You're handsome enough. I'm reasonably endowed. What frightens you the most, Dominic? Are you afraid I'm gonna up and die when you finally realize that you can't live without me? Or is it the kiss of death that scares you?"

"I said that's enough, Bruiser!"

"Do you suppose you could stand to watch yourself dying by the millimeter just like me?"

"Gaddammit! Ya wanna know why? Ya wanna know why I won't fuck you? Because that's who I am! And you wanna know what life is, Bruiser? Ya wanna know? Life is you take whatever you can get. Life is you make the most of whatever you can take."

"Lola's thirsty! Lola's thirsty!"

He's loud and leathermen are straining their necks to witness the scuttle. From across the bar, the doorman mouths the words "Are you okay?" and I shake my head affirmatively in his direction, but I am far from okay. More and more Bruiser is becoming caustic, and it rattles me. Maybe it's the booze, but more likely it's life. Of course, my heart goes out to him because he's sick, but I am not obligated to screw anybody. Nope. Not in my contract. Gay men have confused casual sex with comfort and shelter for so long that these days if you choose to not sleep with someone, you're a hypocrite or a self-hating homophobe, or worse than that, an AIDS-bigot.

I start my closing side work as a distraction. Unstack the cardboard Meat Market coasters and return them to the cabinet, find fresh batteries for the flashlight, and inventory the beers I'll need for tomorrow's restock of the cooler. I make the final drinks of the night, flirt with the leathermen, laugh at their jokes, light their cigarettes, postpone their drunken and salacious advances, and find respite in the more mechanical tasks of my job.

I pour another long slug from the Twenty Year Scotch, and as the smokey booze trickles down the back of my throat, I can feel Bruiser's eyes burning right through me; eyes as blue as they are marred by disease, reticent memory, and wounded confusion. When he realizes I refuse to prepare him another cocktail, he blows me a kiss and stumbles out into the night. Honestly, tomorrow he won't even remember.

Guasparre Gagliardi exits the bar without so much as a "*Caio, Googootz!*" for professional services rendered. And then it hits me —next time I should dump a little blow on his knob to numb up the foreskin.

"Almost ready to call it a night, baby?" asks the doorman as he rests a lumbering lion's paw on my shoulder. I want to say something witty, tousle his graying buzzcut with my fingertips, or simply find repose in his arms—but I'm paralyzed by his close proximity and the Twenty Year Scotch, and I simply smile and give last call.

"Last call! Last call for alcohol, gentlemen! You ain't gotta go home, but you can't stay here!"

When the catch-as-catch-can have departed, the DJ turns a knob and the throbbing music dies a screeching, electronic death right in the middle of The Pointer Sisters' Jump (For My Love). With a single index finger, the doorman flips a switch that transforms all the starlight into soot gray skyline, bare bulbs illuminating black painted plywood walls, scurrying cockroaches, a sea of used condoms littered across the floor, and smoldering cigarette butts in ashtrays across the barroom.

I collect my cash register drawer and head downstairs to rectify my bank. There are those that think a gig tending bar in a gay club is glamorous, but really, it's just a lot of counting. Not in it for the love. He's in it for the loads of cash money.

In the sick-green, fluorescent lighting of the sick-green, windowless basement office, I face and stack piles of fifties, then twenties, then tens, then fives, then singles. I fill a deposit bag with rolls of quarters, then dimes, then nickels. I'm spinning the safe as I cut the power on a tiny transistor radio and Jimmy Sommerville abruptly stops in the center of one fell falsetto swoop, and I'm securing the lock when I hear the doorman admitting the Polish cleaning crew and calling them by American names with ski suffixes and affectionately pulling punches on them and laughing boisterously.

I stuff a generous wad of cash tips into the front pocket of my jeans as I collect my leather jacket and smokes and close and padlock the sick-green, office door on another night. Instinctively, I check for my wallet at my back hip and the keys to my apartment. The doorman is waiting for me as I round the sick-green basement stairs.

"Where are you off to tonight, baby?"

"Home," I tell the doorman. "I'm really beat."

"Uh-huh." And he smiles so confidently that my heart might break in two.

"I'm serious. I'm going home."

"Wha? Oh, yeah? I thought you had extracurricular tail on your mind."

"I did. I mean—I do. I mean—it fell through."

"Well, you have a nice time tonight, baby."

The doorman pulls me close with the weight of his massive arms and for a long minute I allow myself the stillness inside his embrace. His breath is sweet. His torso smells of masculine perspiration and cigarette smoke, and my dick jumps to attention inside my jeans. "Well, well—will ya look at that, eh baby?" And he kisses me on the cheek, slaps me on the ass, and just like that I step out the big, oak door and directly into the purple morning.

The sky is the color of wilted lilacs before they disseminate and fall to the earth. Morning is a transition that happens gradually like flowers that fade petal by excruciating petal. Across West Side Highway, I can see a glimmer of color igniting the Hudson River and extending its path methodically downtown. If you travel with your eyes to the ground, counting sidewalk squares and listening to the glass crunch beneath your combat boots, you can easily miss daybreak. With your hands in your pockets and your eyes fixed on your course, periphery becomes unimportant, but daylight happens on the streets in little ways before it happens in the sky. Shadows drip from street signs and walk-ups until suddenly you survey your strange surroundings and ask, "When did the transition come?" "When did the change happen?" "Where did the time go?"

I blame the poetry on the Twenty Year Scotch and think about hailing a cab until I reach for a Red and find a half-smoked joint in the pocket of my jacket. A constitution is in order. I take in the sweet marijuana, and I can taste it and the early morning at the back of my throat. The predawn air is thick with the perfume of night jasmine and the sweet stench of rotting meat is pervasive throughout the Meatpacking District.

And just like that, I can feel the grass stealing me from reality and rescuing me from my overactive mind. Lately, it's safest to not think too much. Initially, ideas land inside my brain like harmless waves against the West Side Highway, but when I'm not careful to censor myself, the thoughts collect in undertow fashion and drag me beneath the water with their weightiness.

Suffocating scenarios play on repeat. I study the demented beams of moonlight from beneath the surface and emit small bubbles of breath until my lungs are on fire, overcome and about to burst from lack of respiration as I desperately claw at the water around me and furiously propel myself to the surface, gasping for oxygen and grabbing at life.

I turn away from the river and feel the warm evening's breeze on my blue-black buzzcut. A gaggle of leathermen on their way to locate a piss-stained, rickety staircase to a fetid underground sex club, bare bulbs painted red, approach from behind and overtake me on either side. Their masculine laughter, the smell of their leather, and the stomp of their boots against the pavement elicits an immediate response from my crotch.

For a small time, I maintain their stride and we all walk together without words, a tribe, a brotherhood. Then one of them slips an arm around my waist and says, "Excuse me, Handsome," as his fingers trace the crack of my ass with clear intention. They move ahead and I think to follow them, but I recognize one, two, three of them as regulars at The Meat Market and nothing good ever comes of that kinda late-night coupling.

A bored doorman dressed in complete leather gear sits half-cruising, half-reading a paperback copy of Ethan Mordden's *Buddies* outside an abandoned warehouse. I know it's the piss-stained, rickety staircase to a fetid underground sex club, bare bulbs painted red, that the leathermen were headed to, and I feel a persistent tugging in my jeans when I consider stepping inside. But in truth, I'm about as far away as possible from anonymous bodies that crash and retreat, crash and retreat.

I walk two blocks toward shelter. A right and then a left. I ensconce myself in a metal vestibule doorway and take long hits off the joint until I lose myself completely inside the khaki haze. All alone—that's who I am.

The springtime I turned fifteen was the last time my mother uttered a single word to me. At long last, I proved her point that I was of little use because I stalled for too long and mistakenly pissed her off for good. Her crooked, permanent frown sealed up forever.

I'm rounding out Freshman year as I race home from class to catch the Act Two broadcast of Rosalind Russell in *Gypsy* on the three-thirty movie. I pass my sister Anna in the kitchen, grab a sleeve of sandwich cookies, and hurry to throw my book bag on my bed and not miss the entr'acte on the television in the living room.

Suddenly, and seemingly out of nowhere, my mother materializes and menacingly blocks my door frame. Infuriated and imposing, she traps me inside my own bedroom. She sucks her tongue, her eyes aflame, and her mouth grotesquely contorts up in such a way that I think she might laugh, as she gestures with a twisted, arthritic hand toward a stack of unearthed Torso Magazines no longer undercover and secured in mine bomb fashion.

Her words are angry and punctuated with spittle, and never once does she raise her voice. She's been rehearsing this monologue inside her head for years. Calculated, perfunctory, pointed, even poised; my mother's words are intended not to wound a thing but to put it to death. Urgency is no longer necessary because, you see, she has won. She was right. From now on, I am just another disappointment in her gaddammed backyard in this lousy city. No more a need for hysterics, this is routine business. She is simply setting fire to nature.

"I knew there was something wrong with you, Dominic. I knew it from the start. When I saw the other children chasing you home from school, I said to myself, 'Well, kids are kids, and maybe they're just playing a game.' But I knew there was something inside of you—"

"Can I tell you somethi—"

"—and still I cleaned behind your ears, and wiped your nose, and wiped your ass, and took you with me to the market, and to the post office, even when I knew that there was something deeply not right inside of you—"

"But let me—"

"—and when all the other mothers whispered behind my back about you, I pretended as if I didn't hear them. Because that's who I am. Even when I wanted to gaddammed die right there of gaddammed embarrassment I said to myself, 'Well, who the fuck do they think they are,' that they should talk about my son and me—"

"Mama, please."

"—the little fairy that's all the company she can keep?"

"Mama, please."

"And they were right. The children chasing you home from school. They were justified to do so. Those other mothers. They were right, weren't they? And I prayed that it wouldn't be true. Not my son. I prayed to Jesus Christ himself that it wouldn't be true. That he wouldn't look so down on me and plant me in this gaddammed life in this lousy city with a queer for a son."

"Oh, Mama, no—"

"There's a sickness about you, Dominic. A deep-rooted sickness that lives inside you. Something I can't tame. Something I can't break. And it's a punishment to me that I should cry myself to sleep every night because I wish that you were never born. I knew that there was something wrong with you all along and I wish to Jesus Christ that you were never born. Not into my house."

"If you would just listen to me for one moment."

"And I should listen to you? What could you say? Are you gonna tell me you're a queer? Tell Mama. Are you a queer?"

"If you just let me—"

"I said tell me, Dominic. Tell me you are a gaddammed queer."

"Yes, Mama."

"Yes. Well, I knew it all along."

"Mama, it doesn't have to be—"

"I do not want you to call me that name. Not anymore. I should have put you in a home. I should have planted you in a home so fast your gaddammed head turned circles. I do not love you. I will never love you, Dominic. Never again. Now take these filthy, queer magazines out of my house and burn them with the leaves and sticks."

"How do I—"

"You know how. You know how. And don't ever tell your father you're a faggot. Do you hear me? You'll kill him."

As life would have it, shortly after my fifteenth birthday my father was diagnosed with stage four bladder cancer. One evening out of the blue, he pissed a stream of blood and three months later she discovered him dead on the toilet.

My mother was loath to ever look at me again.

Now I've dog-paddled too far from the security of the shoreline. My brain is mired with racing thoughts, and they come at me repeatedly, blindly, furiously as they morph into whitecap waves composed of memories that are ferocious and dangerous and relentless. I'm hiding for cover inside a metal vestibule doorway, pulling my knees against my chest on the cold, concrete door stoop and praying for the purple morning to take shape.

My head is reeling with the marijuana and Scotch, and they never do any gaddammed good anyway because just look at me. Curled up fetal in a random metal vestibule doorway and thrashing to keep my head above the crashing waves, and the purple nighttime, and the undulating tide of tortuous consciousness. Because that's who I am. "Okay, this is who I am now."

After my father died, my mother excluded me from any task that might involve our eyes meeting—even the chores. Not two weeks into summer vacation, solace dotted the milky sunlight with the muscled torso of a seventeen-year-old deaf boy she hired to keep the lawn, broom the fallen crab apples that stained the sidewalk, and manage a tiny city garden filled with wilted tomato plants.

From the complacency of my knotty pine bedroom, I listen to Joni Mitchell sing about Marcie in her coat of flowers on my tinny, portable eight-track player and study the boy as he cuts the grass with a hand mower in sedate diagonal rows, sits bare-chested in the tiny city garden with the fledgling tomato plants, and swipes up dandelions which he fashions into homemade, back-pocket boutonnière.

Every afternoon ends with me touching myself as I picture the deaf boy high on a ladder cleaning the gutters or back behind the stuffy, city garage in the alley smoking cigarettes that he's rolled himself. Marcie's sorrow needs a man, alright. Red is stop and green's for going.

I summon all of my adolescent courage, determined to follow the deaf boy into the stuffy, city garage in the alley and kiss him on the lips before summer's end. I practically wear a groove into the floorboards, where the avocado shag rug had been removed, devising an approach.

When puberty took over, my body immediately discarded the baby fat, and my torso grew thick and squat like so many Italian boys my age. I discovered a set of barbells cast aside with my dead father's things and counted reps aloud—six, seven, eight, nine, ten —and my arms and chest grew sturdy and muscled as I perfected my plan of attack.

One hazy afternoon, I dressed in a muscle shirt, tight jeans, and my father's old work boots, hand-rolled a joint and secured it behind my ear, and initiated my first steps toward touching another man. I stood three feet away from the boy, ready to make my move, and lost my nerve when he naively reached into the back pocket of his jeans and offered up a dandelion bouquet. I never answered to my urgently emerging sexuality that day, but I did learn that the lithe, shirtless deaf boy could read lips and make sounds himself and write out silly non-sequitur sentences on a pad of paper that he carried with him to communicate.

After we became friends, we hung out each day and smoked hand-rolled cigarettes and wrote each other silly incomplete sentences, drew pictures of dicks and giggled immaturely, and wasted hours counting barbell reps aloud—six, seven, eight, nine, ten—with our shirts off. As we grew comfortable with our friendship, we talked a lot of the time without the pad of paper. And when the moody, Midwestern weather followed its predictable course into fall, we were making sloppy, adolescent love in the stuffy, city garage in the alley every day. Red is autumn, green is summer.

One afternoon, after we spent ourselves all over each other's stomachs, we lay half-erect on top of each other, and the deaf boy asked me if I knew what it felt like to be deaf. I knew what it meant to live without words since the time my mother kicked me aside, and my fledgling sexuality had afforded me an understanding of separateness, but I shook my head and mouthed the word, "No," that I did not understand what it felt like to not hear.

He wiped semen from his stomach with an old t-shirt and he said, "It's like you don't..."

"It's like you don't what? What?"

And he repeated himself: "It's like you don't..." and a garbled word that I couldn't make out.

"What? I don't understand."

He softly laughed. I pressed him to repeat, and again he mouthed the same phrase with the indecipherable ending.

"It's like you don't *what*??" I shouted a little too impatiently.

And he pulled out his pad and wrote the letters X Z I Z T.

"It's like you don't exist," said the deaf boy.

For two years, he stayed in employment with my mother: feeding the tiny city lawn in the summertime, shoveling the walkway and spreading layers of salt across the city sidewalk through the winters. And for two years, he placed himself naked on top of me and covered my face and neck with adolescent passion-fueled, wet kisses.

How we kept our affair from my mother, I can't remember. But she'd lost interest in me a lifetime ago, and I had discovered more pressing issues like waking up beside the deaf boy in the stuffy, city garage in the alley and finding the stillness in the waning, harvest moonlight with my nose in the crook of his acrid armpit as I pulled him deep inside of me before sneaking barefoot back to my bedroom.

When he was offered the opportunity of higher education at a specialized school in Wisconsin, the deaf boy promptly set aside his hand mower, snow shovel, and adolescent love. My formative years ended with a sloppy kiss goodbye and an indecipherable grunt in my ear.

My milky white reverie is interrupted by a persistent clubbing sound and the pain of continuous blows against my ankle. I scurry to gather my legs beneath my body and shroud my eyes with my forearm as I scramble backward against a metal vestibule doorway. The glaring sunlight in my eyes makes it impossible to see who or what is attacking me, and when I find my way to my knees, the jabbing continues at my ribcage.

"Hey. Hey, yuh guy. Yuh wit' me so fahr? Wake de fawk up. Whattaya, drunk or somethin'?"

When my eyes find focus, I make out the silhouette of an overweight, New York City beat cop poking his baton into my ribs and spilling coffee from a cardboard cup all over me: thump, splash, trump, sploosh, thump, splosh.

"Am I okay?" Instinctively, I search for the wad of cash in my front pocket, and my wallet at my back hip, and the keys to my apartment. "Was I attacked? Am I alright?"

"Wake de fawk up." He spits when he speaks, and his accent is as populous as all of upstate Rochester.

"I'm up, Officer. I'm up."

"Well, yuh weren't awake one minute ago. Dat much I can tell yuh."

"Who did this to me? Was I attacked?"

"Seems like yuh and me was in a whole different place, yuh guy."

The yellow dawn reverberates off the street signs, the three flats, and the car windows and flares into my line of vision. If I squint toward the horizon, I can make out early-morning joggers and a nanny pushing a stroller and walking some small-breed dog. The glare off the Hudson is fucking lethal. The emerging Sun is devouring the horizon. When did that happen?

"Jesus, my head is pounding."

"Do ya got some place tuh go sleep it off?"

"I'm not drunk, Officer. I was just on my way home and—"

Home is only a couple blocks away, but rest is on another plane.

"Well, ya ain't got tuh go home, butcha can't sleep here. Yuh got me or what?"

"Yeah, I got ya. I'll go home. I'll be good. I'll be good."

"Doan let me find yuh here on my way back, Son. Ya hear me or what?"

"Yeah. I promise."

All around me strays are meowing at Meatpacking District loading docks for their morning meals, and delivery trucks packed with carcasses on ice are arriving at slaughterhouses in convoy fashion. Suits are ordering coffee regular from corner carts and hailing taxi cabs on West Street as I sit for a moment and attempt to retrace my steps, recover the misplaced time.

I spun the safe, I locked the office, I walked out the big, oak door into the purple morning, and then I...and then I...and then I...

My mind is racing and I'm frantically scrolling through remembrances with little luck. And, for just one moment, if I scrunch my eyes closed as tightly as I am able...I'm trapped by my environment and viewing surreal, unfamiliar surroundings, meant to live without words with an astute understanding of separateness. It's like you don't even exist. It's like you don't even exist said the deaf boy. My brow is pouring sweat, and now I'm really frightened, rife with utter dread as I rewind my steps in backward fashion for one reliable memory to cling beside. I watch myself dying by the millimeter and wonder what if this is the time I simply disappear. Forever. I locked the safe, I spun the office...Christ, my head is gonna split in half and spill miniature nightmares all over the cobblestone street.

I locked the safe, I spun the office...and my chest is pounding like a discordant, brass band. My heart is turning flip-flops. Palpitations. Irregular beating. I'm having a heart attack. Uncontrollable trembling in my arms, legs, hands, and feet, and I'm certain this is a medical emergency. I can no longer take full, complete breaths—only loud gasps for air. Lola's thirsty. Lola's thirsty.

One one-thousand, two one-thousand, three one-thousand, four one-thousand. I'm breathing too fast. Shortness of breath, that's a sign. That's a symptom. I'm certain that something horrible took place last night and I don't want to know anymore. I no longer wish to remember. My chest is so tight, so tight, so tight, and I'm going to lose control. Simply disappear. Forever.

My vision is distorted, a brass doorknob throws back the trembling, cartoon-shaped image of me, and maybe I've already lost control, lost my mind, lost my way, because a deep-rooted sickness lives inside me. Something I can't tame. Something I can't break. This is who I am now.

And I sit up tall and shiver in the early morning sunshine, dizzy, unsteady, lightheaded, as I force my mind to focus. I locked the safe, I spun the office. I'll be good, Mama! I promise! I'll be good! I'll keep my shirt off. Always keep my shirt off. Keeps 'em coming back for more.

Somehow, with strength derived from a place I don't recognize, ensconced inside a tableau painting, in midair, and suspended in time, I coerce my trembling limbs to obey—like a floppy, balloon creature at a car lot—and I cull strength from inside to pull myself upright. I climb brick by brick with my bare hands extended on either side of the vestibule.

As soon as I'm steady on my feet, I search again for the wad of cash in my front pocket, and my wallet at my back hip, and the keys to my apartment. When I'm assured that everything vital is in its place, I walk two blocks toward shelter. A left and then a right. And I'm standing in front of the abandoned warehouse with the bored doorman dressed in complete leather gear. Isn't this why I got so frustrated with Bruiser just last night? You see, I do remember. Gay men confusing anonymous, casual sex with comfort and shelter. But I can't go home. It's impossible to sleep when you're afraid to close your eyes.

For me, at this unfortunate place, just as the sunlight spat out the horizon in its wake, there are no choices other than a piss-stained, rickety staircase to a fetid underground sex club, bare bulbs painted red, and deep, deep into the night.

TWO

THE FIRST TIME I wake up, it's nearly noon. Again with the sunlight reflecting off the Hudson River in my eyes. Only now, it's also ricocheting step by stairstep by stairstep off the fire escape outside my bedroom window and following a path downward toward the sidewalk as morning becomes afternoon. I'm still dressed in jeans and combat boots as I let one booted foot fall with a loud clunk and land sole against the seventies-style parquet apartment floor to steady my mind and, hopefully, stop the bed from spinning.

Instinctively, I search for the wad of cash in my front pocket, and my wallet at my back hip, and the keys to my apartment. I lie in the sweaty sheets and breathe deeply—one one-thousand, two one-thousand, three one-thousand—counting aloud to ease the jackhammering inside my head as all the colors of last night collide with my spinning bedroom, and I run to the bathroom and vomit hungover bile, Twenty Year Scotch, and unyielding reality into the toilet.

I let my torso fall against the subway tile, brace my body against the tub, and unlace my combat boots—admittedly an ambitious task in my hungover state. Swollen-eyed and sweating booze, I kick off the left boot, and then the right boot, and let my entire frame fall to the floor and find solace against the cold bathroom tile.

I consider that only a few dormant hours ago I stood assembled among men that huddled against one another to steady themselves at the fetid underground sex club, bare bulbs painted red, each one of us taking our turn to curse and convulse as we spill our seed and then quietly fade away.

And if I trace a path further backward, a flight attendant named César who had also descended the piss-stained, rickety staircase, considered me fortunate to have a predilection for Scotch.

"Jore berrry lucky, ju know Meeester."

"How's that, *Corazón*?"

"Scotch. Theee Scotch eees the onleee juan leeequor that doseeend make ju feeel eeel thee nesssday."

"Then I should probably have another, whaddya say, *Papi Chulo*?"

"Jaaays. Fffooorrr certeeen!" as he reaches down the front of his jockstrap and produces a mini airplane bottle of Johnny Walker Black.

At the time, I didn't realize the protuberance in César's jock consisted of a pilfered American Airlines liquor cart. It is only after having consumed half a dozen mini airplane snorts and lying here this afternoon shivering with hangover that I understand, perhaps, my Portuguese pal's encouragement to imbibe had little to do with professional research and was all consumed with his getting his ass eaten before a morning flight to "Bartheeelona."

And that's all I recall after I spun the safe, I locked the office, and I walked out the big, oak door into the purple morning. Inside my brain, a hazy remembrance plays like a movie of me stumbling into a bodega on Christopher Street, dressed in leather gear and ordering egg salad on toasted rye while suits all around me were gulping coffee regular and dashing to catch the Number 1 train. But that could have been two nights ago, too. Hell, that could have been two weeks ago. My biggest fear is that my black-outs will turn into flashbacks.

The cold bathroom floor tile makes for a suitable makeshift bed and, upon setting aside the nagging disquiet and shabbily negotiating with my unremitting restlessness, I'm content to find rest right here. With my head pounding the Portuguese National Anthem and my quasi-erect member poking sideways in my jeans, for just one moment, I scrunch my eyes closed as tightly as I am able and pray for sleep to take me.

This is the one moment I hate the most and have learned to avoid getting drunk, or stoned, or drunk and stoned, and prefer-ably passed out. I can tolerate the night terrors, but it is the time between activity and rest, life and death, the dying then, when I'm tortured by fright-filled memories of what was and lucid visions of the abominations that will be.

Sleep comes close and I am standing intimidated and sweat-stained facing the awesome responsibility of conducting an enormous orchestra. For as far as my eyes travel, there's row after row after row of tuxedoed gentlemen and ladies—each of them with their ravenous eyes set upon me, all of them eager to consume my slightest gesticula-tion. Poised to perform, they sit tall in their chairs, starved for a cuc as shiny, brass instruments throw back the trembling, cartoon-shaped image of me with no understanding of rhythm, or measure, or tone.

When I shift my hand to mop the perspiration from my forehead, an enraged section of musicians belch a deafening explosion of noise that births countless high-gloss black, miniature music notes that dance in the air. Playful at first and mesmerizing to watch, whole notes and half notes gracefully take flight and rondelet before my eyes until they realize solidarity, amass, and menacingly circle. I'm fascinated until the swarming, razor-sharp, tiny black notes attack my shins and calves, overtake my tarsals, and slither between my toes.

When I kick to free my feet there is trumpeting and the discord birthed by a multitude of offended musical notations. Quarter notes and eighth notes careen in front of me before swarming my ankles and my knees, and bars of barbed wire music immobilize my legs.

They huddle against one another to steady themselves because en masse there is strength and resoluteness. The toxic notations circle and slime in predatory style, crawl on top of, dominate, and sometimes consume each other right there, subdominant as they curse and convulse and spill ribbons of musical score. Stravinsky and Schumann and Shostakovich shackle me.

I struggle to free myself from the ever-enveloping notes, to rescue myself from the imprisonment of this nightmare, to escape the arbitrary cruelty of existence, this terrifying lifetime, and I thoughtlessly conduct more lethal music.

The more full-bodied my fight for freedom, the more prestissimo the music grows. The cacophony is near deafening beside my own labored breathing, and as I raise my hands to shield my eardrums, sixteenth notes and thirty-second notes invade the space of my unpro-

tected waist and tango deliriously atop my suffocating chest. Puccini, Paganini, and Prokofiev paralyze me.

I reach my hands high above me to claw at the air, to escape the impending annihilation, and it is an action that only produces a tsunami surge of staccato sound. My body seizes from the very heft of this wall of music, before it begins to thrust involuntarily in tempo and spew black notes from inside me, thick like ash against my tongue, dripping down the corners of my mouth which is now sealed in a permanent frown—like some malevolent god dropped it right there, crooked and broken.

Still, allegro notes waltz menacingly around my neck and trail the back of my throat. I scream in agony, but no voice comes out of me, solely murderous music that covers my face and takes away the daylight. Mozart, Mahler, and Monteverdi mummify me.

When there's just my arms above my head left unscathed, my elbows to my fingertips and further onward to the heavens, life is distorted, foggy, and I'm outside myself, a lonely, frightened painter armed with a box of paints for protection. Reality is reduced to the insistent din of sixty-fourth notes rattling against my skin...like cicada...like the music of the cicada...bleating before they fall from the trees and die.

My breathing grows raspy and irregular, frightening squalls of an impending storm. With one tremendous clap of thunder the skies open wide, and sheets of rain pelt the battleground and its whimpering, beaten-down infantry. I watch myself dying by the millimeter from inside the cocoon of bars of barbed wire music. It becomes my existence. Why is my breathing this rapid—no, shallow...this shallow—no, rapid? Either it's shallow. Or it's rapid. Which one? Otherwise, you're a gaddammed liar. One one-thousand, two one-thousand, three one-thousand. My body is pins-and-needles sensa-

tions, frozen and numb, my hands, arms, legs, fingers, toes, like a colorless autumn leaf failing and then falling from a tree.

My heart is going to burst from my chest at any moment, the palpitations so persistent, one one-thousand, two—a metronome beating, every clock in the apartment ticking, that keeps a dangerous count of the time on this earth that remains. Time is running out for me. And my mind pounds in time with the perilous beat, throbbing, throbbing, throbbing. This sinuous lifetime is spiraling, inching toward a cumulative climax. Christ, my head is gonna split in half and spill high-gloss black, miniature music notes all over the cold bathroom floor tile.

I am lightheaded. I feel faint. I pray to Jesus Christ himself. Jesus Christ from the 14th Street Y, surrounded by all the men performing unchristian-like sex acts on each other. My left arm goes limp. My fingers tingle. I attempt to pull myself upright, brace my body against the tub, climb brick by brick with my bare hands extended on either side or simply find solace against the cold bathroom floor tiles. This is the time between activity and rest, life and death.

I cannot find full, complete breaths, and I struggle for short breaths accompanied by loud gasps of air. One one-thou...that's my left arm. That's a sign. That's a symptom. The crashing waves, the purple nighttime, and the undulating tide of tortuous consciousness becomes me. I pray to Jesus Christ himself. And I wish to Jesus Christ that I was never born.

And this is how it happens. This is where they find me. All alone —that's who I am. Left out in the cold. Like garbage. Life threw me away just like garbage. Because that's who I am! And you wanna know what life is...ya wanna know? Ya wanna know who I am?

I reach inside and emit a scream that echoes with an entire life of nightmares that delivers me spiraling through the years. And with the sound of flesh and tendons as they're ripped away from the bone, I am transported from some unfamiliar astral level where night terrors are actualities and agreements are secured for many lifetimes—a discarded mass of pizzicato, percussive panic, and labored breathing on the cold bathroom floor tile.

Shattered, panting, and trembling, I weep as I realize all the time—all this fucking time—and I never once closed my eyes.

Flat on my back and desperate for sleep, I stare at the peeling, bathroom ceiling and I can hear every clock in the apartment ticking. I drag my body into a sitting position and crawl on hands and knees across the seventies-style parquet floor into the living room.

I search for a Red and a branded The Meat Market book of matches from the pocket of my leather jacket in a heap where I discarded it hours earlier, and I catch a glimpse of Jerome Cameron, the soap opera stud from *Another Tomorrow*, sculpted and shirtless and lifting weights in his apartment across the courtyard.

I shimmy across the floorboards to dodge the window and the sunlight altogether. I travel in a world beneath David Wojnarowicz posters hung inside flimsy plastic frames, beside a half-eaten, egg salad sandwich on toasted rye discarded on a wooden milk crate end table, and on top of my crumpled leather motorcycle jacket, dirty t-shirts, and worn jockstraps, and mouse droppings hidden in mine bomb fashion.

Brrriiing, brrriiing.

I jump when the phone rings even though I know what to expect. I light my smoke and procure an aluminum ashtray crowded with butts from the windowsill without ever once leaving my position on the seventies-style parquet floor. I lie motionless and inhale long, slow drags off my cigarette as the musical overture recedes inside my brain, as the countdown ticking clocks keep track of the perilous time that remains, and the jangling telephone reverberates throughout the apartment building courtyard.

Brrriiing, brrriiing.

"Dominic! Dominic! Did you wake up, you hungover whore-bag? You gonna answer that call, sweetheart, or do I need to interrupt my workout and act as your personal answering service?"

Maybe if I pretend to not hear him, he'll let me off easy this one time.

Brrriiing, brrriiing.

"Three more rings and I'm coming over there and I ain't wearing a shirt. And I'm warning you now, I've been working out all morning and I am ripe. Positively ripe. I'll bet you'd like that, Mr. Leatherman."

Or maybe Jerome Cameron will come over here and lay his perfect, perspiring soap opera physique on top of me and we'll finally fuck.

Brrriiing, brrriiing.

"Two more rings, my brother. You're really asking for some of my cannoli this time, ain't ya?"

I crawl on hands and knees across the seventies-style parquet floor and burp discarded egg salad sandwich on toasted rye as I recall my plans with Claudia to see the Stanley Stellar thing at The Gay & Lesbian Community Center this afternoon.

Brrriii—

"Hello, hello. Hi, hello—it's me."

"Hey, Girl!"

"Claudia. Don't."

"Wha?"

"Don't call me Girl, Claudia."

And from across the courtyard: "He's a girl, Claudia! A big, ol' girl! You give it to him good, sweetheart!"

"Ooooh, is that that handsome Jerome from across the way? Is he at your apartment?"

"Yes. I mean, no. I mean, yes it's Jerome and no, he's not at my apartment."

"Ooooh, Hi Jerome! Tell him I said hi, Girl!"

"No."

"Well, Jesus Effing Christ, bite my head off why don't ya? How you ever found an apartment directly across the courtyard from that delicious Jerome Cameron of *Another Tomorrow* is—"

"—they have to live somewhere, Claudia."

"*They* are people, Girl. Actors. Actors are people too, Girl."

"I lived here first, remember? And I'm serious. I'm in no mood. Cut the girl crap."

"Alright, alright already. Jesus Effing Christ. Did somebody maybe wake up on the sourpuss side of the bed, Girl?"

"Stop calling me that, Claudia!"

And echoing across the concrete courtyard that's littered with glue traps, down Barrow Street, throughout the West Village, and further onward toward the heavens: "A big, ol' girl, Claudia! That's precisely what he is, sweetheart! And don't you let him forget it neither!"

"Ooooh, hi Jerome! Hi Jerome! Tell him I said hello, Girl!"

"Why don't you just fucking call him yourself?"

"Well, if I had his phone number maybe I just might fucking do so. Jesus Effing Christ, bite my head off—"

"I didn't mean to be short"

"—why don't ya? You sound like you're in bad shape. Are you in bad shape?"

"My head hurts, that's all."

Jerome Cameron is enjoying this. "She's got a headache! Again! The big, ol' girl! Her head hurts, Dollface."

"Ooooh, hi Jerome! Hi Jerome!"

"He can't hear you!"

"Are you for real? The echo chamber in that courtyard rivals the whispering gallery at Grand Central Terminal. Jesus Effing Christ, Girl."

"That's enough. You know I hate that girl shit."

"Fine, Mary."

"Claudia!"

"What? I thought Mary was a boy's name."

"I can't fucking win."

"Oh, come on, now. You win, you win. I'm only pulling your leg. Your big, masculine, hairy third leg. Everybody knows you're not a girl, dear."

"Thank you. I had a rough—"

"—well, of course you did, darling."

"Please don't interrupt me. It isn't what—"

"—now, of course it isn't, darling."

"Listen, I jus—"

"I know. Mommie knows. And Mommie has the perfect remedy for that nasty hangover that somebody maybe, probably, most assuredly picked up at their after hours, underground sex parties. The perfect remedy, I tell you."

"Is it Hemlock?"

"Huh? No."

"Arsenic?"

"Nice try."

"Well, whaddya got to take the sting off?"

"Art!"

"Wha? Huh? Not today."

"Yes, today. Art."

"Art? Today? Oh right, the Stanley Stellar thing at the Community Center. Listen, I don't exactly—"

"Free art. I mean, art that's free. I mean I got those tickets from that producer guy I was telling you about."

"No, Claudia."

"Whaddya mean, no?"

"No art. Free or the other. I'm not feeling well today. I'm not up to walking all the way to 13th Street."

"All the way to 13th Street? Dominic, you live in Greenwich Village. Which is less than a stone's throw. Why, I've seen people crawl to 13th Street on broken cobblestone for a cocktail. And might I remind you that we have had plans in place."

Years ago, when I first started tending bar, I lost track of time in a conventional sense and set aside all but the most essential daytime activities.

"I'm sorry, Claudia, but the answer is no. Not today."

"But through art, we attain a better understanding—"

"Sweetie, no."

"—of ourselves—"

"Nope."

"—and our society."

"No, Claudia."

She calls most mornings, much too early, with plans for cultural rebirth that somehow always transform themselves into lunch, or cocktails. Usually, lunch *and* cocktails.

"Now don't be a stubborn mule."

"She's Dominic the Donkey. The big ol' donkey!"

"My head hurts."

"Nobody told you to drink enough to float Fire Island."

"That's not the line."

"What am I? Judy Garland? At this hour? Well, I'm certain my Midtown piano bar queens would tell you otherwise but still."

"Of course they would. And if you're going to quote Jud—"

"I'm talking about husbands and, Jesus Effing Christ, after five of 'em Judy Garland would most certainly concur. Lots of rich, handsome Daddies at these art affairs."

"I don't care."

"What is that supposed to mean?"

"I don't want a husband."

"What?"

"Or a Daddy."

"Now, that's just crazy talk is what that is."

"Well, it's the truth."

"Nothing could be further from the truth. Horn rimmed glasses, shirts with ties, bulging wallets. Perfect. Husband. Material."

"I. Don't. Want one."

"Don't be silly, Girl. Everybody wants a husband."

"You know she's right, Girl! Everybody does want a husband. Ya big ol' girl!" from across the concrete courtyard.

And so it goes. I plead my case, and she perseveres. I grow annoyed, and she insists. I'm as certain I'll not be ready in the thirty minutes I'll eventually agree to as I am that I'll gain a clearer understanding of Stanley Stellar's time-capsule photography from a bill plastered on Seventh Avenue.

After all, for how many months did we plan to see the Andy Warhol thing only to realize our destiny shooting pool and downing shots in East Village dive bars? While the culturally inerudite, right-wing protested the Mapplethorpe showing at The Gay & Lesbian Community Center, we sucked back nine-ounce martinis with pickled string beans in trendy Chelsea taverns with names like Dirty Dick's and The Filling Station.

"I won't take no for an answer, Girl."

"Just say yes and go, Girl. Ya big ol' girl!"

"Stop. Both of you. I don't feel well."

"We all got pain, Effie."

"This headache is debilitating."

"Oh, you're fine. Don't be such a sissy."

"You sissy, you! Big ol' sissy girl!"

"Jero...I mean, Claudia! Er, Jerome!"

"Wear something cute, Dominic. No leather. This isn't one of your after hours, underground sex parties."

"Yeah, Girl! No leather, ya big, ol' leather girl! You tell her, Claudia."

"Claudia, I haven't said yes yet."

"I'll meet you at Food Bar on Eighth Avenue. We can grab a quick bite and something boozy while we're there. Maybe we can sit in their outdoor cafe...so warm for this late in September."

My stomach turns cartwheels at the notion. And from the apartment window across the way: "Tell her I said goodbye, Dominic. Tell her I'll see her Tuesday night at The Carlyle Room. Tell her I'll see her there. Ya big, ol' girl!"

"Stop that! You, too. I am not a girl."

"Nah. You're a big, ol' girl!"

"Ugh. Jerome says goodbye, Claudia. He'll see you Tuesday."

"Ooooh, goodbye Jerome! Tell him I said goodbye, Girl!"

"I give. I give."

"Thank heavens! I'll see you soon!"

She clicks off the line. For a small time, I sit lifelessly in my easy chair and stare across the courtyard at Jerome, still shirtless and still lifting weights in front of his window.

"Well, whaddya waiting for? You still gotta shower and dress. Ya big, ol' girl!"

Jerome knows I'm studying him from afar. In the past, he's let his hand fall to cup his balls and flop his enormous, flaccid dick in my direction, but today he's content to lift his barbells and water his window boxes all while grinning from one ear to the next with perfect, polished soap opera teeth. He lifts his weights and makes love to his reflection in a full length, stand-up mirror situated prominently in his living room.

Jerome Cameron's physical features are a tribute to the statues that dot his native countryside, and I'd be willing to wager Wednesday night's tips at The Meat Market that his given surname is more along the lines of Cameroni. His chiseled face is perfectly complemented by fat, black curls that fall against his eyebrows, which he's forever pushing out of his silver-blue eyes. His smile is dazzling, and he knows it too well, as perfect for delivering pointed sarcasm as it is pointless soap opera dialogue. Not in it for the love. He's in it for the loads of hot babes.

Michelangelo would have paid to immortalize this body, with its sinewy biceps, powerful pectorals, and a perfectly groomed, vertical stripe of hair extending from his navel to his pubic hair to heaven.

I watch him until I become aroused, tracing my erect dick through my jeans. Jerome drops his eyes to meet my own, spits on his index and middle finger, and uses them to methodically drag a trail of saliva from the base of his throat to the elastic band of his white underwear. He brings his perfect, pink lips close enough to his window to cause a tiny fog on the glass and mouths the words, "Ya big, ol' girl," and howls until he doubles over with laughter and disappears from sight.

Once again time is running out for me. I move to take my place. I chase a cockroach down the bathtub drain with my big toe, spend moments under a shower that knows no temperature more than lukewarm, and brush my teeth. I dress in a tight-fitting white t-shirt and worn-through 501s, grab my Yankees baseball cap, and dash out the cognac-colored vestibule door and down the luminescent aggregate, apartment stair steps to meet the day.

Walking the West Village is always an adventure. The grid that characterizes Manhattan falls off course here, and streets burst into life between other streets, only to twist circuitously and disappear again blocks later. There is no other place with so many stymied tourists, holding their maps sideways and asking for directions.

"How do I get to West 5th?"

"Dere is no West 5th."

West 4th Street tangles up to cross West 10th in a manner that makes absolutely no sense.

"How do I get to West 11th?"

"Just follow West 4th, it's de toid street aftuh West 10th. Yuh got me so fahr?"

I decide to prowl Christopher Street, which is also Stonewall Place depending on which sign you happen to see first. Rife with adult bookstores boasting basements that guarantee twenty-four hour action or the price of admission returned, with racy slogans like 'There's Always Somebody On Hand,' C Street will forever feel like home to me. Slice joints selling pepperoni pie so oil-slicked it renders its paper-plate delivery vehicle translucent in three seconds, always dribbling down my chin. The constant parade of handsome strangers wearing tight-fitting white t-shirts and worn-through 501s—their quantum, tunneling eyes darting from carnivorous gaze and clone style mustache to carnivorous gaze and clone style mustache in the warm September sunshine make it a favorite with the locals. Eyes that connect with urgent reciprocation and bodies that instinctively crash and retreat, crash and retreat. There's no better panacea for a stubborn hangover than Christopher Street for a greasy slice of pie and a darkroom hand job.

A short time after that, Claudia and I are seated at an outdoor cafe on Eighth Avenue. Four blocks from the Stanley Stellar thing at The Center, we're sipping spicy Bloody Marys at Food Bar. She's all energy this afternoon, wearing too much make-up, smoking ultra-thin cigarettes and wildly punctuating the lavender smoke with her exaggerated gesticulation—and almost spilling out of her white flimsy plastic, outdoor cafe chair, not to mention the plunging neckline of her baby-doll pink, rhinestone emblazoned CRAZY FOR SWAYZE t-shirt.

"Claudia! You're making shit up again."

"Jesus Effing Christ, Dominic. Like I would lie to *you!*"

"Alright, then. Start again...but go slowly. I'm still a little boozy from last night."

"Günther. His name is Günther."

"And you met this guy—"

"—at Wild Horse. The Wild Horse Tavern. On Hudson."

"Okay. You met Günther at Wild Horse."

"And we were up until sunrise. My head resting on his perfect pectorals as he read poetry to me in his bed."

"Poetry? Oh, come now."

"Well, kinda poetry. Nietzsche."

"Wha? Huh? Wait a minute—"

"Yes, I'm certain. It was Nietzsche."

"Which Nietzsche?"

"How the hell do I know which Nietzsche? Do I look like a Philosophy Major to you?"

Claudia's most striking feature is her glamorous mane of sultry, soap opera hair; big, bouncy curls colored the perfect hue of Clairol Nice'n Easy No. 6R Light Copper that she flips back and fluffs when she's making a conversational point or flicks over her shoulder when she's performing for the room from her flimsy white plastic outdoor cafe chair.

"So, he reads Nietzsche in bed."

"Aloud. To me. He reads Nietzsche aloud to me in bed."

"No way."

"Yes way. In its original German."

"That is such a New York moment."

"Jesus Effing Christ, right? You know I'm not one for books, sweetie. No, a reader I am not, Dominic—but as soon as he started expounding all those guttural existentialisms, I was ready for my own guttural *pounding*. The next thing you know I was poking around in his boxer shorts and—"

"Aaanddd—"

"Aaanddd what?"

"You know!"

"Oh, I don't know. Six, seven...nine tops. And that's tops.

Definitely uncut. I mean, I think it was uncut. It looked like a tortoise."

"Claudia! You're too much."

"Jesus Effing Christ, Girl! You asked."

Even as we fantasize ourselves to be intellectuals and pretend to assume lofty, cerebral debate when strangers are within earshot, there is no more delightful a dishing session that trickles from our tipsy lips than the one that involves men. Oh, occasionally banter between us transpires that concerns Liza Minnelli falling off the wagon *again* or tabloid pics of Elizabeth Taylor wheeling outta Limelight in a motorized scooter at 8:00 a.m., but it is a comparatively lethargic discussion. Any topic at all that begins with he or his is certain to elicit playful shrieks and rolled-back eyes.

"I'm thinking of switching."

"Teams?"

"Cocktails, Dominic—cocktails. Keep up, Girl. So much sodium. One more of these and I'll be as bloated as a pregnant Pomeranian."

"Ewww."

"Ewww what, Girl? Did I tell you I suspected Mommy's little Pom Pom, Persephone, was knocked up? Did I? Jesus Effing Christ, that slutty bitch. Turns out it was just the bloat. The bloat! Well, that's nature for you. One ginormous fart and she was back to shaking her tail all over 22nd Street."

Even the waiter finds her turn of phrase amusing. At his grimy, outdoor service station, he sets his *Next Magazine* aside and shakes his head with laughter.

"That's grotesque, Claudia."

"That's gross. *That's so gross, Claudia.* It's freaking nature. Well, I'm definitely switching. And I should probably move on to something concocted with Gin. Never mix, never worry. That's what they say. Isn't that what they say, Girl?"

"Purportedly."

"Well, fuck what they say. That's what I say. I wonder what the Martoonis are like at this joint?"

"Half gasoline."

"Well, that's merrier than Perrier."

"Cute."

"One tries."

"One must. Maybe ask our waiter?"

"Ask our waiter what?"

"What people say? How the Martinis rank at this place?"

"You know, I would, Dominic…but I feel bad making him exert himself. He walks oddly. Like he hurt himself. Why do you think he walks like that?"

"War wound."

"Really? He's not all beardy and crazy-eyed. He doesn't look like a vet."

"More like a social veteran. He's actually not that bad a fella. His name is 'Sparre and he's fresh off the boat."

"From Italy?"

"From Staten Island."

"Jesus Effing Christ, do all you Italian people know each other?"

"Just the gay Italians. It's a secret handshake we share."

"He's a gay, too?"

"He works at a bar. In Chelsea. I'm gonna repeat that for you. The man works at a bar in Chelsea, Claudia. He's either a homosexual or he plays one on television."

"Sometimes I don't get your humor."

"Meh. Sometimes I'm not that funny."

"And how do we know this newfound homosexual fellow from Staten Island with the odd gait, Dominic? Hmmm? Do they hold Meet & Greets at your afterhours underground sex parties?"

"By invitation only. Somehow I never make the list."

"Yeah, right, Girl. Like I buy that."

"Claudia! Like I would lie to *you!*"

It's arguable that the incessant talk of men is embarrassingly shallow, unenlightened and socially unaware.

"So, how did you meet him? This Sambuca of Staten Island fame."

"It's Guasparre, if you're formal."

"I most certainly am not."

"I know him from The Meat Market."

"And how did he hurt himself?"

"Speed dating."

The thick, bristles of chin hair that overtake a man's face late in the day. Whether he dresses to the left, whether he dresses to the right. Circumcised, uncircumcised. Something in between the two. The smell of Whiskey and cigarettes on his breath and against your neck as he's shivering on top of you with orgasm. All fitting fodder for libation-fueled tête-à-tête. Never a trivial conversation between Claudia and I is left stones unturned.

"There is nothing—and I mean nothing, Girl—that knots my knickers more than a quick wad blower."

"Ahhh. Popacockaphobia."

"Call it what you might. It's all the same to me. A premature fur burster really chaps my hide."

"Trouser batter from two-stroke Tommy."

"Sheesh! Talk about a short cumming."

"Or a manly misfire."

"Quick draw."

"Speed seed."

"Would youse two like tuh hear about de early bird special, or what?"

"We haven't even looked, 'Sparre. Give us a hair longer, will ya?"

"Just holluh when you're ready."

"Thanks, pal. You know, it's never really mattered, Claudia. Not to me. Ten pumps tops, one ginormous fart, and I'm back to shaking my tail all over 22nd Street."

"Jesus Effing Christ. Slutty bitches—the both of you."

"Also, afterwards I'm always starving for a Prosciutto and Provolone Panini from the nearest bodega."

"Just like a man. One quick orgasm and then the Eleven o'clock Number is a Prosciutto and Provolone sandwich. I wouldn't be sharing that skill set on your resume, Girl."

"I'm not a girl."

"All this talk of Prosciutto. Where's that menu? Now I'm peckish."

"Don't you mean *peckerish*?"

"Huh? Sometimes I don't get your humor."

"It's a curse. Sometimes I'm just an Italian ham."

"As I can only notice yuh are perusin' de menu. Maybe now it is de perfect time dat I can brin' ovuh some chow fawh yuh two lovely people."

"I didn't know you worked here, 'Sparre. Since when have you waited tables at Food Bar?"

"It's a new adventure fawh me. Ya' dig? It's only my toid shift on de floawh. Yuh know, waitin' de tables."

"How interesting, Doll. Now, I'll take a—"

"Since I was a young boy, I wawhked as a meatball selluh. On de Staten Island side. I sold de Meatball Submarines at de St. Geawhge Ferry Terminal. And de othuh day I said de time has come fawh yuh tuh make an adventure, Guasparre. Yuh with me? So, I boarded de boat tuh South Ferry. When I arrived, I felt it was time tuh look fawh a new job. I took de MTA Bus from de tip of Manhattan to Chelsea. Yuh with me? That's how I ended up on de floawh here. Waitin' de tables."

"Fascinating. Do you think I might be able to—"

"Dis might be all tempawhary. Ya' dig? All I know is from wawhkin' in de service industry. It's de only wawhk I have evuh perfawhmed. From hawkin' meatballs at de ferry terminal tuh meetin' homos at de fairy central here in Chelsea. I could be bettuh at somethin' else, too. Okay? I'm still findin' myself. Yuh with me? Always lookin' tuh be a bigguh man. Okay? One day I have my dream tuh go tuh college. At de CUNY College of Staten Island. Ya' dig? Dis I am fully aware of fawh certain. Dere I will study medical procedures and such impawhtant tings like dat dere. Yuh got me so fahr?"

"That's wonderful, man. Everybody's got a dream."

"Indeed, they do. I'm dreaming of a Martini right now. Drinks, Girl, drinks! Now, Spumoni, I'll have a frosty cold Gin Martini, if you please. Extra, extra dirty. No olives, thank you very much. I've got a figure to look out—ooohhh, Girl, get him! Across the street. Polka dot umbrella, pinstripe suit..."

Should it ever happen that conversation falters, which is rare, all we need to do is find our inspiration in the studs that saunter the sidewalks situated with trendy Chelsea taverns.

"I'll have a dark beer. Anything in a bottle please, 'Sparre."

"I'm aftuh it, friends. Yuh with me? Let me just write dis down and—"

"You see, Claudia, now that's what I'm talking about. Him right there! Now, that's a man. The one wearing the motorcycle boots. There's something about a man in motorcycle boots."

"If I offered up a guess, I would have tuh say it is becawze yuh picture him ridin' around wit' a hog between his legs all day. Yuh with me? Ya' dig, or what? *Che palle!* Do yuh know what I mean, Brudduh, or what?"

"Lovely thought, Doll. Yes, thanks a lot. Now, might we get those drinkies, Spumoni?"

"Claudia! Take a look at this guy."

"Who him?"

"No, *himmm*! The man I pointed out to you. Across the street, rounding the corner of 17th Street. He's built like a—"

"Like a proverbial brick shithouse. Look at those shoulders. Hubba hubba."

"Look at those enormous delts with the tattoo sleeves. Just the kinda arms you could rest inside forever, protected and warm and safe."

"Don't look now, Girl, but he's smiling at you from across Eighth Avenue."

"Christ, that jawline. Just look at his smile, so benevolent...and the slightest bit lewd. Sexy. Familiar. Oh, this man has got it going on, alright."

Claudia flips back and fluffs her perfect, Clairol Nice'n Easy No. 6R Light Copper soap opera hair and flicks it over her shoulder as she's preparing to perform for the room from her flimsy white plastic outdoor cafe chair. Her ultra-thin cigarette creates halos around her head, and she wildly punctuates the lavender smoke with her exaggerated gesticulation, and all I can see is this handsome man with the sexy smile growing closer and closer.

His gray buzzcut glints in the late September sunshine. His amber eyes dance alongside my own. This guy exudes masculinity with an ever-broadening, seductive grin as he grows closer, motor-cycle boot step by motorcycle boot step. I digest him with my eyes, knowing nothing more than to breathe this man deep inside me until I feel ribbons of him expanding in my chest and intoxicating my brain.

So mesmerized am I by him that I barely notice my heart beating in my ears, and the tiny hairs at the scruff of my neck stand tall with anticipation. As I reach to receive his lumbering lion's paw, I inadvertently disengage the flimsy white plastic outdoor umbrella, as Guasparre Gagliardi stumbles, and fumbles, and empties the contents of his waiter's tray made up of frosty cold Gin Martini, if you please, extra, extra dirty, no olives thank you very much all over my lap.

"Aye! Aye! Aye! *Vaffanculo*!"

"For fucks' sake, that's cold!"

"Jesus Effing Christ."

Moments later, Claudia is full-throttle expelling a monologue from *Iphigenia*—exhaling billows of lavender smoke that could prohibit the expeditionary force against Troy.

"Sambuca, you dolt, this is my good date night outfit!"

In a consummate exemplification of karmic contrition, 'Sparre is now on his knees in front of me. Returning the favor, blotting at my saturated crotch with a barrage of beverage napkins, and all I can think to stammer is, "What are you doing here?"

"Well, it's nice to see you too, baby."

"I'm sorry...hi, hello, hi there, ummm—for fucks'sake, I'm all wet."

"I can see that. Baby, here lemme help."

"Nah, I'm good. I'm good. Ummm—what are you doing here? 'Sparre, stop that. I'm fine. I said I'm fine, for fucks'sake! Now...where did you say you're coming from?"

"I just finished working out at Chels—"

"—Chelsea Gym. 17th Street. Of course, now it makes sense."

"Uh-huh. And I was walking up Eighth Avenue, minding my own business, listening to Lisa Stansfield on my Walkman Cassette, when out of the corner of my eye I noticed *the* most handsome man on the entire island of Manhattan."

"Clearly you didn't get to the *All Around the World* song yet."

"Wha? Oh, good one, baby! And I thought to myself, what kind of self-respecting, homosexual man in good standing would I be if I didn't—"

"Oh, so you're in good standing, are you? You're the one! How do you do? Dominic can be so unmannered. My name is Claudia."

"Hello, Claudia. My name...sayyyy, where do I know you from? Now, don't tell me. Did I meet you at Lucy Badalamenti's kid's christening in Astoria last week?"

"She's right. I can be so rude sometimes. This is Claudia. And you'd have a better chance meeting her on Fire Island than at Immaculate Conception on 29th Street."

"I do a Cabaret Show. On Fire Island. At The Blue Whale. Just this side of the Pavillion...or that side of Judy Garland Memorial Park. Depending which way you're going. Or coming!"

"Ha! That's very clever, but no—no, that's not it—"

"She's de pad. She's de pad."

"Wha? Oh, heya Gagliardi. Shit, I didn't know you worked here. The lovely Ms. Claudia and I were jus—"

"*Maddon' mi!* She's de freakin' pad, Brudduh. Okay? She's de feminine unnerwears protecshun fawh de lady privates. Right? Ya' dig, or what? She dances on de television."

"And you watch too many soap operas, Staten Island! Don't you have cocktails to spill on unsuspecting customers somewhere?"

"The pad? What pad?"

"I play a tap-dancing maxi pad in a feminine hygiene ad spot on daytime television. And, Jesus Effing Christ, let me tell you one thing. That costume was a bitch. I'm all but lame from that gig and ought to strangle my agent—the gobsmacked fool. But he does get me work."

"Well, I will tell yuh in all truth dat I tink yuh are very wonderful and dance like a fuckin' rock star, young lady. Yuh got me so fahr? On my mudduh—may she rest in peace, of cawhse. Yuh got me so fahr? Yuh wit' me, or what?"

"Thanks, Doll. Now, do you suppose we can get some drinks? Perhaps something that we don't have to wear home this time? Was it Spumoni? No. Sambuca? Am I right?"

"*Si, si.*"

"Well, I think it's wonderful, too! I've never met a television star in person."

"Oh, and Sambuca, bring something refreshing and *cocktailiscious* for my new friend."

"Well, I'll be damned. Baby, you never told me you hung out with famous actors."

"I, ummm. Well, I guess it never really came up."

"I also do the voiceover for Scrubby Bubble Number Two during Prime Time."

"Excellent!"

"I was up for Scrubby Bubble Number One, but Number Two is actually more of a nuanced character."

"They were lucky to book you."

"And you're a mensch. Also, Jesus Effing Christ, just look at you—easy on the eyes is an understatement. Listen, the Dow Chemical Company is paying for lunch this afternoon if you care to join us?"

"Oh, I'd hate to interrupt."

"Nonsense. We'd be delighted. In fact, Dominic was just reminding me how you two kids know each other."

"I'm certain he's already got his afternoon planned out, Claudia. We wouldn't—"

"—we work together at The Meat Market. I'm the doorman there."

"Well, Jesus Effing Christ, clearly I'm hanging out at the wrong bars."

"Clearly, my dear."

Instantly, they are old friends—the vainglorious Massengill starlet and the freshly scrubbed, muscle-ripped stud from Chelsea Gym on 17th Street. He borrows a flimsy white plastic outdoor cafe chair from a neighboring table and saddles up beside me. Instantly, I feel my heart swell in my boxer briefs.

Claudia is talking about peeing in the stall next to Phyllis Diller at an AIDS Benefit Concert and the doorman is enthralled: communicating with his massive hands, every third moment resting a paw on my knee, tugging on my earlobe, and bellowing his benevolent laughter.

Up close, he is ruggedly handsome. I've known the man for ten years, maybe more, and this is the first time I've seen him in the daylight. The dappled autumn sunlight dances on his skin, reflecting deep within the hazel flecks of his doting eyes and picking up the tiny golden hairs that trail his forearms, his wrists, and the backs of his fingers.

I think about nudging my torso against his own, into the crook of his arm so he'll rest his muscled arm across my shoulder, his thumb and forefinger at the nape of my neck. But for now, it's all I can do to keep up with conversation and pressure my hungover, Twenty Year Scotch paralyzed brain to produce an occasional witticism.

"So, do the two of you often share the same shifts at The Meat Market?"

"He's the doorman. At the bar, ummm...The Meat Market bar where I work. You know, I've told you about—"

"Yes, dear. This we've previously established. That Martini slapped you right upside the head, didn't it? Maybe you should always drink them from down below. You know, with your little head instead."

"Claudia!"

"Relax, baby. She's making a joke. She's being funny. She's very funny."

"And you, my handsome new friend, should really take in my cabaret act. If you find *this* funny, you should hear it all set to music!"

"She really is quite extraordinary."

"Thank you, Dominic. For that, we can all thank The Brooklyn Academy of Music. As I was saying, I play The Blue Whale on weekends. Because, as we all know, summer weekends are when all the well-to-do queens pack their poodles and their speedos and their well-to-do poodles in speedos and make the journey to Mecca. The Island of Fire, as it is most commonly referred to in such circles. And this city becomes a ghost town."

"Absolutely it does."

"A girl's gotta make an honest buck someplace. Some place where she can make a difference, ya know?"

"She also plays The Carlyle Room on Tuesday nights."

"Thank you, Dominic. Yes, she does. And how kind it is of you to recall. Jesus Effing Christ, I can't remember the last time I saw you there! I know, I know—that would entail getting you into a shirt with a collar. Ahem. Oh, how I adore my Midtown piano bar queens. And how my Midtown piano bar queens love me right back."

"I'll bet you're fantastic."

"You really should come see for yourself. It's a standing gig—Tuesday nights at The Carlyle Room—but anymore it feels more like a Revival Meeting. I gather all my Midtown piano bar queens next to me and help them to feel better. I am a healer of sorrow-filled souls. Oh, we drink, and we laugh. It really is quite an evening...and evidently, the more the boys drink, the funnier I become."

"Excellent!"

"Exactly. You know the drill. I sing 'em all and they stay all night. And then they roll out feeling somehow lighter, happier. For a short while at least."

"You're just like an overnight attending physician at Saint Vincent's Hospital."

"Laugh all you like, Girl. It's a gift. One day I will be recognized for my gifts. *Recognized*. Jesus Effing Christ, where is Sambuca with those cocktails?"

The doorman's breath is sweet as he shares his tales. His freshly scrubbed body smells faintly of perspiration from his workout and cigarette smoke from the walk over, and my manhood betrays me inside my jeans. Each time he gestures, he traces my forearm with a rough-fingered touch, lumbers his arm across my shoulders, pulls me close into him, and clumsily slaps his muscled thigh against my own.

"Now, this has gotta be going back two years, maybe even three years—am I right, baby? Jeez, where does the time go? Anyway. This sexy guy—this one sitting right here next to me—is behind the bar all night just like always, mixing cocktails and having conversations."

"Always preferable to having cocktails and mixing conversations."

"Wha? Oh, yeah. Good one, baby. Yeah, I'm pretty certain this story goes back three years. The time when we ended up in the Emergency Room at Saint Vincent's."

"Girl! You never told me about this?"

"Oh, it's nothing. It was nothing."

"Paronychia is what the doctor called it. This fifteen-year-old punk of an overnight attending physician who looked exactly like Neil Patrick Harrison, but only gay."

"It's Harris. I think it's Harris. Bar Rot. I'm pretty sure he called it Bar Rot. That much I know for certain. A fungal, bacterial infection that most commonly occurs from hands and fingers that are constantly wet. The moisture mixes with the citric acid from lemons and limes and breaks down the cuticle of the nail, allowing bacteria into the nail bed, blah, blah, blah."

"Ewww, Girl."

"His fingers were swollen like Italian sausages at The Feast of San Gennaro."

"Ohhh, I love that festival. Those cannoli are to die!"

"Wha? Oh, yeah. So good. Anyway, I have to laugh when I think of wrapping Dominic's *cannolis* with prophylactics procured from the coin-operated condom machine in the tiny john at The Meat Market. Remember, baby? Do ya remember? One for every Paronychia filled piggy."

"No expense is too great. The non-lubricated variety of prophylactic to boot. And whether they're Paronychia filled or not, I believe piggies are toes. Anyhow, Doogie Howser instructed me that a stern dose of antifungal salve and keeping my hands dry and moisture free for seven to ten days was the only path to non-Paronychia piggy-filled salvation. But I was saving tips to pay my rent which was due in a week."

"I believe you were saving your tips toward a decent share on Fire Island that year."

"Well, honestly, who could blame me? A good share is the only way to fly. There's more to find on Fire Island than dicks in the Meat Rack. Some say in the perfect share you might just find yourself."

"I went to the Underwear Party once."

"Oh, Claudia, you did not."

"I did so. It was one night after my midnight show at The Blue Whale. Somehow, I lost my very inebriated friend, and someone told me they saw him at the Underwear Party. So, I marched right in and found him wandering the hollows. And we clung to each other for dear life—one tentative step at a time for what seemed like an eternity, ultimately feeling our way back to the Sayville Ferry."

"Claudia, you are too much."

"Quite possibly, Girl. But I realized something that night. There's a lesson to be learned. Experiencing the Underwear Party is a lot like living in Queens. No one can hear you scream, it's difficult to breathe, and you step into a world of working stiffs only to end up desperate to be home and safe."

"Dis one time I did mushrooms on Fire Island. Which, of cawhse, I had nevuh even heard of befawh. Yuh got me so fahr? And I just started wanderin' all ovuh de boardwawhk. From Cherry Grove tuh de Pines. From de Pines tuh Cherry Grove. Ya' dig? Soonuh than latuh, I decided tuh lay down right on de boardwawhk becawze I was exhausted. Also, it felt like de best tin' tuh do becawze, of cawhse, I was extremely high. Okay? I really wanted a cigarette. So, I meandered ovuh tuh dis house wit' lights on where I saw dis leadduh daddy smokin' a cigarette. Okay? Well, he was like, 'Can I help yuh, or what?' And I told him I really needed a cigarette. I'd even give him a dollar. Right? And he was like, 'No, sawhry, we have nuttin' fawh yuh,' and slammed de doawh right in my face".

"Sambuca—that is the saddest story I have ever heard."

"Well, anyway. Here we go! Fresh drinks fawh de table, ya dig? And de one dat belongs tuh de young lady—well, dat one is from me, okay? Fawh bein' such a clumsy *strunz*."

"Well, thank you! You're never too successful an actress to not accept a complementary and frosty cold Gin Martini, extra, extra dirty if you please, no olives thank you very much that happens your wray. For that, we can all thank The Brooklyn Academy of Music."

"So dis here refreshin' cocktail is cawhtesy of me. *Saluti!* May yuh always *foonah* your bread in de pot of gravy or yuh will be considered a real *mezzo-finocchio*. Right? *Saluti, saluti!*"

"Yes, Gracias. I'm certain."

"And can I possibly get a beverage fawh my good friend de doawhman, or what? Dominic, *chat il tuo ragazzo dovrebbe bere?* What is it dat I can get for your boyfriend dis fine afternoon?"

"No, no. It isn't like that—"

"Wha? Oh, yeah. Well, what's it like then, baby?" He playfully tugs on my nipple ring.

Suddenly, I find myself without words, struggling for breath. Trapped twenty feet below sea level and petrified to open my mouth because water will overtake my lungs, without taking action, between activity and rest, life and death, the dying then. I examine the sooty clouds above me as they eclipse the Blue Harvest Moon. I have an unfounded fear of open water. Senseless because I am an accomplished swimmer, even earned my first coin working as a life-guard at the Pulaski Park Public Pool.

Covering the nighttime shift as a teenager, I wait all evening for the community jocks to depart, watching the Moon modulate from orange to yellow to harvest blue as it makes its hesitant ascent into the evening sky. And then I venture to the deep end of the pool with graceful, intention-filled strokes and float motionlessly on top of the water.

On clear nights, after the sooty clouds depart, my body drifts without direction as I listen to the cicada chirp, brekekekex brekekekex, and far off in the distance the haunting chooga chooga chooga of an elevated train, and stare down the Blue Harvest Moon. I expel all the air from my body, and I sink methodically, spirit-lessly, to the floor of the Pulaski Park Public Pool.

I study the demented beams of moonlight from beneath the surface and emit small bubbles of breath until my lungs are on fire, overcome and about to burst from lack of oxygen, and wish to Jesus Christ that I was never born. One one-thousand, two one-thousand, three one-thousand. Then, with the disquiet and angst that only a young man can summon, I desperately claw at the water around me and furiously propel myself to the surface, gasping for oxygen and grabbing at life.

Claudia rescues me from the sooty clouds of reverie with an especially robust "Jesus Effing Christ!" as she flicks her mane of sultry, Clairol Nice'n Easy No. 6R Light Copper soap opera hair over her shoulder and executes a choreographed dance, performance art, for the room from her flimsy white plastic outdoor cafe chair.

"What? What's the matter?"

"The time! Look at the time!" she cries as she exhibits a stage wink they notice in Poughkeepsie. Now I'm getting nervous.

"Wha? Huh?"

"I completely forgot about my audition!"

"But you don't have an audit—"

"I most certainly do too have an audition. The one I was telling you about."

"I have no recollection of any new audition."

"Well, of course you do. I told you all about it. Dorothy in *The Wizard of Oz*. Summer Stock in Westchester."

"Dorothy?"

"Gale. As in Gale, Girl. Admittedly, I'm a little long in the tooth for the role. But it is Westchester, after all. And I'm terribly late. Terribly, terribly late."

"I'll bet you'll be fantastic."

"She doesn't have an audition. She never told me about any audit—"

"Oh, I did too. And I don't have time to argue with you, Girl."

"I'm not a—"

"I've got to grab a...ummm, er...I mean, I've got to catch a—"

"—a train?"

"Exactly! Exactly that, Mr. Doorman. I'm terribly, terribly late and I've got to catch a train. A train to Westchester. Spumoni! Sambuca! Jesus Effing Christ! Where the hell has he gotten off to now?" She waves her credit card in the air, creating lavender smoke rings around her head.

"*Sì, bella signora?*"

"Sambuca, I'm going to need the check, puhleeese."

"I'll secure dat fawh yuh in a New Yawhk moment. Yuh with me? Right, or what? Do yuh get it, or what? I sometimes considuh dat I should be on de stage myself. Like perhaps it is my true callin'. Operatin' on de stage. Yuh got me so fahr? Yuh wit' me, or what?"

Claudia is stubbing out her ultra-thin cigarette, collecting her Gucci Marmont Matelassé bag, fitting her pink Christian Dior Cat Eye Sunglasses, and smiling so wide she can barely contain herself. She wildly punctuates the halo of lavender smoke around her with exaggerated gesticulation as she autographs the check with all the exuberance and dramatic flair of Patti LuPone outside a stage door.

Before I can protest any further, she slips tickets to the Stanley Stellar thing at The Gay & Lesbian Community Center into the doorman's hands. With a kiss that leaves a perfect, pink imprint on each of our cheeks, including 'Sparre, and a wave of her manicured French tips, she makes her exit down Eighth Avenue, giggling to herself, and humming something by Harold Arlen. Off to see the wizard, indeed. Westchester, my ass.

One final, futile outcry. "You're headed the wrong direction to Grand Central, ya know!"

"Goodbye, Girrrrrlllllll."

And just like that, we are two.

"Oh, boy. Do I murder her now or wait until later?"

"Wha? Oh, I think she's adorable."

"Now. Definitely now."

Ten minutes later, the doorman and I are strolling side by side through history. Established in a stunning, brick Italianate structure originally built as Public School 16, The Gay & Lesbian Community Center has been a resource for the community since its founding in the early eighties. The building served as maritime trade schools for more than a century until a ragtag activist group of gays and lesbians offered to purchase 208 West 13th Street from the City of New York. At the time, *The New York Times* published an article with the headline 'Sale of Site to Homosexuals Planned.' And upon amassing approximately $1.5 million dollars in private donations, the founders paid cash for the property and incorporated the premiere center for gay and lesbian services.

The Center organized to rally around the AIDS crisis as well as to provide a physical space for the community to hold events and meetings. From its central location, it incubated numerous, small grassroots organizations—many of which are still active today, and its initial cultural programs featured prominent figures from the arts, politics, and academia such as Audre Lorde, Fran Lebowitz, and Quentin Crisp among others. Near the end of the 1980s, activist and playwright Larry Kramer raged at the government's unresponsiveness to the epidemic from the steps on the building and motivated the crowd to create ACT UP, the AIDS Coalition to Unleash Power. Today, the operation has grown to become the largest Gay and Lesbian Multi-Service Organization on the East Coast.

Once inside, we saunter shoulder to shoulder taking in Stellar's erotically charged photography. I can feel the heat of his body next to mine, the hair on his forearms brushing against my own, and occasionally his fingertips at the small of my spine. Not for one solitary moment does this stallion's touch pass me unnoticed. It's time for liberation alright. Oh, how I yearn.

At first we peruse the prolific imagery in silence. Studying our forefathers and then some. Standing in front of Stellar's evocative *Peter at the Door*, our conversation shifts to include some of the most personally revealing thoughts we've shared.

"You really like this, baby, dontcha?"

"Well, you can't argue with photos of half-naked men."

"Half-naked?"

"Well, some of them have shirts on."

"It's more than that for you though, isn't it? Like you could lose yourself in these pictures. I can see that in your eyes."

"History, I suppose. Our history. It fascinates me."

"Ahhh. Stonewall. The riots and all that."

"More than Gay Liberation. More than Stonewall. I mean, just look at these photographs. The fear, the desperation, the rebellion—sure, I see that. But also the beauty, the love, the sense of community."

"The brotherhood."

"Exactly. One day somebody has gotta write it down...record all the intimate observations—before they're gone and nobody remembers it right. The way it actually went down, ya know?"

"I'm not certain the general public is ready for all that reality, half-naked or not half-naked. This isn't The Guggenheim and these ain't Picassos we're perusing. Oh, not that the art is any less important. It's just that when it comes down to facts, we're still looking at pictures of naked men in our community center. From the comfort of our own living room, ya know?"

"I think it's profound."

"Sure, it's great camera work. What I'm saying is this isn't a Fifth Avenue exhibition. Sometimes I'm shocked the masses are as comfortable as they are—or as comfortable as they *say* they are—with our antics. You know, I've seen change happen. Acceptance. I've watched acceptance come to pass. Things I never fathomed that I would witness as a kid. But when it comes right down to it, we've only progressed a finite—"

"History in motion. These photographs are the proof in the pudding. And whether we take them in at some art gallery uptown or right here in our own digs, these courageous souls...these men found the fearlessness inside themselves to document their surroundings. So that one day we could better understand them. And, in turn, learn more about ourselves. Where we came from, ya know? This is the genesis of us. Our fear and desperation, our rebellion, our love, our beauty. Our history. Our brotherhood. Talk about nakedness. Mark my words—one day they'll teach these lessons in school."

"To me that seems...well, I dunno—that's a far away future, baby. You and I see these photographs with different eyes. To us these pictures are more than a huddle of randy homos on the Christopher Street Piers. Maybe it's just meant for us. For our appreciation alone. I don't see Mrs. Miller in Cedar Rapids teaching her sixth-grade classroom the importance of understanding a system of hanky codes...or...or the intricacies of knowing which button left unbuttoned on your 501s is code for your favorite sexual position."

"Wait! There's a code for that?"

"Wha? Oh, good one, baby. You know what I'm saying. My question is what does a handful of horny, shirtless fellas posing in front of the camera on our own turf, our playground, the piers for chris'sakes—prove to anybody? What does that teach others about us as gay men? You know, about the way we lived?"

"It documents the way we survived. The way we survive still. And that's for everybody to see."

"Agreed. But who else is gonna see it showcased in the middle of The Gay & Lesbian Community Center except us?"

"Word will get out. You see, it's this universal language that these men discovered. The horny, shirtless fellas posing in front of the camera at the Christopher Street Piers, and the men before them, and the men before them even—they stumbled upon the secret, too. An entire language of gemstone discoveries that exists between the lines, both hidden and heart-touching. The history was passed down. We learned it. We teach each other. It's written on the walls of the caves. Hieroglyphics."

"What caves? Hieroglyphics?"

"Our caves. The walls of the piers. Our words. Proof that we existed. David Wojnarowicz drew us a map, for fucks'sake. Keith Haring spelled it out in bright, primary colors. Stanley Stellar captures our life in motion. Proof that we exist still. Our own hieroglyphics for future generations to see and comprehend, and a day will come when our words will be their words, too. Everybody's language, ya see? The masses ain't gonna be such an exclusive crew for long."

"That's some dream, baby."

"All languages have the same structure. It's just different words. All of us are gonna speak the same language one day."

"You're optimistic, baby."

"Listen, if they can swallow half-naked Marky Mark grabbing his junk on an oversized tribute billboard in Times Square, then they can certainly learn the vernacular. It was the gay interest in Marky Mark that fueled his career as a rapper and secured him a contract with Calvin Kein. Our own icon immortalized in his underwear by Herb Ritts himself *and* showcased at the crossroads of the nation—that's certainly bigger than our living room. More prominently displayed than the art at any museum on Fifth Avenue, too. We're almost full circle, don't ya see?"

"I see, baby. I see."

"The future isn't that far away. I just know it. It's like...well, it's like inside of me I just gotta believe it for true. It's up to us to remember our history. To record it, and to retell it—one million or more times if we need to do so. The way it actually went down."

"Man, you're handsome when you get passionate about a thing. There is no bigger turn-on than a man compelled by his beliefs. There's this glint that starts in your eyes that hijacks your smile. It sends me spiraling to the Moon every time it happens. Over the fucking Moon, baby."

"Nah. It's just talk, that's all."

"No—no, no. Are you listening, baby? Do you hear the words I'm trying to say to—"

"Shhh! *If you pleassse!* Some of us are here trying to take in the art, Gentlemen." from a lispy number in a black Calvin Klein turtleneck. Oh, you know the type. His real name is Albert, but he wants everyone to call him Chase. Really? Chase?

"Sorry, pal."

"What I'm trying to articulate, baby, is that it feels incredible to have you all to my own. Even for this little lesson in history. I was hoping to take a moment to tell you—"

"To tell me what?"

In truth, there may not be a bar rail or customers between us, but we are anything but on our own. Horn-rim wearing, black Calvin Klein turtleneck sporting queens are all around us, gulping at plastic glasses of cheap Chablis and cruising each other and the art, in that order. All of the fine gentlemen are craning their necks to flirt with the just-a-little-bit too too tooty fruity fine gentleman. Meandering West Village nannies, who've seen it all, are traipsing through the erotica with blank stares as their wards in Aprica strollers nod off with complete boredom.

"Better yet. Here. Take my hand and follow me, baby. No more words."

Horn-rim wearing, black Calvin Klein turtleneck sporting queens roll their fake blue contact lenses into the back of their heads and Aprica enveloped toddlers yawn and reposition themselves. The muscle-ripped, doorman leads me toward the gay community's halcyon days of free love, where eyes connect with urgent reciprocation and bodies instinctively crash and retreat, crash and retreat.

Just nine months before his death from AIDS, Keith Haring painted his most audacious, masterful mural celebrating homosexuality in the men's bathroom at The Gay & Lesbian Community Center. Over the course of just a couple weeks, he covered every untiled surface of the bathroom with turgid, squirting penises of all sizes. Some are attached to buff male bodies tangled together in pleasure, others float like happy clouds or hungry dragons.

The doorman escorts me beyond Haring figures dancing the conga and enjoying an orgy and passed a real-life bearded fellow with his baseball cap turned backward, fellating his bearish sex partner with admirable, dedicated gusto. The genesis of us. Just more history revealing itself. Crashing and retreating, crashing and retreating, skillful blowjob by skillful blowjob through time.

When we arrive at the furthest wall from the frosted glass bathroom door, directly beneath one impressively large, veined phallus, he turns me around to face him. I move to take my place. He intertwines his meaty fingers from both hands with my own, palm to palm, and confidently, assuredly, he lifts my hands well above my head until I'm almost standing tiptoe. He leans his body into me and my back arches to meet him as he pins me against the wall with the weight of his strapping torso.

This close, his breath is sweet, and his body smells of masculine perspiration and cigarette smoke and his kind smile grows mischievous, lascivious even. A huge toothy grin masks a carnal growl, and a dangerous laugh in the back of his throat. A raised eyebrow reveals his intention, his amber eyes dancing alongside my own, as we achingly press against each other. He teases by grazing his hardness against my hardness and laughs willfully as he tells me he's going to make me beg for it. And the doorman makes his move. He kisses me with urgency as his tongue probes my mouth hard and without abandon.

My brain is aflame, knowing nothing more than to breathe this man deep inside me until I feel ribbons of him expanding in my chest and intoxicating my brain. I leverage my restrained hands, arms, and shoulders against the lewd Haring masterwork to gain balance and thrust my groin longingly, greedily, repeatedly against his own and pray to Jesus Christ himself that the two of us will stay this way forever.

Oh, how I breathe him inside me, ravenous to take him deeper and starving for the masculine scent of him, pungent sweat, musky smoke, all the beauty, the fear, the love—the very real sense of brotherhood, the history, our history, inside my airway until I require it for sustenance, to survive, to survive still.

And with his teeth against my neck, I squirm. I writhe like so many horny, shirtless fellas posing in front of the camera at the Christopher Street Piers before me, huddled and randy and communicating in our learned, exclusive language. Little bites initially, lingering longer, harder, rougher. He breathlessly delivers a litany of foul words inside my ear—rhythmically, hypnotically, grinding his manhood against me as he traces his coarse beard stubble along my collarbone. I struggle to free my arms, my hands, my fingers, but I am no match for this muscle-ripped man. I gasp for breath, hungrily bite at the air, and straddle his massive thigh. He growls, and snarls, chews on my lips, spits hard in my mouth, and his own saliva drips from the corners of my breathless jaws as I instinctually, helplessly, purposefully buck my dick against his dick, one one-thousand, two one-thousand, three one-thousand, as—

"Ooo, that's a Princess! That's a Buttercup. Uh-huh. That's a Cutie Pie."

Followed by an indistinguishable "urrrmmmpgh" from the sweat-soaked, real-life bearded fellow with his baseball cap turned backward, sprawled across the Keith Haring showpiece tile floor.

"Ooo, you go, Princess! That's my Princess. Uh-huh. You want it, Princess? You want your brawny Daddy Bear's special sauce, dontcha now? Uh-huh. Ooo, that's my Princess! You get it, girlfriend! That's right! You get it, girlfriend! You get it, Princess Buttercup! You get that special sauce! Uh-huh, uh-huh, uh-huh—"

"Aaarrrgggghhh-uh-uh-uh-uh."

"Uh-huh, uh-huh, uh-huh—"

"Urrragggooopmmmh."

"Ooooooooo, Paaahhhrrrrincessssss! You got it, girlfriend!"

We let our bodies collapse into each other. With labored and heavy breaths, we fall into an embrace and laugh until our lungs ache for oxygen. Eventually, after we've finally calmed ourselves, I hear every Swatch at The Gay & Lesbian Community Center ticking, and then: "Mmmph. C'mon, Dale. We didn't come here to be the main course for a couple of old, nasty leather queens. They should probably go back to The Ramrod or wherever it is they came from."

"Yeah. With all the other old, nasty leather queens."

Once you've been served up by Princess Buttercup, it's probably best to excuse yourself from the dinner party post haste. After all, the main course has already been special-sauced. Uh-huh, uh-huh, uh-huh. And who's she calling old, anyway? Brotherhood indeed.

Beyond the horn-rim wearing, black Calvin Klein turtleneck sporting queens, the blank stares of the meandering West Village nannies who've seen it all tending to their nodded off Aprica stroller encased wards, and the turgid, squirting penises of all sizes, the transition into sunshine is a relatively easy one. We ditch the history lesson and make like schoolboys, rib-tickling, ass-grabbing, and laughing uproariously, out the grand ornate, Italianate front doors of The Gay & Lesbian Community Center.

Standing on 13th Street beside the doorman, I feel the warm

September sunshine on my face. I take stock and can smell him on my fingers and forearms, taste him on my lips, and feel the redness rising on my collarbone from the brush with his coarse beard stubble.

Filthy fragments of sentences he uttered echo in my brain: "If we do this, there will be rules. Do you think you can play by the rules, sexy fucker?" as I replay our intimate interaction—before it's gone, and I don't remember it right. The way it actually went down, ya know? My lips ache to taste him. My arms long to pull him close, right here, right now, on the steps of The Center, deep inside of me, and my hardness threatens to burst from my worn-through 501s.

So enamored am I of him that I can hear my heart beating in my ears. The tiny hairs at the scruff of my neck stand tall with yearning anticipation still. Yes, I see it, Doorman. *Yes, I hear the words you're trying to say to me.*

"Man, I am ravenous, Doorman. Whaddya say we take the train to Chinatown? Better than that, we can walk...so warm for this late in September. We can take our time and stroll through Washington Square. The leaves are just beginning to do their thing, red and amber, and—"

"Oh boy, does that sound sweet—"

"I know this place on Canal Street that serves dim sum twenty-four seven. Canal and Orchard. Jing Fong, it's called."

"Now, dim sum I definitely do dig, but..."

"They wrap peanut butter and shrimp in a big, black mushroom. It's crazy delicious! And they serve these beautiful, intricately designed Tea Cakes made of plum and ginger and basil."

"We'll have to make a point to go there some time."

"Most times, I could eat a half dozen of 'em in one sitting.

That's a true story. The way I'm feeling right now, so fucking hungry—like I haven't eaten in weeks...I'll bet I could eat one dozen or more."

"...but I'm covering the door at The Meat Market tonight, baby."

"Wha? Huh? Oh."

"Walk me to the subway, huh?"

"Yeah. You betcha, Doorman."

"You'll see me soon enough, mister."

"Sure thing."

"We've got our own history to write. A history of you and me."

"C'mon, man—why do I gotta wait so long?" I plead.

"Awww, the future isn't that far away, baby. I just know it."

"So, you were paying attention all along, eh?"

"Baby, I couldn't ignore you if I tried. I'll see ya tomorrow night at work."

"Yes. Yes, you will. Bye."

The doorman kisses me softly on the cheek, slaps me on the ass, and grins as confidently as all his promises for tomorrow. I hear the blood pounding in my ears and feel my heart thumping in my chest as I study his gray buzzcut glinting in the late September sunshine and watch as his chiseled torso and tattoo sleeves, and his perfect, cantaloupe ass disappear down the steps of the West 4th Street Washington Square Subway.

THREE

AFTER WALKING home from the West 4th Street Washington Square Subway, I unlace my combat boots and kick them off, first the left, then the right, and with two consecutive clunks, they land loud against the seventies-style parquet floor. Distracted by daydreams of what tomorrow holds, I sit down heavily in my favorite cowhide tuxedo chair to roll a joint. The setting Sun draws sharp amber and red shadows across the courtyard apartments on Barrow Street, and from my perspective, enveloped in the waning evening sunset, only the brightest celestial objects can be observed by the naked eye.

That's precisely when I spot Jerome in the yellow, lamp-lit windows of his apartment across the way. I break apart the fragrant grass until my fingertips are sticky, pinch the joint paper between my thumb and forefingers, and roll it back and forth to pack the herb. I lick the top edge of the paper and seal it with one final roll and pull hard hits off the sweet marijuana cigarette.

Slumped lazily in my favorite cowhide tuxedo chair, I rest my feet on the windowsill, and wait for my favorite story to begin.

Jerome Cameron is no artist, but he plays a consummately shirtless Neurosurgeon on daytime television. The first time I noticed him, his precise diction was ringing off the courtyard walls as he rehearsed his lines, experimented with intonation, and practiced all the big words: Arteriovenous Malformation, Cerebrospinal Fluid, Hypothalamus, and Trigeminal Neuralgia. It wasn't until I spotted him staring me down with silver-blue eyes from across the courtyard that I recognized him from the soaps. I still get a kick out of the fact that women across America sit down each day to salivate over Jerome during his scenes on *Another Tomorrow* as regularly as I study him naked and feeding his Basset Hound, Frank, or chasing a mouse across his apartment with a Doc Marten lace-up shoe, or lifting weights in his underwear while making love to his reflection in a full length, stand-up mirror situated prominently in his living room.

This evening as the Sun sets over the West Village, disco music pulses from his open windows as he hustles, three-step turns and claps, and electric slides as he cleans his apartment with a feather duster like a titillated, time-traveled maid from a Molière farce. *Le freak, c'est chic, freak out!*

His body is toned to perfection, and each muscle performs its solo in a scintillating, symphonic overture as, dressed only in his Calvin Klein tighty-whities, he feathers the bookcase shelves, a mammoth Bowflex home gym machine, and the full length, stand-up mirror situated prominently in his living room. He scatters dust motes that Bump and Grapevine right along with him, Alicia Bridges, and Cheryl Lynn, that catch the last light of the waning dusk before touching down caressingly on his fat, black curls that fall against his eyebrows, which he's forever pushing out of his silver-blue eyes, his exaggerated cheekbones, and his tiny brown nipples.

For just one moment, if I scrunch my eyes closed as tightly as I am able, I can spot tiny beads of sweat forming at his armpits and collecting in the center of his chest and making a slow, methodical descent down his torso as they cascade to follow a path between his powerful pectorals, and deposit themselves in the perfectly groomed, vertical stripe of hair extending from his navel to his pubic hair to heaven.

I pull one final, hard hit off the sweet marijuana cigarette, and my brain careens as his silver-blue eyes catch my own. I let my hand fall to my crotch as Jerome trails his hand along the flat terrain of his torso. Instantly, he grows stiff in his CK underwear as disco music side-steps off the courtyard walls.

Jerome fingers his tiny brown nipple and thrusts his groin toward the windowpane while grinning from one ear to the next with perfect, polished soap opera teeth. He slips his hand just beneath the elastic band of his Calvin Klein tighty-whities as The O'Jays break into Love Train, and his laughter bellows as if projected by an on-set boom mike as he pushes his fat, black curls out of his silver-blue eyes, feather dusts his bulging underwear, and pulls out of the station to clean the remainder of his apartment. *People all over the world join hands, start a love train, it's the love train.*

I'm deflating in my jeans as I lean my head back in my favorite cowhide tuxedo chair, close my eyes, and search for rest. With my eyes pressed shut, my brain teeter-totters with the marijuana, with the day...so warm for this late in September, and with the break-neck pace of life charging forward.

In a lucid dream, the leaves are just beginning to do their thing, red and amber, as Curtis Champa chases me home from middle school. I maneuver my fat twelve-year-old body through a courtyard of sharp shadows and apartments, stuffy, city garage filled alley-ways, tiny city gardens filled with wilted, tomato plants, and fallen crab apple stained sidewalks—crooked and broken, and cracked-in-half.

It happens this way every day. The children chase me home from school. And they are right, aren't they? Justified to do so. One day, somebody has gotta write it down...record all the intimate observations—before they're gone, and nobody remembers it right. One day they'll teach these lessons in school. The way it actually went down, ya know?

When I falter with breathlessness, Curtis Champa easily finds my pace, walks right alongside me, pedestrians cross the street, and feral cats cascade lithely from rusted-out garbage drums to stuffy, soot gray city garage roofs to avoid the impending scuffle. Maybe if I pretend to not hear him, he'll let me off easy this one time.

Colorless, failing leaves rain from twisted arthritic branches, whipping up tiny chaotic cyclones, the squalls of an impending autumn storm along gravelly city alleyways. Curtis Champa torments me with filthy fragments of sentences that echo in my brain: "Ya big, ol' girl! You're a big, ol' girl!" Give it to him good, sweetheart!

He drills my ribcage with the pointed knuckles of his closed fist repeatedly, rhythmically, hypnotically, as he derides me to reveal my clumsy knowledge of all things masculine. With his blows, he scatters dead leaves and damp twigs that Bump and Grapevine right along with him that boogie in the air until they realize solidarity, amass, and menacingly circle.

"Are the Cubs in the American League or the National League, Dominic?"

"National."

"Wrong, Faggot." He jabs my ribcage painfully with his knuckles.

"American."

"Wrong, Faggot." He jabs my ribcage painfully with his knuckles.

"Ouch! You're hurting me!"

"Whaddya gonna do? Hit me with your purse?"

"I told you to stop it, Curtis!"

"I sure do feel sorry for your parents on account of them having a little sissy for a son!"

"Leave me alone."

"Sissy! You sissy, you!"

My skin is gooseflesh in the cool, cruel, colorless autumn. He jabs my ribcage painfully with his knuckles, and my only recourse is to run away. Curtis Champa chases me through twisted arthritic alleyways as I propel my school books to the street side, and middle school homework swirls in tiny chaotic cyclones outlined against the soot gray sky. I dodge tiny city gardens and rusted-out garbage drums and emit small bubbles of breath until my lungs are on fire, overcome and about to burst from lack of oxygen.

Just as I consider that I actually might reach the walkway to my front door unscathed, I feel his hot breath on my face, and he is on top of me. A crooked and broken, cracked-in-half grin masks a carnal growl and dangerous laugh in the back of his throat. A raised eyebrow reveals his intention. He teases by grazing his hardness against me, laughs willfully, and makes his move.

He barrels into me ceaselessly with punches and kicks and bucks his rough denim-clad crotch in my face, grinding his manhood against me. Uh-huh, uh-huh, uh-huh—you want it, princess? Our bodies collapse into each other with labored and heavy breaths. And I struggle to free my arms, my hands, my fingers, but I am no match for Curtis Champa.

I gasp for breath, hungrily bite at the air, and he growls, and snarls, spits hard in my face, and his own saliva drips from the corners of my broken, cracked-in-half mouth. And I taste dirt, pebbles, and tiny colorless, failing leaves stuffed between my lips, against my tongue, at the back of my throat, inside my airway until I require it to survive—one one-thousand, two one-thousand, three one-thousand—to survive still.

He finishes his task expeditiously and flees down a gravelly city alleyway of sharp shadows, no more a need for hysterics, this is routine business; simply setting fire to nature. Slumped lazily, I leverage my restrained hands, arms and shoulders against the broken, cracked-in-half pavement, through all of the years, and I search for rescue just in time to observe my mother's eyes—mean, miserable, cold, sealed in a permanent frown, as she draws the lace curtains of our apartment living room abruptly closed. Where I came from, ya know? This is the genesis of me.

With the dull scrape of a branch against the windowpane, I am again deposited in my favorite cowhide tuxedo chair. I quietly reach for a Red from the pack on a wooden milk crate end table and light it with a branded The Meat Market book of matches that reads *A Butcher Bar*. I sit without movement, barely breathing, and watch the blue smoke pierce the tangible darkness of my apartment. All around me, sharp amber and red shadows have melted into an all too familiar plane of existence.

For a long moment, I reverberate with reflection of the terrifying recollections. I realize that I could stay this way forever until the darkness consumes me too, when the shadows at long last paralyze me with their weight, and then I jump up and pull myself into the present tense.

I lace my combat boots, first the right, then the left, and grab my crumpled leather motorcycle jacket from the seventies-style parquet floor. Instinctively, I search for cash in my front pocket, my wallet at my back hip, and the keys to my apartment. I close the door on everything I care about and hurriedly make my way down the cognac-colored vestibule stairwell, without time to trace the pattern of penny wall tile with my fingertips.

I take inventory on the luminescent aggregate stairsteps of my apartment building on Barrow Street. After the Sun goes down, when the denizens walk the land, meandering these streets is a revelatory experience. Streetlight shadows drip from street signs and walk-ups as I ask myself, "When did the transition come?" "When did the change happen?" "Where did the time go?"

I pace Christopher Street from the West Street Pier to Sixth Avenue with unfocused eyes, flicking back and forth like a caged animal. I don't know what I'm looking for, but I know to keep moving at all costs. The future isn't that far away. I just know it. It's like...well, it's like inside of me I just gotta believe it for true. I learn new things, talk to strangers, make new friends, and feel most alive tracing these streets—above all, I never sit still.

My neighborhood is distinguished by avenues that are set at an angle to the other streets in Manhattan. The streets of the West Village are disobedient. West 4th Street crosses West 10th, 11th, and 12th Streets, ending at an intersection with West 13th Street. West 12th Street is separated by three blocks from Little West 12th Street, which in turn is one block south of West 13th Street.

I travel this idiosyncratic network, sometimes parallel or sometimes perpendicular to the Hudson, beneath brownstones built in the mid-19th century, beside twisting Gingko tree-lined streets with tiny restaurants, and among purposeful, tight-fitting flannel-shirt and worn-through 501 wearing men who pose themselves, crotches protruding, on luminous granite steps, in vestibule doorways, and huddled in threes and fours around glowing orange hash pipes. They're the proof in the pudding. These courageous souls clad in flannel and button-flies are the brothers with whom I've created this place to live. Mark my words—one day they'll teach these lessons in school.

The counterculture, a band of randy bohemians, and the homosexual alliance named this small section of the world, this ghetto, their home in the early and mid-twentieth century. The neighborhood became known for its colorful, artistic residents and the alternative culture they propagated.

Due in part to the progressive attitudes of many of its residents, the West Village became a focal point of new movements and ideas, whether political, artistic, or cultural. To this day, you can still find late-night jazz, see an art film at midnight, and connect the dots between slice joints from West 14th Street to West Houston Street.

I love the history and the security of belonging to someplace. The real reason homosexuals relocate to metropolises is not to wallow in anonymity as some would have you believe, rather it is to search out the fear, the desperation, but also the beauty, the love, the sense of community. The brotherhood, I see it.

"Where are yuh headed in such a hurry, Mistuh Leadderman?"

"Just getting some fresh air, man. Taking a walk."

Under the haze of golden streetlight, shadows intersect across his face angularly, accenting his searching eyes, Al Parker porn-stache, and a chipped front tooth. A leather jacket, a Muir cap, and motorcycle boots—the uniform of heightened masculinity and formidable appropriation of sexual power—will always turn my head, and I reach in my jacket pocket for a Red and light it from a branded The Meat Market book of matches that reads *A Butcher Bar.*

"Yuh, uh, got a place around here yuh'd like tuh show me?"

"Nope."

Above us, two muscle men share their time, a cigarette, and a can of beer in a paper sack on a fire escape. Music drifts down from their third-floor walk-up and hangs thick in the warm September night, something cool and sexy by Janet Jackson.

Come with me, don't you worry, I'm gonna make you crazy. I'll give you the time of your life.

The aesthetic sensibilities couldn't have been scripted more astutely by Joe Gage himself, the first filmmaker who dared to suggest that sex between men was more about camaraderie than romance. Gage aimed to replicate the narratives, characters, and authenticity of mainstream gay life in his pornography and notoriously opposed romance focus in his films.

That's the way love. That's the way love. That's the way love goes.

I trail the stranger casually and watch the blue smoke of my cigarette pierce the tangible darkness and the twisting Gingko tree-lined streets. Together we walk toward shelter, from the pub that was the site of the Stonewall uprising, to the legendary Smalls Jazz Club, a left and then a right, and six stairsteps beneath street level in the damp, darkened alcove of a garden apartment, between puddles of urine and greasy brick walls, he unzips his fly and I blow him.

He leans over and pushes me deeper onto his dick, a deliberate motion as he emits inarticulate grunts from the back of his throat, and whispers in my ear that he wants to finish in my mouth. He ensures his intention with a firm grip on my earlobe and a rough, calloused hand around my neck, and I scrunch my eyes closed as tightly as I am able to regain balance. He finds his rhythm and bucks briskly, as I vaguely remember a time when it was easier than this to find distraction from the night terrors.

And then I think about the doorman. I've known him for so long—ten years, maybe eleven, maybe longer. What is this newfound desire in me to find rest, seek shelter, in his benevolent arms? I consider all the comfort I realized inside his embrace earlier this afternoon, the safety I felt in realizing the brotherhood. History, I suppose. Our history. It fascinates me. In my mind's eye, I replay our time together before it's gone, and I don't remember it right. The way it actually went down, ya know? My arms ache to have him close, right here, right now, deep inside of me, and my hardness threatens to burst from my worn-through 501s. Yes, I see it, Doorman. Oh, how I yearn.

I'm seventeen years old and sitting tall on a ripped, red leather bar stool at The Gold Coast Tavern, a dive bar where all the hustlers hang out in the gaddammed seediest part of the lousy city of Chicago. At three in the afternoon, I'm taking my time with a Scotch that I don't have the dough to pay for, fingering the names, telephone numbers, and assorted graffiti carved into the bar counter—so many exaggeratedly-sized phalli, 'Call Jesus for a good blowjob,' and 'Prince is living proof that Liberace fucked Little Richard,'—and staring straight ahead at the cigarette stained mirrors and the knock-off red velvet wallpaper.

A bored bartender dressed in complete leather gear sits half-

cruising, half-reading a paperback copy of Andrew Holleran's Dancer from the Dance by the light of a blue hockey game that plays on a wall-mounted television. The sound is turned down and nobody pays attention—a diversion in case the law should arrive. Sleazy men of business sit with liquor dribbling down their chins, never losing track of the constant parade of available young men dressed in tight-fitting clothes, some of them shirtless, many of them missing teeth inside the filthy dive bar—their quantum eyes darting from chubby businessman in dribbled on button-down shirt, to chubby businessman in dribbled on button-down shirt. Eyes that connect with urgent reciprocation and bodies that instinctively crash and retreat, crash and retreat.

Distraction arrives in the form of a gratis Scotch rocks served with a yellowed, paper beverage napkin. Across the bar sits a rumpled character in desperate need of a haircut and shave dressed in a crumpled business suit. His greedy, soot gray eyes leer at me with obvious intention as he plays a wooden toothpick between his broken, yellow teeth. And he smirks as if we two could possibly share some commonality. These are the fearless men who document their surroundings so that...well, so that one day, we could better understand them. And, in turn, learn more about ourselves.

Dusty Springfield sings something drifting and distracted, on a tinny, old juke—a song about a woman who rises up, then dies, then comes back to life again. One swallow of cheap Scotch and suddenly he appears on the ripped, red leather bar stool right beside me.

"Ya wanna see the whole world, kid?"

"Fifty bucks would make me happier."

At this, the rumpled character dressed in the crumpled business suit smirks as he fingers the toothpick between his lips and proceeds to call up mucus from his lungs for a full five minutes.

He spits disgusting brown phlegm on the sticky brown, cigarette burned floor. He steadies himself with an inquisitive hand on my thigh as he produces two twenties and one ten, which he folds in half and crams in the front pocket of my jeans. He sucks his tongue, his eyes aflame, and his mouth grotesquely contorts up in such a way that I think he might smile as he gestures with a twisted, arthritic hand toward the doorway which leads to the whole world.

We exit into the gaddammed frigid air in this lousy city, and my stomach turns cartwheels from the cheap Scotch and with terrifying anticipation of what tomorrow holds. We walk in single file fashion for many blocks. I could make a run for it at any moment, push the rumpled character dressed in the crumpled business suit down and steal the money, or take him easily should a scuffle come to pass. Yet, I choose to follow him in the milky sunlight until we stand beneath the yellowed and blinking neon lights of an adult bookstore that boasts private booths.

Beyond the entrance everything is damaged and fractured. The air is motionless, and the same foul stench has been inhaled and exhaled for a million damaged, foul lifetimes. Yellowed and blinking neon hustlers pose in jockstraps at distorted angles, mooching cigarettes, scratching their exposed asses, and trading slovenly, withdrawn sexual acts for any commodity they can get their hands on—cash money, needles, or pilfered wallets. With disinterested eyes, they offer up broken-toothed, stale breath smiles, and welcome strangers close with forearms bruised and bloody with track marks.

I follow the rumpled character dressed in the crumpled business suit as he leads me confidently through a network of rancid hallways that appear identical and all end up at the same place. My tempo-

rary employer indicates a room of his particular liking and pulls aside a black felt drape. I move to take my place.

He lists in a corner, hacks and calls up mucus from his lungs for a full five minutes, spits disgusting brown phlegm on the sticky brown floor, and gestures with a twisted, arthritic hand for me to begin my obligation. I finger two folded in half twenties and one ten in the front pocket of my jeans, and as I unbutton them my dick is shriveled and disinterested. I think to push past the rumpled character dressed in the crumpled business suit, and the yellowed and blinking neon hustlers, and the gaddammed frigid air in this lousy city, when he expels a singular croak and a gasp for oxygen arrives in his throat.

He brings himself to climax with three lifeless strokes and flees down a gravelly city alleyway of sharp shadows more quickly than I can erase his grotesque, yellow semen from my thigh and reach to pull my jeans up. At seventeen, I'm on my knees with my pants around my ankles on the cigarette-stained floor of an adult bookstore that boasts private booths. So, this is the whole world, eh? All lit by yellowed and blinking neon, bare bulbs painted red.

I bolt from the maudlin memories and force myself to concentrate on the task at hand, one one-thousand, two one-thousand, three one-thousand, as his grip on my earlobe and the rough, calloused hand around my neck begins to seize. He's bucking hard now, involuntary noises from the back of his throat, the distant echo in my brain of, "If we do this, there will be rules. Do you think you can play by the rules, sexy fucker?" and his knees collapse against my chest as he takes his turn to curse and convulse and spill his seed.

That's the way love, that's the way love goes.

In the achromatic time of safe sex, I have incautiously—willfully committed the most shameful of sins and swallowed a stranger's load. The fucking doesn't include kisses on the cheek or a fake punch on my chin as gentle as a breeze off the Hudson as he slips in to playfully tug on my nipple ring—but it is dangerous and harmful and that delivers me more completely than the Twenty Year Scotch or the marijuana cigarettes. Life is you take whatever you can get. Life is you make the most of whatever you can take. Because that's who I am!

I retrieve my jeans from around my ankles, taking desperate care to avoid contact with the puddles of urine and the greasy brick walls in the damp darkened alcove of the garden apartment. I fasten my fly in such haste that I must pursue the action three separate times to steady my fingers to match the correct buttons with their respective buttonholes.

I coerce my trembling limbs to obey—like a floppy, balloon creature at a car lot—and I cull strength to climb step by step with my bare hands against the greasy, urine-puddled pavement. Instinctively, I search for a small wad of cash in my front pocket, my wallet at my back hip, and the keys to my apartment.

Before my sex partner with the searching eyes, Al Parker porn-stache, and a chipped front tooth can adjust his leather jacket, secure his Muir cap, and step aside in his motorcycle boots, I push past him and run deep into the light of the dark black night.

I run through amber and red shadows across the concrete court-yard littered with glue traps, where only the brightest celestial objects can be observed by the naked eye, stuffy, city garage filled alleyways, tiny city gardens filled with wilted, tomato plants, and fallen crab apple-stained sidewalks—crooked and broken and cracked-in-half. I emit small bubbles of breath until my lungs are on fire, overcome and about to burst from lack of oxygen. I travel in a world beyond cruisy tourists searching for Christopher Street, beside men who couple themselves in twos and threes to immodestly fuck in vestibules, and beyond addicts with syringes out in the open.

I run until there is no breath inside me. I steady myself against the cognac-colored vestibule doorway with one hand on my knee, as a tiny chaotic cyclone of colorless, falling leaves menacingly circles around my combat boots.

When I begin to breathe more regularly, I stand tall and methodically inhale the damp, late September evening and exhale tiny colorless, falling leaves stuffed between my lips, against my tongue, at the back of my throat, and inside my airway. I've lost track of time in a conventional sense. The perfunctory, masochistic acts of the damp, darkened alcove of the garden apartment could have been two nights ago. Hell, that could have been two weeks ago, too. All I know is counting, counting—one one-thousand, two one-thousand, three one-thousand, a metronome beating, every clock in the West Village ticking, that keeps dangerous notice of the time on this earth that remains. Time is running out for me. One day you look around and think, "Okay, this is who I am now."

I take inventory from the steps of my apartment building on Barrow Street. Instinctively, for a second time, I search for a small wad of cash in my front pocket, and my wallet at my back hip, and the keys to my apartment.

I'm miles away from everything I care about, somewhere beyond the luminescent aggregate stairsteps and the cognac-colored vestibule stairwell, when I spot Jerome Cameron approaching, and he tickles the tiny hairs at the scruff of my neck that stand tall with mock-petulance and tugs firmly on my previously firmly tugged upon earlobe. He motions to key into the building with take-out Chinese food, and I nearly vault outta my combat boots as a little scream catches in the back of my throat.

"Goodness, we're a little jumpy this evening. You gotta take it easy on that stepped-all-over, leather bar blow there, sweetheart. Or maybe splurge for a higher grade of goods, ya know? You're not above splurging, are ya, ya big, ol' girl? Such a big, ol' girl!" as he pushes the fat, black curls that fall against his eyebrows out of his silver-blue eyes, and smiles his perfect, polished soap opera teeth from one ear to the next.

Ever a gentleman, for a purported big, ol' girl anyway, I move aside and leave him to deliver his exit line and afford his stage entrance into Number Eighty-Five Barrow Street. He blows me a kiss, leaving a trail of hot mustard condiment packets, as I reach in the pocket of my motorcycle jacket for a Red and light it from a branded The Meat Market book of matches that reads *A Butcher Bar*.

In an instant without notice, a cordovan maroon Pontiac Bonneville Firebird Trans Am careens up onto the sidewalk, rendering it crooked and broken and cracked-in-half, and immobilizes my body against the mid-19th century brownstone bricks. I propel the keys to my apartment and the pack of Reds to the streetside, and colorless, fallen leaves, gray soot, and alleyway gravel swirls in tiny chaotic cyclones. I feel the hot engine of the car breathing on my face, burning against my torso and groin, and it is nearly on top of me.

My only recourse is to run away, but with every movement, the driver inches the vehicle closer toward me. I feel the exhalation of its exhaust against my groin. When I shift my hand to mop the perspiration from my forehead, an enraged section of car pollution and a deafening, explosive *vrrrooommm, vrrrooommm* births dust motes that Bump and Grapevine, and miniature razor-sharp music notes that dance in the air.

"Ju fuckeen' *mariposa*. Look at theees one, *hermanos mío*. We found a *mariposita* dressed like a fuckeen' leather *puta*. Why don' ju waaahhhtch wheeere ju're walkin', *puta?*"

Seconds drip like lifetimes. And this is how it happens. This is where they find me. All alone—that's who I am. My mind pounds in time with the perilous breathing of the car engine, vrrrooommm, vrrrooommm, vrrrooommm. This sinuous lifetime is spiraling, inching toward a cumulative climax, and any moment the car will roar to life.

My heart is turning flip-flops. Where is Jerome Cameron and how did he negotiate the cognac-colored, vestibule stairwell with the penny tile walls so quickly?

I examine the sooty clouds above me as they eclipse the Blue Harvest Moon, and I study the demented beams of light from beneath the surface of unsullied dread as I realize this is the time between activity and rest, life and death, the dying then.

And what's become of the chirping abuelas that gather on these stairsteps to share neighborhood *el chismorreo* and play Ten Penny Rummy? Are they securely ensconced behind lace curtains in city apartment living rooms abruptly drawn closed? They're justified to do so. Those other mothers. They were right, weren't they?

Then I think about the doorman—and how I found reassurance and comfort in his words. I replay our time together before it's gone, one one-thousand, two one-thousand, three one-thousand. My arms ache to have him close, right here, right now, deep inside of me.

My body is pins-and-needles sensations, frozen and numb, my hands, arms, legs, fingers, toes, like a colorless autumn leaf failing and then falling from a tree. I watch myself dying by the millimeter from inside the cocoon of bars of barbed wire music. I hear my heart thumping in my ears. We've still got some history to write, the doorman and me. Yes, I see it. Yes, I hear the words you're trying to say to me. Over the fucking Moon.

From the passenger window of the cordovan maroon Pontiac Bonneville Firebird Trans Am, an empty beer bottle is hurled through the sooty, evening air and strikes me square in the chest. The force of it knocks me off my feet, and I crawl backwards to ensconce myself beside the mid-19th century brownstone bricks. The aesthetic sensibilities couldn't have been scripted more astutely by Joe Gage himself. Raucous laughter from inside the vehicle as it inches ever closer.

I scream in agony, but no voice comes out of me, solely murderous music that covers my face and takes away the daylight. Time is running out for me. And you wanna know what life is...ya wanna know?

Vrrrooommm, vrrrooommm as the cordovan maroon Trans Am squeals backward and peels off into the soot gray horizon, leaving behind it a noxious cloud of exhaust and the fumes of uncomely laughter that perforates the late September evening. The sound of it echoes in my brain as I crawl on hands and knees to the luminescent aggregate stairsteps of my apartment building and sob.

FOUR

I TAKE my place behind the bar and mentally prepare for a busy work shift. Thursday nights can be tough. Leathermen stand on line for an hour, sometimes more...so warm for this late in September, on the shadowy cobblestone streets of the Meatpacking District, flirting with each and furtively smoking weed, clandestinely selecting sex partners, crashing and retreating, and edging their way ever closer inside the big, oak door.

The first thing I do is reach for the pack of Reds that I keep to the right of the cash register. I light a smoke with a branded The Meat Market book of matches that reads *A Butcher Bar*, and I search for answers inside the enormous gilt mirror behind the shelves of booze. Inside the glass, deep circles of sleeplessness overtake my eyes, reflections of the last few days haphazardly ricochet against one another inside my brain, and yet still a smile forms easily, handsome—just so fucking tired. Steps away, a formidable group of leather-clad, beer-swilling customers stand on line to gather at my station.

Stack the cardboard Meat Market coasters, flashlight for the cooler, clean bar towel tucked into the back of my jeans at the small of my back. Just like any other shift, but there's also special Thursday night setup, too. Additional side work includes procuring cases of condoms from the sick-green, windowless basement office, and posting hand-designed instructional signboards.

Once a week, contraceptives are donated by the New York City Department of Health and Mental Hygiene, along with reams of glossy educational flyers that convey the importance of safe sex. The signboards and pamphlets are covered in sexual imagery, no different than a Torso Magazine, and are born from a demand for action that my tight-fitting white t-shirt and worn-through 501 wearing brothers and I fostered and fought like hell to bring to life. You gotta educate the masses. And you gotta catch the eye of the beholder if you want him to pay attention to your mission.

Free tools for sexual protection and educational campaigns are unsupported by government bodies these days. In fact, The United States Congress explicitly banned the use of federal funds for AIDS-prevention as well as all informational campaigns that promote homosexual activities. The legislation was spearheaded by conservative senator Jesse Helms and signed into law by President Reagan.

Much of the government's $600 million AIDS-prevention budget was spent on advertising campaigns that demonize gays for the epidemic smite they brought upon themselves. These posters portray ominous images of graves and caskets behind large headline proclamations of danger. A very different strategy than the irreverent, erotically-charged handbills brought forth by the gay community themselves, featuring chiseled muscle-men dressed solely in jockstraps and rain boots with clever calls to action such as 'Every Good Boy Wears His Rubbers.'

Over the past decade, the AIDS pandemic has baffled government officials and stung politicians into a shocking display of denial and avoidance. Ronald Reagan was president for nearly five years before he said the word AIDS in public. As a response, a ceaseless network of New York City gay men have taken action to create and promote a safe sex message of AIDS prevention on our own. The AIDS Coalition to Unleash Power. We work together as a community, reaffirming our beliefs and brotherhood, as we take care of our own at grassroots political coalitions that target treatment, advocacy, and change to legislation and public awareness.

So now we have home-grown, large-scale placards that focus on sexual pleasure, health, and positive awareness to get people to affect change in their behavior pasted right on top of government-issued posters of gallows, deathbeds, and graveyards. Ultimately, it's up to each of us to teach awareness, left alone to educate our own kin. To record it and retell it. One million or more times if we need to do so. The way it actually went down, ya know?

We've even recruited figures from the worlds of art and fashion to lend their voices to our movement. Just last week, a public campaign more resembling a citywide gallery exhibit was put in place titled SAFE SEX IS HOT SEX. A series of steamy, sexually-explicit large-scale photographs by Steven Meisel began infiltrating Manhattan—replicated inside slice joint windows from West 14th Street to West Houston Street, framed as wall art inside tiny restaurants beside twisted Ginko lined city streets, wonder-glued on West Village, Chelsea, and Hell's Kitchen buildings, and even celebrated on one oversized tribute billboard in Times Square. Our own hieroglyphics for all the future generations to see.

History, I suppose. Our history. It fascinates me. And being a part of history as it happens affords me a place to belong. These posters—no different than a Torso Magazine, the community initiatives and the advocacy, and the demand for change are the proof in the pudding.

I inhale hard and take in cigarette smoke, and the men in their leather gear who assemble here at one of the last remaining public spaces for cruising and exploration of backroom sex. I exhale a cloud of smoke into the night, the blue-black lights, the throbbing primal rites, and turn to face a collection of leathermen who all look the same—same haircut, same harness, same probing eyes, and off we go.

Wipe the bar, Meat Market coaster, smile handsome for tips to pay my electric bill.

"Heya. What can I get ya?"

"I can never make up my mind. It's like I'm always chasing my tail."

"Sorry to rush you, man, but there's a little bit of a line."

"Okay. Okay. I'm not a common cur. No need to be so *Rrrufff*."

"How about a Greyhound? You know—Vodka with grapefruit?"

"*Rrrufff, rrrufff*."

"No? Hmmm. Salty Chihuahua?"

Into puppy play. Not all the way paper-trained. Sadly, no one will adopt him.

"Would you make me a Pink Poodle?"

"No."

"Fine. Stolichnaya Vodka. *Rrrufff, rrrufff*. Neat."

Rocks glass with my left hand, Stolichnaya from the shelf

behind me, second up from the counter, without even turning my torso, three-count pour—one one-thousand, two one-thousand, three one-thousand.

"Who's a good boy? Who's a good boy? *You*'re a good boy! *Yes, you are!* Yes, *you are! Here, boy.* Have a Vodka!"

"Bitch, please. *Grrrowl.*"

Wipe the bar, Meat Market coaster, smile handsome for tips to pay my gas bill.

"Heya. What can I get ya?"

"Beer me, Butch."

"I got Bud Lite, Coors Lite, Keystone Lite, Miller Lite, Michelob Ultra, Amstel Light, Corona Light Mexican Lager, and Wachusett Light IPA."

"I'll have an Amstel Light. Hey, pal, I got a small question. Is there a Lost and Found at this joint?"

"Nah. Believe me, man—anything that falls to the floor in this place you don't wanna pick up. Unless, of course, it's your boyfriend."

Made a big commotion by going from Kenny to Kenneth when he came out. Threw himself a Coming Out Party. So did every other Kenneth.

Grab the flashlight, Amstel Light from the cooler on the left.

"You ain't kidding, pal. This one time I lost my wristwatch up some guy's *tuchkis* in that very backroom. It was an anniversary present from my boyfriend. Sadly, I never saw it again."

"Wha? Huh?"

"Yeah, I know, right? Thank goodness it was only a knockoff Rolex from 14th Street. Ever since then I leave my good jewelry at home. And my boyfriend."

Wipe the bar, Meat Market coaster, smile handsome for tips to pay my rent which is due in a week.

"Heya. What can I get ya?"

"I'll take a beer, brother. I'm working up a buzz to check out the backroom. Is it *all that*?"

"Men slip in and out of the shadows. Sometimes they're dancing. Sometimes they're choking on a dick. Sometimes they're fucking. It's all that."

"I feel at home already."

"Desire led us all here."

"People call me Grunt."

"Good to know you, man. You got this, Grunt. Before backroom bars, we screwed each other in alleys and beneath trucks. Dilapidated warehouses at the piers. This is nothing you ain't seen, brother. Okay, so I got Bud Lite, Coors Lite, Keystone Lite, Miller Lite, Michelob Ultra, Amstel Light, Corona Light Mexican Lager, and Wachusett Light IPA."

"I'll take a Bud Lite. I remember that entire scene like it was yesterday."

"Oh yeah?"

"Oh yeahhh. All the fucking underneath the overnight rigs parked at the meatpacking slaughterhouses. All those dark alleys."

"The decaying, cavernous rooms at the piers. Filled with all that dangerous sex."

"What a fucking time it was. Always the risk of being mugged or, even worse, falling right through the slippery, rotting wooden pier into the Hudson River—thump, splash, trump, sploosh, thump, splosh. I miss the danger of the good old days. What a fucking bore sex is anymore."

He's seen everything. Fat septum ring in his nose. Goateed and handsome.

"Look at it this way. Maybe the police will raid the bar tonight. We'll all be arrested for sucking and fucking in public and finally live out our fantasy of a no holds barred orgy at Rikers Island. Did you ever think of that? Talk about getting lucky. Am I right?"

"You're making my dick hard, man."

"Always happy to lend a hand, Grunt."

Grab the flashlight, Bud Lite from the cooler on...now, where the fuck did he disappear to so quickly?

Wipe the bar, Meat Market coaster, smile handsome for tips toward a decent share on Fire Island this year.

"What can I—well, look who's here!"

"Who might dat be, or what? Which ways are we lookin'?"

"You, 'Sparre. I'm talking about you. What can I get ya?"

"One Drambuie wit' a long pour of house Scotch of de rocks, please. Do yuh got any Angostura Bitters fawh dat? Only if it ain't no kinda problem, *paisano* of mine. Yuh got me so fahr?"

"So far I got ya, man."

Rocks glass with my left hand, Drambuie from the shelf behind me, third up from the counter, without even turning my torso, cheap-ass house Scotch from the speed rack, two-count pour of both—one one-thousand, two one-thousand, skip the Angostura Bitters altogether.

"How's your night going, killer?"

"Killuh? Ain't dat a kick tuh de meatballs! Okay? So far at dis particular moment, I must say dat dis has been a very pleasant evenin' fawh me. Ya' dig? Ya' dig?"

"I dig. I dig. It's all fun and games until somebody gets their foreskin tangled up into a knot, huh 'Sparrc?"

"Yuh Manhattanite homosexual types are so freakin' funny, Brudduh!"

Dink. All the lights at The Meat Market dissolve to pitch black. Except for the miniature blue gleam of a 6-watt cash register bulb and the red-yellow glow of random lit cigarettes scattered across the bar, the darkness is palpable. Silence. Nary a boot-strapped motorcycle boot dares to jangle.

The doorman and I flick the battery switches on our Underground Miner Hard Hats with attached battery lamps, and the music kicks in, something sultry with deep beats by Bronski Beat, and beneath that the resonance of random shuffling, zipper adjusting, and carnal gasps for breath.

Wipe the bar, Meat Market coaster, smile handsome for tips to pay my electric bill.

"Heya. What can I get ya?"

"Yuh got Bourbon?"

"I do indeed."

"Yuh got Coca-Cola or what?"

"I do."

Needy and aggressive at the same time. Always looking for an extra ticket to the Pier Dance. He'll fuck you for it.

Highball glass with my left hand, house Bourbon from the speed rack, cola from the soda gun, three-count pour—one one-thousand, two one-thousand, three one-thousand.

"There you have it, friend. One Bourbon and Coke."

"Yuh know I said absolutely nuttin' about mixin' dem togethuh."

"Wha? Huh? Well...sure, that I can do. I'm gonna have to charge you for a cocktail *and* a soda, though."

"What a rip-off. What a fawkin' rip-off. It's fine. It's fine. I'll drink it de way it is. Sheesh, gay bars, am I right? Fawkin' gay bars."

"So, we're good to go with your cocktail, right?"

"Listen, do yuh know where a guy might be able to scawh a ticket to the dance at de pier?"

"Sorry. I do not."

"I'm willin' tuh trade fawh me poppin' a load off up your ass. What time do yuh get off, Stud?"

"I gotta go, man."

Wipe the bar, Meat Market coaster, smile handsome for tips to pay my gas bill.

"Heya. What can I get ya?"

"Well, let me ssseee...Lisssen, can I be completely honessst? I'm jussst looking for the toiletsss. The ladiesss toiletsss. Sssee, I prefer to sssit."

Graduated lauding cum from The Paul Lynde College of Effete Effects.

"It's past the pool table and just beyond the cigarette machine. Two doors. Right is for tops. Bottoms is left. There's probably a line. After that, the darkroom with the red light is...well, don't pee in there. Unless you're into that."

"Thanksss, Doll."

Wipe the bar, Meat Market coaster, smile handsome for tips to pay my rent which is due in a week.

"Heya. What can I get ya?"

"Hey, I'm Matthew."

"Yes, I know. Hi, Matthew."

"Matthew Musgrove."

"Again, fully aware. What can I—"

"It's good to mcct me, right?"

Magazine gossip columnist. Handsome. Sexy at first glance. I learned my lesson the hard way. Two times.

"So, what can I offer you, Matthew?"

"Something watered-down, I imagine. Ultimately, that's what you'll serve me anyway. Does it really matter what I order, Daddy? Or do you prefer I call you Mr. Daddy? Honestly, after last night's floorshow, I can hardly raise a glass to my lips. I said I can *hardly* raise a glass—make it a double. I'm meeting my friends Robyn and Joey. Byrd and Steffano. In that order. Is there a private celebrity room here or...?"

Rocks glass with my left hand, Bacardi from the shelf behind me, third up from the counter, without even turning my torso, five-count pour—one one-thousand, two one-thousand, three one-thousand, four one-thousand, five one-thousand.

"This one is on me, Matt."

"I *said* it's Matthew. Burning bridges is my shtick."

"Again, fully aware. You should probably see someone for that."

"Droll, Daddy. Droll. Yesterday's news."

"Lemme know when Robyn Byrd gets here. That girl knows how to *par-tay*."

"Maybe you could bang her box."

"Thanks. Now that song is gonna be stuck circling in my brain all night."

"Sorry. Not."

Wipe the bar, Meat Market coaster, smile handsome for tips toward a decent share on Fire Island this year.

"Heya. What can I—well, of all people!"

"Who is it dis time, *Googootz*, or what?"

"What can I get ya, 'Sparre?"

"One Drambuie wit' a long pour of house Scotch of de rocks, please. Yuh must realize my cocktail by dis time. Right? Yuh got me so fahr?"

"So far I got ya, man."

"*Paisano*, can yuh explain it tuh me again how dis adventure here wawhks dis evenin' or what?"

"There's really not a lot to tell. It's completely random."

"Tuh tell de truth I'm not really comprehendin' what you're layin' down. Okay? If yuh was askin' me what a Meatball Parm wit' extra red sauce might cost ya I'd happily explain it tuh yuh. And here I am askin' a simple inquiry and I feel as though perhaps you're not tellin' me everythin' yuh know about de situashun at hand, *Googootz*. Yuh with me?"

"It happens when it happens. It's completely out of my control."

Rocks glass with my left hand, Drambuie from the shelf behind me, third up from the counter, without even turning my torso, cheap-ass house Scotch from the speed rack, two-count pour of both—one one-thousand, two one-thousand, skip the Angostura Bitters altogether.

"You've got your hand on de pulse of dis place. Yuh with me? Dat certainly is a mattuh of fact dat I would catergawhize as remarkable. Somethin' tells me dere's mawh tuh dis here party than you're lettin' on tuh me. Yuh got me so fahr?"

"Yeah, it's all fun and games until somebody drops their poppers on the dance floor. Suddenly every Leather Queen in the room gets the vapors."

"Yuh Manhattanite homosexual types are so freakin' funny, Brudduh!"

Dink. All the lights at The Meat Market dissolve to pitch

black. Except for the miniature blue gleam of a 6-watt cash register bulb and the red-yellow glow of random lit cigarettes scattered across the bar, the darkness is unmistakable. Secrecy. Nary a hand-built pair of leather chaps dares to unsnap.

The doorman and I flick the battery switches on our Underground Miner Hard Hats with attached battery lamps, and the music kicks in, something sultry with deep beats by Frankie Goes To Hollywood, and beneath that the reverberation of anonymous scuffling, flannel shirt unbuttoning, and intimate heaves of exhalation.

Every Thursday, The Meat Market hosts a Blackout Party. The event is exclusive, a big draw, and I accumulate a good thirty percent of my weekly tip revenue during these sex parties. The bar offers two-dollar select canned beer all night through and, beginning at about 9:00 p.m., the DJ douses the lights for random twenty-minute intervals. Anything goes.

The Meat Market occupies a long-closed, former slaughterhouse and meat packaging plant. Boasting several obtuse corners, a winding maze through abandoned business offices, and refurbished cattle stalls that are often pitch-black, the barroom itself is dim enough to ensure anonymity, ass-grabbing, crotch grinding, and even more intimate forms of leather play.

The parties are sweat-fests to encourage the leather brothers of our tribe—pros and first-timers, kinks and more vanilla-types, the old and the young—to dance and fornicate, crash and retreat, crash and retreat, with hundreds of other guys. Pretty much everything goes down at a Blackout Party, at least in twenty-minute intervals.

I can hear him breathing next to me in the dark behind the bar. Before he speaks a word, I feel the warmth from his torso beside me. Filthy fragments of sentences he uttered echo in my brain: "If we do this, there will be rules. Do you think you can play by the rules, sexy fucker?"

His body smells of perspiration and cigarette smoke. He stands completely still, and I notice his thick mustache, ribcage, thighs, and crotch pressing into me. His lumbering lion's paw rests at the beltloop near the crack of my ass. I breathe the scent of him inside, in and out, in and out, in and out, until I require it for sustenance, to survive.

"Hi, baby."

"Hi, hello, hi there, ummm..."

Distracted and lost for words, I drop my eyes and the projectile beam from my Miner Hard Hat with attached battery lamp illuminates a path down his muscle-ripped torso and lands at his crotch. I look too long. He smiles too big, fully aware. And instantly, I am revealed.

"When you're done checking out my dick, I really gotta make rounds, baby," he growls.

"Wha? Huh?"

"I'll stand here as long as you want, sexy fucker. I just stepped behind the bar because I need supplies. But I'm in no rush to depart. Lights are out anyway."

"Take whatever you need. I mean...what kinda supplies? Can I grab you a beer? You got condoms to hand out?"

"No beer. I got my hands full. Yeah, baby—I grabbed an extra case of prophylactics from the basement because I had a feeling it was gonna be a busy evening. The fucking New York City Department of Health only sent us one size. I hope everybody is okay with magnums."

"Sounds about right to me."

"Oh, yeah? Is that what you like, baby?"

"I...uh, yeah. Are you sure I can't get you something to drink or—"

"Lucky for you. Things seem to be working out to your advantage."

"Oh, yeah. Er, yeah?"

"Oh, yeah"

"I...uhhh—"

"You got any batteries back here? This damn hard hat is fucked. Light keeps going in and out, in and out, first in, then out."

"Sure thing. Check the drawer with the recipe dictionary. I think I saw some extra batteries in there underneath the drop envelope with the rolls of quarters, dimes, and nickels."

Given that the bar is built from a former slaughterhouse and meat packaging plant, The Meat Market is an enormous place. Men are sucking and fucking all around us. Behind the bar, however, there is barely enough room for one man to negotiate—let alone two grown men to untangle successfully in the pitch-black darkness.

"Where was I to look?"

"In the drawer, Doorman. Just underneath the cash register there's a—"

"Jeez, I can be so clumsy. Was that me? That's my bad."

"No, no. That is not a problem."

"If I could just step behind you for one moment," as the sweat and heat from his lion's paws rests at my waist above either hip.

"Oh, I, er...yeah, of course. Cool."

"Fuck, baby, I had no intention at all of being so personal."

"Really? Because it's alright. It's alright if you—"

"I know what I want. It's not for you to say. When the time is right, I'll just fucking take it."

"Lemme see...ummm, batteries, batteries...er, batteries, drop bag, pack of Reds. Where are those fucking batteries?"

"Nobody told you to move. There are rules, fucker."

"Usually...I keep...everything so organized. I've just been a little preoccupied lately, ya know?"

"Tell me, baby. What's on your mind?"

"You'd be surprised by the thoughts that circle my imagination."

"Wha? Oh, yeah? Oh yeah, baby?"

"Oh, yeahhh."

An energy begins at the soles of my feet, and I feel it racing like mercury inside of me. My face is on fire. His hands at the small of my back are burning. The stubble of his beard brushes against my nipples, and suddenly he's tugging hard at my leatherman's harness. I can feel where his fingers are moving, and my head falls backward, with his teeth against my neck, and...Whhhrrr. The lights come up.

"Wha? Oh, yeah? Must be just my dumbbell luck or something."

"Wha? Huh?"

"I cannot wait to have you all to my own, baby. I think I'll make you beg for it first. I could make you beg for hours. You gonna take orders like an obedient fucker?"

"I ummm, uh-huh. Uh-huh."

"Right now, I gotta get back to work, baby."

"Yeah. There's gonna be a line of...ummm, leathermen looking for me."

"I will see you later. I got plans for us, baby. Wait'll you see what I got in store for us. I got plans you're gonna dig, baby."

"That's something I can get behind...I mean, ummm, in front of—well, you know what I mean."

Wipe the bar, Meat Market coaster, smile handsome for tips to pay my electric bill.

"Heya. What can I get ya?"

"Scotch rocks. Stet."

Jewish doctor. Looking to marry a Jewish lawyer.

Rocks glass with my left hand, house Scotch from the speed rack, three-count pour—one one-thousand, two one-thousand, three one-thousand.

"Here's looking at ya."

"Bartender, you haven't happened to see a fellow about my age, shorter...er, on the shorter side, maybe this tall. He's got a winning smile. You haven't seen him, have ya?"

"All night long, man. All night long."

"This guy might be wearing a tie. I dunno, we had plans to meet here for a couple weeks now, and well, nobody said anything about there being some kinda drug-fueled, Bacchanalian love-fest sex party taking over the place tonight."

"Look, if I see him, I'll send him your way. In the meantime, why not try to enjoy yourself?"

"Oh, I would. I will. It's just that I'm afraid to touch anything. And then the lights go out and I'm afraid to move."

Wipe the bar, Meat Market coaster, smile handsome for tips to pay my gas bill.

"Heya. What can I get ya?"

"I'm Kevin. Kevin's my name. From the Bronx. I came from El Bronx."

"Whatcha drinking, Boogie Down?"

"Whassup? You up? You up for it? Looking? For now? Free now? Are you off soon? That's hot. You're hot."

Perpetual nose wiper. Slicks his tongue across his teeth. Practically polishes away the enamel.

"How about a drink?"

"Yeah? Oh yeah. Lemme get. Lemme take. Tequila. Decent Tequila. I'll take Tequila."

Rocks glass with my left hand, Tequila from the shelf behind me, third up from the counter, without even turning my torso, three-count pour—one one-thousand, two one-thousand, three one-thousand.

"Here ya go."

"Lime? Got a lime? Any limes? Any lime to go with this, please? Ya got limes?"

"Here ya go, man. Slice of lime. Sorry to rush you, El Bronx. There's a line this evening."

"I got lines. You want lines? You want a bump. I'll sell ya a bump? Primo shit. Never been stepped on. Pure shit, man. I got bumps. Are you off soon? You're hot."

Wipe the bar, Meat Market coaster, smile handsome for tips to pay my rent which is due in a week.

"Heya. What can I get ya?"

"Duuude! Can I get a Vodka, Dudesicle?"

Went to Columbia. Won't shut up about it.

"I'm on it like Donkey Kong, Frat Boy."

"Right on, Dudearoooni!"

Rocks glass with my left hand, house Vodka from the speed rack, four-count pour just because he's cute—one one-thousand, two one-thousand, three one-thousand, four one-thousand.

"That's four bucks, man."

"Thanks, Chief. Go Lions! Yeah!"

Wipe the bar, Meat Market coaster, smile handsome for tips toward a decent share on Fire Island this year.

"What a surprise! If it isn't 'Sparre."

"It ain't like yuh din't notice me just a minute ago. Right? Which I'm certain yuh did. Right? You've been makin' me drinks all night. Ya' dig? Dis I am certain yuh realize by dis point. I mean I do unnerstand how busy yuh must be, *Googootz*. But I've been here all night, my Brudduh. Right? We've already had dis same conversashun."

"Sure. What can I get ya, 'Sparre?"

"One Drambuie wit' a long pour of house Scotch of de rocks, please. Yuh got me so fahr? Right, or what? Do yuh got any Angostura Bitters fawh dat, or what? Yuh got me so fahr?"

"So far I got ya, man."

"So, tell me somethin' I've been wonderin', Dominic. Is dis your *novio*, or what?"

Rocks glass with my left hand, Drambuie from the shelf behind me, third up from the counter, without even turning my torso, cheap-ass house Scotch from the speed rack, two-count pour of both—one one-thousand, two one-thousand, skip the Angostura Bitters altogether.

"Wha? Huh? Who?"

"De man I saw yuh wit' at my restaurant. Well, ya know, at my restaurant where I wait tables. On Eighth Avenue. Of cawhse, I doan own de place. Right? I've got othuh plans. Okay? Yuh wit' me, or what? One day I'm gonna go tuh college. We all stab our meatball wit' a fawhk, yuh fuwhk. Ya' dig? But that's anudduh stawhy. Okay? A stawhy fawh anudduh daytime. So, de man dat wawhks de doawh. De doawhman de fuwhk. Right? Yuh wit' me, or what? *Googootz*, is he your boyfriend, or what?"

"No, 'Sparre. He is not my boyfriend."

"Becawze I can see it. Okay, or what? I can see de way he touches yuh. Yuh got me so fahr? De way he makes yuh feel inside yawhself. Right? If perhaps dat ain't too personal a ting tuh say. Right? Which, when I tink about it, I do not believe it is too personal a ting tuh say becawze aftuh all, yuh and I are friends. Right?"

"Right. We're friends. And the same goes for me and the doorman. We're just buddies. Ya dig?"

"Yuh Manhattanite homosexual types are so freakin' funny, Brudduh!"

Dink. All the lights at The Meat Market dissolve to pitch black. Except for the miniature blue gleam of a 6-watt cash register bulb and the red-yellow glow of random lit cigarettes scattered across the bar, the darkness is substantial. Restraint. Nary a leatherman's harness dares to unhinge.

The doorman and I flick the battery switches on our Underground Miner Hard Hats with attached battery lamps, and the music kicks in, something sultry with deep beats by Eurythmics, and beneath that the vacillation of stealthy padding, poppers inhalation, and passionate pants for breath.

Wipe the bar, Meat Market coaster, smile handsome for tips to pay my electric bill.

"Heya. What can I get ya?"

"I'm feeling a Vodka Martini. Yes, a Vodka Martini is in order. But first I'm feeling my bladder—and during this brief intermission, I think I should most likely take the opportunity to eliminate."

Broadway Queen. Can recite Lorna Luft's tour dates. Also, her complete setlist.

"It's past the pool table and just beyond the cigarette machine. Two doors. Right is for tops. Bottoms is left. There's probably a line. After that the darkroom with the red light is...well, don't pee in there. Unless you're into that."

"Bravo!" Indeed.

Wipe the bar, Meat Market coaster, smile handsome for tips to pay my gas bill.

"Heya. What can I get ya?"

"Just a simple beer for a simple man who needs sustenance and fortitude."

Elijah. The poet, not the prophet. Struggling East Village artist.

"I got Bud Lite, Coors Lite, Keystone Lite, Miller Lite, Michelob Ultra, Amstel Light, Corona Light Mexican Lager, and Wachusett Light IPA."

"Well, in that case, I shall opt for a Corona Light Mexican Lager, kind sir."

"Sir is fine. I ain't that kind."

"Whoa. Well, you certainly seem like the type."

Grab the flashlight, Corona Light Mexican Lager from the cooler on the left.

Wipe the bar, Meat Market coaster, smile handsome for tips to pay my rent which is due in a week.

"Heya. What can I get ya?"

"Mariposita! Hermano mío!"

"What?"

"Maybeee ju neeet to waaahhhtch wheeere ju'are walkin', puta?"

"Who are you? Who are you! Listen—you don't belong here!"

Rocks glass in my left hand that I'm prepared to use as a weapon. With my right hand, I finger a bottle from the speed rack that I can easily shatter over the bar rail if I need to protect myself. Seconds drip like lifetimes. I scream in agony, but no voice comes out of me.

My skin is gooseflesh in the cool, cruel, colorless autumn. After the Sun goes down, the denizens walk the land. Out the big, oak door and directly into the purple morning, overcome and about to burst from lack of oxygen, vrrrooommm, vrrrooommm, vrrrooommm. My body is pins-and-needles sensations, frozen and numb. My hands, arms, legs, fingers, toes—all like a colorless autumn leaf failing and then falling from a colorless autumn tree. In this gaddammed backyard in this lousy city.

I struggle to free my arms, my hands, my fingers, but I am no match. Time is running out for me. Maybe if I pretend to not hear him, he'll let me off easy this one time. Wrong, faggot. Wrong, faggot. In the squalls of an impending autumn storm, I scan the room for the doorman.

One one-thousand, I ummm, uh...I replay our time together before it's gone. One one-thousand, two one-thousand, three one-thousand. I hear my heart thumping in my ears. We've still got some history to write, the doorman and me. Yes, I see it. Yes, I see it. Yes, I see it. Plans I'm gonna dig. Just the way I like.

This sinuous lifetime is spiraling, inching toward a cumulative climax. And this is how it happens. This is where they find me. Dusty Springfield sings something drifting and distracted, on a tinny, old juke. Something about a woman who rises up, then dies, and I can hear him breathing next to me, behind the bar, before he says one word.

Raucous laughter rings in the air. I search for the wad of cash in my front pocket, and my wallet at my back hip, and the keys to my apartment. One one-thousand, two one-thousand, three one-thousand. With the disquiet and angst that only a young man can summon, I furiously propel myself to the surface, gasping for oxygen and grabbing at life. I pray to Jesus Christ himself.

And when I look for a second time, he is gone. All alone—that's who I am.

Wipe the bar, Meat Market coaster, smile handsome for tips toward a decent share on Fire Island this year.

"What can I get ya?"

"One Drambuie wit' a long pour of house Scotch of de rocks, please. *Paisano* of mine."

"Who was in front of you?"

"What de fuwhk are yuh tawhkin' about?"

"In front of you, Guasparre. Who the fuck was standing on line in front of you?"

"I ain't moved, Brudduh. I ain't moved fawh one inch from dis red leadduh bar stool. De whole time I've been right here. Yuh got me so fahr? Ya' dig, or what?"

"That isn't true. I saw him."

"So freakin' funny, Brudduh!"

I'm lost somewhere in the sooty clouds above me when I notice the slobbering noises. The aesthetic sensibilities couldn't have been scripted more astutely by Joe Gage himself, the first filmmaker who dared to suggest that sex between men was more about camaraderie than romance. Guasparre Gagliardi is sitting tall on a ripped, red leather bar stool having a conversation with me, and getting his dick sucked at the same time.

"Oh my fuckin' merciful gawd on heaven dat mouth is like fuckin' velvet, Brudduh."

"I can see that you're having a good time there, but maybe you should zip up your fly. At least until the lights go down again."

"I cannot becawze dese are button fly jeans. Okay?"

"Then take a moment to button your pants, please."

"Nah. I'm fine ovuh here. One Drambuie wit' a long pour of house Scotch of de rocks, please. Right?"

The rocks glass is already in my left hand. I was prepared to propel it at a stranger. Drambuie from the shelf behind me, third up from the counter, without even turning my torso—do not dare look in the mirror—cheap-ass house Scotch from the speed rack, two-count pour of both—skip the Angostura Bitters altogether.

"Listen to me. I thought I asked you to put your junk away while the lights are up."

"Now I get it! Okay? Okay! I finally unnerstand why it is you're always so happy tuh see me. All night long. Yuh with me? Yuh like tuh watch, doan yuh? Yuh dig watchin' me get my fat, uncut dick sucked off. I cannot say dat I blame yuh. It is a pretty dick. *Un pene così bello!* And den yuh wanna know who it is in front of me becawze you're jealous. But dere is mawh than enough of my *cazzo* tuh go around. Okay? Ya' dig? Let me tell yuh dat yuh are free tuh watch anytime yuh like tuh do so, *mio amico Nicolo*. Right?"

"I'm only gonna say it one more time, Gagliardi."

"*Maddon' Mi! Meengya! Tiempo! Tiempo!*"

"Wha? Huh?"

"De time! Okay? What is de mudder fuwhkin' time?"

"A little after 1:00 a.m."

"I'm very late. Ya' dig? Tuh meet my boyfriend. Yuh got me so fahr? De love of my life. On de Staten Island of New Yawhk City. Ya' dig? Yuh with me?"

"You have a boyfriend?"

And with a resounding pop that echoes from The Meat Market to the South Ferry to the Staten Island side, Guasparre forcibly yanks his pretty, uncut dick from his fervent admirer's mouth. His chest deflates and thrusts involuntarily as he spews a hot stream of Italian curses guaranteed to rouse his dead mother. "*Va fongool! Vai a fare in culo! Facia-brota skifosa. Mi Meengya, Stonato!*" and he forcefully ejaculates, a tiny chaotic cyclone that targets the dicksucker, the ripped, red leather bar stool, and the bar top itself.

"Well, it's all fun and games until somebody brings Butter Flavored Crisco to the orgy. Suddenly, all the leathermen pull out their recipe caddies."

"*Maddon' Mi!* So freakin' fun, Brudduh."

He stands abruptly. The dicksucker chokes on his foreskin. Dink. All the lights at The Meat Market dissolve to pitch black. Except for the miniature blue gleam of a 6-watt cash register bulb and the red-yellow glow of random lit cigarettes scattered across the bar, the darkness is noticeable. Stillness. Nary a five-speed cock ring dares to snap unclosed.

The doorman and I flick the battery switches on our Underground Miner Hard Hats with attached battery lamps, and the music kicks in, something sultry with deep beats by Soft Cell, and beneath that the vibration of deliberate scuffling, belt buckles clanking against the floor, and sensual gulps for air.

FIVE

THIS MORNING I wake up feeling rested. Strangely centered, as if growth has transpired during sleep and I stand tall at the precipice of something larger than I can comprehend. I lie in the sweaty sheets and breathe the morning deeply into my lungs, the salty Hudson River, the twisting Ginkgo tree-lined streets, the rusted-out iron fire escape outside my bedroom window that follows a path toward the future. I consider that maybe the terrifying nightmares and the daydreams of what tomorrow holds have arrived at a compromise. I can see the experiences of my youth in Chicago and my growing up years in New York City all collated in precise, cataloged fashion.

Such a curious sense of calm is eerie and leaves me ruffled. My first steps out of bed are tentative and exploratory. I search the apartment for staple comforts—David Wojnarowicz posters hung inside flimsy plastic frames, my crumpled leather motorcycle jacket, dirty t-shirts and worn jockstraps in a heap on the seventies-style parquet floor, my combat boots beside my favorite cowhide tuxedo chair, mouse droppings hidden in mine bomb fashion. Small familiarities prove I am indeed awake and moving through real life.

I spring the yellowed, paper window shade and look for Jerome, but his apartment is quiet and lifeless. As I do so, white-hot morning time sunshine bursts into the apartment like a flooded dam. From one chirping abuela to another, "*Mira*, Betty! Ju got waaater?" ricochets off the bricked courtyard windows of Barrow Street, as I turn my face and catch the time on a digital clock atop a makeshift end table of Paul Monette hardcovers. The crimson numerals read 9:15 a.m. I've not been awake this early in lifetimes.

In the past—man, especially these last few weeks, nine in the morning was the hour when I'd scrunch my eyes closed as tightly as I was able with sheer exhaustion, after a difficult shift of tending bar, avoiding the premonitions and night terrors, engaging in drunken behavior and careless sex, with whatever mix of alcohol and illicit drugs swirling in my brain it took to secure rest.

This morning, however, finds me with the Sun painting my body through the yellowed, paper window shades, and a curious sense of growth empowers me. I search the pocket of my motor-cycle jacket for a Red and light it from a branded The Meat Market book of matches that reads *A Butcher Bar*. I pad barefoot around the seventies-style parquet floor, step out of and kick aside my underwear, and move toward a shower—determined to discover precisely what it is that people do at this hour of the day.

The water spray of a shower that knows no temperature more than lukewarm is pins and needles on my skin. I menace a cock-roach in the bathtub with my big toe, and watch it and the night-mares circle the drain and disappear. I lather my biceps and my armpits and finger a yellowing bruise beneath my pierced nipple where I was pelted with the beer bottle the other night. Strangely, even the recollection of the incident with the cordovan maroon Pontiac Bonneville Firebird Trans Am lives outside the periphery of contemplation this morning.

On the other side of the glass brick shower window, a mother pigeon sits watchful guard atop a nest she's constructed for her soon-to-be hatchlings. The enterprising pigeons of New York City are forever on the move. They build flimsy platform nests of sticks undercover on the window ledges of apartment buildings. The females lay blue speckled eggs which hatch with consistent sitting, and then they abandon their flying-rat babies to get knocked up and again begin the process on a different window ledge of a different apartment building. It's their answer to the ever-increasing cost of housing across the city. Without rent control laws in place, these industrious flying tenants typically relocate every three weeks. One of the advantages to traveling light, I suppose. When I reach to replace the soap to its recessed subway tile shower window, the mother pigeon squawks a warning and flaps her expansive wings against the glass—patiently waiting for the day when she can take flight from responsibility to soar away to a higher plane.

The water trickle tickles my flat tummy and the hairs around my treasure trail as steam rises around me in fat, drippy clouds. It reminds me of the scene when Dorothy liquidates her evil, green nemesis and watches her woes dissipate before her eyes.

I towel myself in front of the mirror and, as I erase a spot of steam, I almost catch myself smiling at the silly *The Wizard of Oz* metaphor. I search my brown eyes but dare not to look for answers —even this morning that's more than I'll allow. Having arrived at the unprecedented bluff of what tomorrow holds, I digest each moment with suspicion and tentative toe-dipping. All mirrors get cloudy and lose reflectiveness over time. Best to not press my good fortune.

Inside the glass, I recognize the familiar traces of an attractive man and a smile that forms easily with a space between my two front teeth big enough to pass a dime. The thick mustache that extends well beyond the corners of my mouth and trails the smile lines to touch my chin is modeled after Glenn Hughes of Village People fame. I laugh aloud when I consider all the adolescent time lost in my second-floor bedroom, knotty pine and avocado shag rug, with my hand stuffed down my jeans, studying his image on album covers and posters hung with shiny brass tacks, and growing up to mix the man Tequila and Cokes and share conversation with him from three feet across the bar rail at The Meat Market. "Okay, this is who I am now."

I dress in a tight-fitting white t-shirt and worn-through 501s and my Yankees baseball cap. I steal *The New York Post* from across the hallway and sit down heavily in my favorite cowhide tuxedo chair to roll a joint and pore over Reid Miller's theatre chatter; a galvanizing production of Stephen Sondheim's *Passion*, a lengthy liturgy on *Angels in America* and its epochal heft, and a prediction that newcomer Audra Ann McDonald will win a Tony Award for *Carousel* head the stories.

For a second time, I peruse my private, proscenium, courtyard window for Jerome, but the dust motes Bump and Grapevine all alone this morning. Must be an early call to set day for him.

I digest one, two, three forks full of leftover Pork Fried Rice. I empty three overflowing, pilfered, and branded The Meat Market ashtrays into the toilet. I retrieve two glue traps occupied with squeaky rodent inhabitants and toss them out the courtyard window aiming for somewhere close to the dumpster. Who cares, I think. Everyone else in the building does it. It's our enterprising answer to West Village housing without rent control laws in place.

I clear a path of dirty t-shirts and worn jockstraps in a heap on the seventies-style parquet floor. I make the sweaty bed. I pad barefoot through the rooms without one terrifying thought passing through my brain and consider that maybe I am making progress. Most simply put, I suffer with premonitions guided by fear. And If I accept fear, there's no room to be frightened. I can just toss it out the courtyard window and aim for the dumpster. For right now, with the protection of a flimsy platform nest built of sticks, what would be the point for concern? So, I'm no longer afraid because ensconced in the most secret inner-working of me, I believe it will all be over soon anyway.

I scan the room for something to occupy my time, anything to fill the quiet. I'm ambitious enough to dust the nightstand with a dirty t-shirt procured from the seventies-style parquet floor. My wallet, the keys to my apartment, a wad of cash, poppers, a steel cock ring, and a couple licked-clean baggies of cocaine—the remnants of the purple dawn's amusements—are all relegated to their proper places of rest. Red is autumn, green is summer.

I think to call Claudia, but she's been my alarm clock for so long I don't even know her telephone number. I need to ask her for it and write it down the next time we speak. Does it begin with 212 or was she assigned one of the dreaded bridge-and-tunnel exchanges? Christ, the embarrassment of having to pay some skyrocketing Manhattan rent and being branded by Bell Atlantic with an outer-borough area code. Mortifying when one meets a prospective employer or potential sex partner only to offer up your digits and receive a dreaded eyeroll in return—as if life happened in any of the other boroughs.

So I'm checking to see if the gas range actually ignites, because in truth I'm not certain the gas bill has been satisfied—all that smiling at strangers, all those pleasant, "What can I get ya's," for naught—when the phone rings, and in my haste to answer it, I trip over my combat boots standing tall beside my favorite cowhide tuxedo chair, and all but face plant in a glue trap hidden just to the left of the radiator.

Brrriiing, brrriiing.

"For fucks'sake, that was a close one!"

"Huh?"

"I was nearly trapped in one of my own devices: a tray coated with sticky adhesive, destined to suffer a slow death by starvation."

"At one of your afterhours underground sex parties?"

"Wha? Huh?"

"Some things I do not wish to know, Girl."

"Never mind, never mind. Good morning, Claudia."

"Good what? Girl? Girl—is that you?"

"It's me. And I'm not a girl."

"Ummm, wait one moment...I believe I've dialed the wrong number."

"Nope. It is I. Listen, are you a 212?"

"Who are you and what have you done with Dominic?"

"...or a 718? Surely, you're not a 347. You're not a 347, are you?"

"Jesus Effing Christ, what are you blathering on about? Look, you put my best friend on the horn this very minute or I will be forced to hang up and dial New York's fattest...er, finest."

"Call them should you choose. Have them send a handsome one, please. It will still be me when he arrives."

"Huh. Get a load of that, will ya? It *is* you."

"Precisely what I've been trying to tell you."

"Are you still up from last night? Jesus Effing Christ! Are you *still* up? Please tell me you're not still awake from last night, Girl."

"I am neither still up partying from last evening nor am I a—"

"Girl—how did you know it was me?"

"Who else would it be? You call me every morning, Claudia. Honestly, you're probably the only reason I keep this line. Which reminds me—I need to get your telephone number. I don't even recall your area code. Are you a 212, too?"

"Are you certain you're not as high as a kite? You sound kinda as high as a kite. You haven't ingested something at one of your afterhours underground sex parties, now have you, Girl?"

"Nope. Not stoned. I've been outta bed and awake for hours."

"Oh, you have not."

"Sorry to disagree. Made coffee. Ate a nutritious breakfast. Finished the crossword. It was a Friday crossword too, may I add. And I finished it in pen."

"You did what?"

"Uh-huh. Showered, even thought about shaving. Blew my handsome, soap opera husband and got him off to his early call to set day. "

"You and Jerome? Oh, you did not. That I will not believe. That man is as masculine as Bruce Jenner. A gold medal-winning straight boy. Are you certain you're not high? You sound high. Did you wake and bake this morning?"

I'm still forking leftover Pork Fried Rice, spitting the peas out the courtyard window, intriguing the fickle pigeon, and watching the tiny green dots disappear from my third-floor window, bounce once, and land hard against the concrete courtyard that's littered with glue traps.

"I am not high, Claudia. I just...well, I woke up feeling good today."

"Well, that's a shocker. It's gonna take a minute or several for me to digest this new and improved you."

"How could something be both new and improved? An oxymoron."

"Girl, you're a moron."

"You take that back."

"Fine, fine. I rescind the name calling. Any judgment, however, I shall continue to stand behind."

"At least I know your heart is in a good place."

"Speaking of matters of the heart. Ahem. Sooo, tell me. How was the Stanley Stellar thing at The Gay & Lesbian Community Center?"

"Which reminds *me*—"

"Oh, come now. There's no need to thank me, Girl. I did you a little favor, that's all. That's what best friends do for each other. That Doorman certainly is a looker."

"That he is. I'll give you that much. And your audition, my dear—how did all that *mishigas* work out?"

"Oh, that entire *mashugana* mess. The role of Dorothy Gale was awarded to a fourteen-year-old girl! I'd like to see her belt a B Flat. Typical typecasting. Can you believe it?"

"Barely."

"Well, it's true. And for that, we can all thank—"

"Certainly not your agent. That guy needs to be destroyed."

"Destroyed? Oh, I can't! I mustn't. Feh. It's too early for me to start quoting Judy Garland films. They'll only be wasted on the likes of you this morning. You're high, Toto."

"Am not. I'm as straight as—wait one moment, strike that turn of phrase...I'm as sober as Liza Minnelli introducing herself to the crowd at a Hazelden mixer."

"And no doubt as egregiously costumed, Girl. You can hide a flask beneath as many sequins as it takes. When I think of poor Bob Mackie practically sewing on beads and bangles, bangles and beads, until he was all but blind."

"Those were the Sisters of St. Joseph, dear. Not the Sequined Sheik of Seventh Avenue."

"Whatevs. Now, where were we? Oh, that's right. The Stanley Stellar thing at The Gay & Lesbian Community Center. So, how was the art?"

"Evocative. Somewhat precious. But with a historical bent."

"Girl!"

"Wha?"

"Details. I want details!"

"Ahhh. Mostly black and white portraits. Photographs of the Christopher Street Piers. You know the stuff. Muscled, shirtless homos against a backdrop of Wojnarowicz's puking cow."

"What? Ewww. Dominic, you know the dirt I'm after."

"Ahhh. Of course. Did you hear Audra Ann McDonald is gonna win a Tony Award for *Carousel*?"

"Not that—the good dirt. Wait one moment. Who? Never mind. C'mon, spill the beans. Get to the good stuff!"

It's perfectly quiet without Jerome interrupting. I've rather grown accustomed to our party line telephone conversations each morning. I reach for a Red and light it from a branded The Meat Market book of matches that reads *A Butcher Bar* and flip on the tube, and it's there that I find Barrow Street's own Romeo shirt-less and covered in television blood, valiantly resuscitating a busty woman in a frilly camisole who's out cold on a gurney.

"Oh, *that stuff*. The good stuff, eh? There's not a lot to tell. We went to the exhibit, Claudia. We looked at the art."

"There's gotta be more to the story than simply that much. Why are you playing so...so hard to get? I'm after information, Girl."

Jerome is wearing a stethoscope and scrub bottoms and little more as the camera caresses the fat, black curls that fall against his eyebrows, which he's forever pushing out of his silver-blue eyes, his exaggerated cheekbones, and his tiny brown nipples.

"What's to tell? There's little more to it."

The Neurosurgeon heartthrob is informing his patient she's suffering from a temporary case of Guillain-Barré Syndrome, and if I scrunch my eyes closed as tightly as I'm able, I can spot tiny beads of sweat forming at his armpits and collecting in the center of his chest and making a slow, methodical descent down his torso. Jerome Cameron stares into the camera with the same concen-trated attention he offers me from across the concrete courtyard that's littered with glue traps.

"Start with the sexy stuff and I'll stop you when I'm embar-rassed. Now, don't leave anything out—not one tidbit of gossip."

"Gotcha. After we meandered through the exhibition, I walked him to the West 4th Street Washington Square Subway, and we said goodbye."

"You what?"

"Um-hmmm."

"That's it?"

"Pretty much."

"Wait one moment, Girl! That's not you. Not at all like you. No kissy-kissy? No elaborately staged sexual encounter in the darkest corners of the subway station?"

"Hardly that, I'm afraid."

"Well...I mean...are you going to see him again?"

"I suppose so. We do work at the same bar."

"Girl, this man is perfect for you. And he's crazy about you, too! Jesus Effing Christ, the way he looks at you—can't you see that? I mean...do you not notice that?"

The busty woman in the frilly camisole on the gurney with the temporary case of Guillain-Barré Syndrome is cooing as she feathers her nest beneath her handsome surgeon suitor. The mother pigeon in the recessed subway tile shower window sighs with boredom, shifts her weight, and rolls her head provocatively.

"Silliness. Things like this happen all the time between gay men. I'll see him at work, and it'll be like—"

"What will it be like? If you do not give this a chance, then what will it be like? Girl, I'm losing faith in you."

"Claudia, I appreciate the concern. It was cute of you to try and fix the two of us up. We had some drinks and a couple laughs, but I'm just not at a place to date right now."

"Uh-huh. And exactly what place would you be at, Dominic?"

"I've been trying to tell you. I woke up feeling different this morning, centered even. Like I'm on the verge of something momentous."

"And you're trying to tell me six foot something of silver buzz-cut, blue eyed, motorcycle boot sporting muscle man ain't momentous? I saw him touch you. I saw him *touch* you. Inside, ya know?"

"They're hazel."

"What is?"

"His eyes. The doorman's eyes are not blue. They're hazel."

"Uh-huh. Well, of course they are, Girl."

At that very moment, Jerome discovers the cure for temporary Guillain-Barré Syndrome is emergency mouth to mouth resuscitation. He climbs on top of his frilly-camisoled patient for easy access to administer necessary medical attention. The mother pigeon squawks a willful warning at life, and she leans into it, and flaps her expansive wings as she betrays her unborn hatchlings in favor of the mushy peas in the concrete courtyard.

"Hazel with flecks of gold."

"I love you with all my heart, Girl. And Jesus Effing Christ, you know I want what's best for you. I truly do. You're making a mistake ignoring his overtures. If a man ever looked at me with so much unadulterated affection in his eyes, the way that doorman looks at you...well, I'd push you under a bus on Eighth Avenue and 17th Street just to stand next to him. I would do that, too."

"Honey, how many times have I said you ain't gonna meet a man that plays for your team at a bus stop in Chelsea."

"Right under the M-11, Girl. Squashed like a stuffed olive trailing blue cheese all the way to the World Trade Center."

"Charming visuals."

"Call them what you may. I've been told I have a way with wordage."

"Listen, Claudia, what are you up to this afternoon? I was thinking we could maybe blow a j and hang out in Central Park...so warm for this late in September. The leaves are just beginning to do their thing, red and amber, and—"

"Doesn't that sound davoon! Now, Central Park I definitely do dig, but..."

"We could climb that great big rock by the boathouse—you know the one, and just waste the afternoon watching the clouds roll by."

"I have a gig."

"Not another audition in Westchester I hope."

"When you're a working actress, your first priority is the theatre. Also, all that other crap to boot, because the theatre *is* my life. For that, we can all thank The Brooklyn Academy of Music. And this afternoon, the duty most definitively calls."

"What are you doing?"

"I'm playing Barney at Francine Goldfarb's kid's birthday extravaganza on 73rd and CPW."

"Barney whom? You don't mean—not the children's purple television dinosaur."

"The very same. And that tyrannosaur happens to be a headliner."

"Sweetie, you really need a new agent."

"Tell me about it. And someplace Audra Ann somebody-or-other is gonna win a Tony Award."

"McDonald. Reid Miller wrote it in the—"

"—never heard of her. Probably a one hit wonder."

"Listen, I need your number."

"Huh? What?"

"Your telephone number. Somehow I lost it and I need to write it down."

"Girl! For how long have we been friends?"

"I know, I know. I just—now, lemme find a pen."

I scribble the digits on the cover of a *Next Magazine*, and chat with Claudia until it's time for her to pick up her Barney costume for Francine Goldfarb's kid's birthday extravaganza.

"Okay then. I'm off to the theatre."

"The theatre of the absurd is more like it."

"It's 73rd Street, Girl. Not Queens."

"Goodbye, Claudia. Break a leg, doll."

"Yo Holmes, smell ya later!"

On the television, Jerome completes his medical procedure, dismounts, and stares into the camera breathlessly. The mother pigeon circles the sky for less populated, soot gray concrete canyons; her hatchlings have stalled for too long and mistakenly pissed her off for good. And I stuff a generous wad of cash tips into the front pocket of my jeans as I collect my leather jacket and smokes and close the door on everything I care about.

I rumble down the vestibule stairwell steps, without a thought to trace the pattern of penny wall tile with my fingertips. Then I follow the twisting Gingko tree-lined streets to Christopher Street Pier, specifically to Pier 45 opposite West 10th Street.

The yellow leaves turn concentric circles in the air and land on the graffitied concrete pier surface beneath my combat boots and atop the shimmering, sunlit Hudson River. Since before the Stonewall riots, when these abandoned shipping docks were covered in thatched wood and served as vessels for import, homosexuals have gathered here to trade sex and drugs and deposit their seed into each other and the churning river beneath the cracks of the creaky floorboards.

Even after the city was forced to pave the wooden piers numbered 42, 45, 46, and 51 from so many years of spilled sperm, gay men still use this waterfront as their playground. Gays, you see, innately understand the importance of atmosphere and how to create it. And where better to affirm our existence than in the shadowy piers of the Meatpacking District? Just the thought conjures images of stevedore, blue collar dockworkers—bare-chested with faded tattoos and cigarette-stained fingers, dressed in fishermen's skullies and work boots.

It seems only natural that enterprising gay men in their ever-broadening search for sexual release should choose the piers to stomp around on. The history. I love it. It was passed down. We learned it. We teach each other. Proof that we existed. Our own filmstrips for all the future generations to see, and comprehend, and a day will come when our words will be their words, too.

Today, these graffitied concrete pier walkways are a tanning bed for naked sunworshippers, an amusement park for frivolous public sex, and provide the backdrop for the most exalted community events: Sunday Tea, Wigstock, and the elaborate Pier Dance and Fireworks at the close of Gay Pride Day. I survey my surroundings and smile large as I recall standing on Pier 45, dressed in a jockstrap, combat boots, and a Muir cap, watching Patti LuPone sing a medley of The Star-Spangled Banner and Heaven is a Disco to an adoring mass of admirers just last June. To me, Gay Pride Day is the epitome of belonging to someplace.

I pick the perfect spot, face downtown where the Statue of Liberty is no larger than a quarter, and remove my motorcycle jacket and white t-shirt, and rest my back against the chain link fence with the warm September Sun on my face and the sea air invading my nostrils. I close my eyes and listen as the turbulent river repeatedly smacks against the highway, crashing and retreating, crashing and retreating.

When distraction comes close it is a party given in my honor, and all the guests are friends and relations. There are cousins I attended Catholic school with mingling alongside customers from The Meat Market. There are familiar faces of spiritual acquain-

tances with whom I've shared agreement for many lifetimes. These are the courageous souls that found the fearlessness inside themselves, a huddle of randy homos sporting oversized baskets and modeling for each other at the piers. All the guests gather beside me today to bear witness as I stand tall at the precipice of something larger than I can comprehend.

The amber-colored, late September daydream is dressed in milky sunlight, and the salt sea air is motionless, has been inhaled and exhaled for a million lifetimes. The children who chase me home from school. They are here. And they are right, aren't they? Justified to do so. Leathermen stand on line on the shadowy cobblestone streets, flirting with each and furtively smoking weed, clandestinely selecting sex partners, crashing and retreating, and edging their way ever closer. They are here, too. Yellowed and blinking neon hustlers pose in jockstraps at distorted angles, mooching cigarettes, scratching their exposed asses, and trading slovenly, withdrawn sexual acts for any commodity they can get their hands on.

A stampede of mustached men in plaid lumberjack shirts and tight-fitting jeans, some of them shirtless, gobble Black Beauties and boogie to live performances by The Ritchie Family and Vickie Sue Robinson, to celebrate the very notion of me on the verge of something momentous. They've all arrived to see me off.

We converse, my ascendants and I, and share little jokes and tiny lies. Silliness. Things like this happen all the time between gay men. The way we survived. The way we survive still. Yes, survive still. But what are we saying? What's the lesson? One one-thousand, two one-thousand, three one-thousand, a metronome beating, every clock in the West Village ticking, that keeps dangerous notice of the time on this earth that remains. One one-thou...that's my left arm. Girl, I'm losing faith in you.

With every movement, the guests of this funeralistic affair inch closer toward me. When I shift my hand to mop the perspiration from my forehead, enraged friends and relations, Catholic school cousins, the children who chase me home from school, a huddle of randy homos, spiritual acquaintances, yellowed and blinking neon hustlers, The Ritchie Family, Vickie Sue Robinson, Glenn Hughes of Village People fame, and mustached men in plaid lumberjack shirts Bump and Grapevine as they descend upon me.

Miniature razor-sharp music notes dance in the air. I cannot find full, complete breaths, and I struggle for short breaths accompanied by loud gasps of air. One one-thou...that's my left arm. That's a sign. That's a symptom.

I woke up this morning feeling different. Evaded the drunken behavior and careless sex, avoided the premonitions and nightmares, with whatever mix of alcohol and illicit drugs swirling in my brain. Blew my handsome, soap opera husband and got him off to his early call to set day. One one-thousand, two one-thousand, three one-thousand, inching toward a cumulative climax. Gone. Forever. And this is how it happens.

A rhythmic, hypnotic saxophone plays in the air, the squalls of an impending autumn storm along gravelly city alleyways. Raucous laughter rings in the air, and I search for the wad of cash in my front pocket, and my wallet at my back hip, and the keys to my apartment. This is where they find me. Because that's who I am.

Enveloped in these dark, decaying cavernous rooms that are filled with glorious pier sex. What a dreamy time. There's always the risk of being mugged or falling right through the slippery, rotting wooden pier into the Hudson River—thump, splash, thump, sploosh, thump, splosh.

These courageous souls clad in flannel and button-flies, the brothers with whom I've created this place to live, communicate with me from sitting up positions in their caskets. Everybody chatters at the same time. And alongside every first, second, third word one of them loses a rotting appendage with an empty thud against the wooden, graffitied piers numbered 42, 45, 46, and 51. Believe me, man—anything that falls to the floor in this place, you don't wanna pick up. Unless, of course, it's your boyfriend. So many years of spilled sperm. Buff male bodies tangled together in pleasure float above me like hungry dragons. This AIDS pandemic has baffled officials and stung politicians into a shocking display of denial and avoidance. Ultimately, it's up to us—to you, to me, to remember our history.

I face downtown and the Statue of Liberty appears no larger than a quarter, steam off the Hudson rises around me in fat, drippy clouds, and I study the demented beams of light from beneath the graffitied concrete pier walkway as I realize this is the time between activity and rest, life and death, the dying then.

Bruiser floats through the crowd of attendees toward a ripped, red leather bar stool, and I gather him in my arms only to suffocate him with the aggressiveness of my embrace. I squeeze the life right out of him. Dink. All the lights dissolve to pitch black. What frightens you the most, Dominic? Is it the kiss of death that scares you? I scream in agony, but no voice comes out of me, solely murderous music.

My only recourse is to run away. I scurry to gather my legs beneath my body. I scramble backward, pushing hard into the chain link fence. The crisscross pattern is like ink on a pin, underneath the skin, against my bare back, the redness rising, and the force of my body leaves a sizable gap between the graffitied concrete pier walkway and the flimsy protective barrier exposing the churning, brown Hudson below me.

The glaring sunlight makes it impossible to see who or what is attacking me as finger snaps, sequins, and feathers dance menacingly in the air, and I shroud my eyes with my forearm as I protect myself in a concerted attempt to get out of the way. Maybe if I pretend to not notice the sequins and feathers, she'll let me off easy this one time.

"You give dat back to me, you cock-sucking, cum-swallowin' bitch!"

"Whoa!" as I duck my head to avoid a silk stiletto the size of a West New York Ferry Boat hurled in my direction. It clacks loudly for a full minute before it lands with a theatrical stop against the graffitied concrete pier walkway—but not nearly as dramatically as the shriek-emitting African drag queen whose shadow shades the sunlight.

"Honey, I gonna be need dat back. Dat glamorous, size thirteen Needless Markups silk stiletto riverboat came my way from heaven. And you about to find yo fool-self in de stink-ass Hudson Riveh if you don't stop yo tryin' to run away from me. Lorell ain't gonna hurt you! This be between Deena and me!"

The other queen, the tall African that everybody calls Deena, snatches the size thirteen Needless Markups silk stiletto from the graffitied concrete pier walkway and dances off toward the end of Pier 45, performing perfect split leaps in the air. Deena leaves a trail of finger snaps, sequins, and feathers in the air as she makes her escape.

"I don't know who dat crab-laddered bitch thinks she be fuckin' with, but I sure as shit ain't no white-ass Hella Lawson wanna-be. I'll fuckin' plant a tree right up heh ass, she thinks she gonna play me like dat."

"I'm sorry...hi, hello, hi there, ummm—"

"Girl, what dey got you on dat you so spooked and scared as a rabbit? I tol you twice now. Lorell ain't gonna hurt you. And why you not sharing none with me, baby? You got sumthang fly, Boo?"

"I ummm—"

"Oh, Lorell ain't gonna bite, you white-ass leatheh man. Whateveh you boys be callin' you damned-fool selves this week. I just came fo my shoe. What an unfortunate thing to happen to a great drag queen like me. Well, shiiit. I gon' go out de way I came in."

Lorell gently clears her throat, lights a long brown Moore cigarette with a Lady Zippo lighter, and removes a Canal Street-Special Golden Yellow and Opalescent Blue Hermès Silk Head-scarf from her brocade clutch kimono purse. Those poor, blind Sisters of St. Joseph. She snaps her headscarf at New Jersey prior to fastidiously securing it, and spits unfiltered cigarette against the graffitied concrete pier walkway. And with a puckered air-smooch in my direction, she saunters regally toward West Street—one foot high in a size thirteen Needless Markups silk stiletto and the other foot flat against the graffitied concrete pier walkway. Click clack, slap, clack clack, slap, click clack, slap, click clack, slap.

The sobering premonition, the *Dreamgirls* drag fight, the Apple Blossom Hermès Headscarf, and me very nearly floating in the Hudson with the other garbage; none of it is enough to distract me from the reality that this morning I have arrived precariously, precisely at the place I'm meant to be.

I tuck my t-shirt into the back of my jeans at the small of my back, carry my leather jacket slung over my right shoulder, and follow a semen-stained path of finger snaps, sequins, and feathers back to where Pier 45 begins, opposite West 10th Street. I explore the twisting Gingko tree-lined streets further, as yellow leaves turn concentric circles in the air, with my chest hair ruffling in the warm breeze and my nipple ring glinting in the sunlight.

I travel in a world beneath handbill posters advertising a double bill of Talking Heads and The Patti Smith Group in miniscule West Village basement venues, beside the sweet stink of New Jersey emanating from the Path Train, and on top of cracked sidewalks littered with used prophylactics and empty poppers bottles.

The warm Sun feels amazing on my bare shoulders and chest, and I gather the attention of more than a few of my flannel shirted, button-flied brothers craning their necks and lowering their mirrored sunglasses to have a closer inspection and to hopefully catch my eye. Cruising for sex between men in public, anonymously and without exchanging names, inhabits a comfort that far outweighs the fleeting pleasures of the predictable fornicating which almost always inevitably follows. The future isn't that far away. I just know it. I learn new things, talk to strangers, make new friends, and feel most alive tracing these streets—above all, I never sit still.

I nab a peach from an outdoor bodega on Hudson Street just because I can, and hand it off to a homeless man who's realized temporary digs outside the Garden of St. Luke in the Fields, a West Village oasis filled with leafy trees, wildflowers, blooming bushes, and carefully manicured gardens. He grabs greedily at the offering, and when he opens his mouth to give thanks, no words come out but his eyes burn right through me. Eyes as blue as they are marred by disease, reticent memory, and wounded confusion.

So many years of spilled sperm. Honestly, tomorrow he won't even remember.

I count sidewalk squares on my final steps home. I stand for a long moment on the luminescent aggregate stairsteps of my apartment building and take stock. Inhaling and exhaling, with an urgent beckoning from somewhere inside me to memorize this setting down to the details, in these the moments of quiet before the impending storm; brownstones built in the mid-19th century, tiny restaurants, and purposeful, tight-fitting flannel-shirt and worn-through 501 wearing men who pose themselves, crotches protruding in vestibule doorways. They're the proof in the pudding.

Yellow leaves turn concentric circles and whip up tiny chaotic cyclones at my feet. The first chill of autumn travels the length of my spine as a tiny shiver follows its course. I gather myself trembling in a pile of dead, brown leaves that crashes against my face as I ask, "Where did the time go?" One one-thou...but there is no longer time left to count. The time is now. The past collides forcefully into the daydreams of what tomorrow—no, today, today—this exact moment holds forth, and I'm no longer lost somewhere in the sooty clouds above me. "Okay, this is who I am now."

I key into the cognac-colored vestibule doorway of Number Eighty-Five Barrow Street without urgency. I climb the cognac-colored vestibule stairwell, without desire to trace the pattern of penny wall tile with my fingertips. Ensconced in a hazy white memory for all the steps, I can taste dirt, pebbles, and tiny colorless, falling leaves stuffed between my lips, against my tongue, at the back of my throat. Ya wanna see the whole world, kid? Urgency is no longer necessary. You win, Mama. You win. No more a need for hysterics—this is routine business.

Inside my apartment, I slump lazily in my favorite cowhide tuxedo chair. I unlace my combat boots and kick them off, first the left, then the right, and with two consecutive clunks they land loud against the seventies-style parquet floor. I rest my feet on the windowsill, and wait for my favorite story to begin.

I reach in the pocket of my motorcycle jacket for a Red and light it from a branded The Meat Market book of matches that reads *A Butcher Bar.* That's all the time it takes until Jerome Cameron notices me noticing him and blows me a kiss—only to snatch it mid-air before it travels across the concrete courtyard, pretend to stuff it down the front of his jeans, and howl until he doubles over with laughter.

"Oh, lookeee, lookeee. A big, ol' girl! How goes it, ya big, ol' girl?"

"There's a chill."

"What? Huh?"

"The first chill of the season. Autumn. It appears autumn has arrived."

"Well, natch, Nicky. That's how the seasons happen."

"How was your day at the office, dear?"

"Oh, you know—saved a few lives, broke a few hearts, kibitzed at the craft table."

"You might wanna watch those carbohydrates."

All through our conversation, he makes love to his reflection in a full length, stand-up mirror situated prominently in his living room. He traces a finger along his prominent jawline, first from the left, next from the right. The dialogue he performs completely to his reflection, except for the punchlines which he delivers as asides to me, with a singular raised and perfectly coiffed eyebrow, all while grinning from one ear to the next.

"Listen, I've been meaning to ask you—"

"Gimme five minutes. I'll cut across the courtyard."

"You *wish*, ya big, ol' girl."

"I could rock your fuckin' world, man."

"Yeah, yeah. You and a shitload of overweight, middle-aged housewives across the country. Evidently that's my demo...well, my character's demographic. Dinosaurs and Joy Boys. Anyways, this place of yours, this leather discotheque where you work—"

"The Meat Market."

"Sure. Whatever. Is there a door charge? You know, like a cover to get in? An entrance fee?"

"It's a secret handshake. Or you gotta know someone. Lucky for you, you know me."

"Very funny, ya big, ol' girl."

"Nope. Never a cover."

"Good to know. I walked past the joint the other night when I couldn't sleep. There was a line around the block to get in the front door."

"So, now we're cruising the Meatpacking District at all hours of the night, are we?"

"The fresh air does me good. And I made no mention of cruising. That sort of behavior I'll leave to your tribe."

"Well, you needn't worry. You're not our demographic."

"Just my luck. You got beer there?"

"Where? Here?"

"No. There! The Meaty Store."

"Meat *Market*. The Meat Market. And didn't we just have a conversation about your carbohydrate intake, Jerome? Yes, of course, there's beer. I got Bud Lite, Coors Lite, Keystone Lite,

Miller Lite, Michelob Ultra, Amstel Light, Corona Light Mexican Lager, and Wachusett Light IPA."

As we speak, he disrobes without modesty or inhibition. He removes a tank top undershirt, and each muscle performs a sonata, reverberates in scintillating, symphonic style before traveling with resonance to the next section, rippling and reflexing poetically, from clavicle to deltoid to trapezius to adductor longus. Jerome pulls back the fat, black curls that fall against his eyebrows, which he's forever pushing out of his silver-blue eyes, and the yellow, lamp-lit windows of his apartment exaggerate his cheekbones, and his tiny brown nipples.

"I'm thinking of getting a Caesar Haircut. You know like—"

"—like Julius Caesar?"

"Who? No. Like George Clooney. The actor from *ER*. As president of my fan club, how do you think me sporting a Caesar Haircut would make you feel?"

"Betrayed. Just like Brutus."

"Brutus from Popeye?"

"No, that's Bluto."

"Who? C'mon, I'm serious. How do you suppose I'd look with a Caesar Haircut?"

"If you get a Caesar Haircut, are you still gonna parade around your apartment in your tighty-whities all the time?"

"That's the plan, Stan."

"I'm down. Works for me."

He sniffs his armpits, first the left, next the right, and fingers the fluff of palindromic curls before bringing the finger in charge to his nostril, inhaling deeply, approvingly, and nonchalantly offering me a whiff—like any good neighbor might. He traces his nipples in gentle concentric circles, breathes in sharply with pleasure, and exhales a private, raspy moan from his core as he instinctually throws his head back and shakes his lion's mane.

"Sometimes I wonder why I have such a special connection with you. I mean, I've known plenty of homos. I played Provincetown one summer."

"You know, we gay guys don't talk about you nearly as much as you talk about us."

"I even did a benefit reading for the HRC. That stands for The Human Rights Campaign, ya big, ol' girl."

"Really? How interesting. We should harness some of that star power, Jerome. Do you wanna come with me to my ACT UP meeting on Wednesday? Steve Meisel is gonna be there. He's looking for muscly straight boys to photograph for a second series of posters to raise money and awareness to fight AIDS."

"I can't Wednesday. I have Salsa lessons. And don't even ask about the weekend. Shopping at Balducci's is my Zen Time."

"You are a true Renaissance man."

Jerome pets the perfectly groomed, vertical stripe of hair extending from his navel to his pubic hair to heaven, coils the expertly styled hairs around his forefinger several times, and tugs hard, refracts in quiet contortion, and simultaneously arches his back and flexes the muscles of his six pack.

"Seriously, man—I wish I was gay. I'd get laid like every single day."

"It's a chore, Jerome. But we all have to play our part."

"Right? I mean, no wonder you Joy Boys get so much action. You're all guys! You're *all* horny *all* the time."

"Add to that, in between flower arranging and gourmet cooking classes, we've an overabundance of free time on our hands."

"Wait—so isn't, like, every guy your type?"

"Pretty much. That's why we invented the Broadway Theatre. You know, so we'd have something else to occupy our minds."

"I so get that. Everybody needs a hobby. For instance, if I didn't have my Bowflex Xtreme Body Tower SE2000...well, I'd probably rub myself raw."

"What a way to go, though. Am I right?"

He pulls the ripcord on his Adidas mesh-lined gym shorts, causing them to cascade gracefully like a scrim and land around his ankles on the floor. He is clearly aroused from studying his reflection. Jerome's stiff manhood preens against his sculpted stomach and points directly toward Inwood, and he wets two fingertips with his tongue and lets an overflow of saliva drip achingly from his soft pink lips to his chiseled chin, that forms a delicate string of spittle all the way to his rock-hard dick.

"Yeah, well I should probably...ummm...be signing off here."

"No way. Not fair. The show's just beginning."

"Well, this ain't...ummm...one of your...ummm...one of your afterhours underground sex parties, ya big...ummm...girl."

"I'm not gonna tell anybody. It'll stay between you and me."

"Nah. I'm gonna have to ask that you...ummm...step out of the Operating Theatre, pal."

"Awww, come on. Now I wanna see how the episode ends!"

Jerome pulls hard on his balls, and even harder on the yellowed, paper window shade to find privacy. The setting Sun draws sharp amber and red shadows across the courtyard apartments on Barrow Street, and from my perspective I watch him through the transparent rental spring shade. The yellow, lamp-lit windows of his apartment silhouette his perfectly muscled physique as he sways and gasps for air and manipulates his body.

He plants his feet, he bucks his hips, and grabs the pane of the window when his knees begin to buckle. Feral cats cascade lithely from rusted-out garbage drums to soot gray, courtyard rooftops to avoid the impending scuffle.

Jerome's chest heaves, and his head rocks first to the left, next to the right, and if I scrunch my eyes closed as tightly as I am able, I can spot tiny beads of sweat forming at his armpits and collecting in the center of his chest and making a slow, methodical descent down his torso as he takes his turn to curse and convulse and bring his character to life.

I remain motionless in my favorite cowhide tuxedo chair, like when the credits roll at the movie theatre and you stay on with hopes that they'll include a blooper reel at the end—always so much fun. And not five minutes later, I hear him spring the yellowed, paper window shade, trip over his Basset Hound, Frank, and order stromboli and a tossed salad with creamy garlic dressing on the side from Village Pizza on West 4th Street.

SIX

TIME IS RUNNING out and I need to take my place. I shower but do not shave. A cockroach travels the hairline fractured, glazed steel bucket bathroom sink and, on the other side of the glass brick shower window, a returned mother pigeon wages a battle against the Sun for setting before she's completed her courtyard work.

I dress in a sleeveless, blue flannel shirt that pays tribute to my delts and biceps, and tight-fitting worn-through 501s. I lace my combat boots, first the right, then the left, and grab my crumpled leather motorcycle jacket from the seventies-style parquet floor. Instinctively, I search for cash in my front pocket, and my wallet at my back hip, and the keys to my apartment.

I secure the apartment door, follow the cognac-colored vestibule stairwell, and count the penny wall tiles with my fingertips: one, two, three, four, five, six, sev—but what's the point? Here I stand having arrived at the moment. I search my jacket pocket for a Red, and realize I need to buy smokes on the way to The Meat Market. I mutter to myself that I just purchased two packs and should one day consider quitting. One day, not *today*. For now, I'll have to detour to Village Cigars and catch the subway at the West 4th Street Washington Square Subway.

Chirping abuelas are gathered on the luminescent aggregate stairsteps to share neighborhood *el chismorreo* and play Ten Penny Rummy. They snack on guava paste and queso blanco on saltine crackers, and they sing along with music coming from a Spanish radio station that filters out of their first-floor apartments. The reverberation of their happy laughter takes over Barrow Street, and their bright eyes and warm greetings light up the neighborhood.

Dressed in A-line smocks with fine-print red and white flowers, lathered in sweet-smelling gardenia perfume, not one of them blinks an eye at my work uniform. What do they care about how I dress? Rather, they ask if I've time for a quick game of dominoes and inquire whether I've been having any trouble with mice in my apartment.

"Ju habe to be berrry cerrrtain de basurrra goes out eberrry night. Eberrry night beforrre bedtime, *Chacho*. Ju masssst take out de basurrra. Dats hwhen dey come arrround—"

"—*y mira, Maaami*, juan daaay dey come to jourrr house ant dey neberrr want to go home—"

"Hwad basurrra? How much basurrra coult he possibleee make? Look at dis! He's all muscles, *Maaami*. Ant too skeeenny. *Tan muy flaco. Chacho*, do ju eberrr eat?"

My Spanish language skills are embarrassing, but I try. I really try: "*Escuchen, señoras, me gusta comer tantas veces. Como demasiadas veces.* I eat like a horse. I really do. *Puedo pedir prestado un*...ummm, er...a Lucky Strike *hasta que llegue al*...ummm...ummm, bodega—how do you say bodega? I guess you just say bodega, is that right?...*de la Séptima Avenida?"*

"Ju help jourrrself, *mijo*."

"Here, now. Ju take from me. Dis one! She eees alrrready on de fooot stamps."

"La piña está agria."

"Well, hwaaat? Ju are, *Maaami*. Ju are!"

"Gracias, mis amores."

"Gooniiight, *Chacho*. Gooniiight."

Brownstones built in the mid-19th century ignite with yellow, lamp-lit windows as I make my way up West 10th Street. Lines are forming outside tiny restaurants on twisting Gingko tree-lined streets as I follow a path toward Village Cigars, where I purchase smokes, and cross the street to disappear down the steps of the West 4th Street Washington Square Subway.

The concrete railway beneath Christopher Street is cruisy at this time on a Friday evening. At peak hours at this particular station—well, practically any station—all the MTA needs to do is drop a disco ball and serve up Margaritas. They'd certainly increase ridership, and not find a need to raise the fare every six months. Or, more likely, they would still find a reason to raise the fare every six months. I mean, it is New York City, after all. The commuters deserve punishment. Even so, a buck and a quarter to ride the train for six blocks is outrageous.

When my line arrives, it's filled with overdressed, West Village matriarchs on their way to uptown pre-theatre dinner reservations accompanied by their just-a-little-bit too too escorts wearing their just-a-little-bit too too expensive suits and flamboyant ties with matching pocket squares. Their Gucci Marmont Matelassé bags and faux rabbit autumn capes occupy the seats on either side of them, and all of their fine gentlemen companions stand craning their necks to flirt with the just-a-little-bit too too tooty fruity fine gentleman standing at the strap next door.

With nowhere in sight to sit, I grip the greasy subway pole and purposefully arch my bicep to show off my well-developed, muscular arm, and I pretend to lose myself reading the comic strip above the windows between the advertisements for hemorrhoids, hernias, and foot doctors. I study the hand drawn art thoughtfully even though I've already read this particular edition.

It's the newest episode of *Decision*, the city Health Department's cartoon for straphangers that's one part steamy soap opera and two parts AIDS education. Just weeks ago, the serial began with a grant from the Federal Centers for Disease Control and Prevention as public service announcements. So, we are making progress. The Health Department hired an advertising agency to produce photo-novellas to reach New Yorkers who, officials feared, were ignoring other posters and televised commercials about preventing the lethal citywide spread of AIDS.

In this installment, Julio drops in on his friends Marco and Miguel, tank-topped and muscled to reinforce their sexuality, who deliver the news that Raul is sick and Raul's girlfriend, Anita, has died. Sobering stuff for sure. An HIV photo-novella. Also, an important tool for fostering education about reducing transmission of the virus, and an entertaining time-filler between subway stops. A day will come when our words will be their words, too. Everybody's words, ya see? The masses ain't gonna be such an exclusive crew for long.

Above ground at 23rd Street, Eighth Avenue explodes with commuters hurrying home from another day at the office and enterprising homosexuals scurrying closer toward happy hour at any number of Chelsea destinations. I'm onto something with my MTA Margarita disco party concept: 'Ride the Number 9. Why Wait Until Happy Hour to Get Your Buzz On?' Now, who do I know in marketing?

I walk toward The Meat Market and the stink of the pungent Hudson River drifts across the avenues to take over the West Side of Manhattan. The streets are tree-lined, and the leaves are just beginning to do their thing, red and amber, as the September dusk dapples the red brick low-income housing and the densely populated basketball courts and cordoned-off city parks.

The leaves on the sidewalk crunch beneath my combat boots as I step inside the drawing amber shadows, and the avenues grow larger and more crowded with traffic, a sea of yellow taxi cabs, the further West I progress. I reach in my jacket pocket for a Red and light it from a branded The Meat Market book of matches that reads *A Butcher Bar*, and exhale a long stream of billowy smoke into the gradient orange, lilac, blue sky. The Sun has yet to fully disappear into the hungry Hudson River as the very first stars of evening find their place. A left and then a right, and I'm standing in front of the bar where I work.

As I enter the big, oak door to The Meat Market, the doorman is toting cases of liquor and stocking the bar with his shirt off. I stand in the shadows for a long moment just to watch him perform the tasks. The muscles on his back dance a ballet as he lifts the heavy wooden crates and sorts the spirits.

When he notices me, he sets aside his work duties and pulls on his t-shirt. The sweat from his torso soaks through it with immediacy, and he smiles wide with his thick, graying mustache dripping over the corners of his self-assured grin.

"Hey, baby."

"Heya."

I wipe the perspiration from his temples with an open palm and he pulls me into his arms and kisses me full on the lips. His breath is sweet, and his insistent arms guide my torso closer into his own. The heat from his sweat-soaked t-shirt is slightly acrid and wet against my chest. My heart is in my throat when I step back from his warm embrace, and I trip over a bar stool, and laugh clumsily as I move to begin my side work.

One spirit after the next, the doorman hands me the bottles and I wipe each one down, affix it with a pourer, and situate it in its respective spot in the speed rack; Vodka, Gin, Rum, Scotch, Whiskey, Tequila, Triple Sec in front of the ice bin within fingertip reach, so I can access the ingredients to mix drinks without having to turn my back to customers, browse through shelves, or move around the bar too much.

"So, how are you? What'd you do with your day, baby?"

"I'm good. I'm pretty good. Had a walk to the pier, took my shirt off and caught the last rays of sunshine for the season."

"Sounds nice. Cruising the Christopher Street Pier for a rando hummer, were ya?"

He pantomimes giving a blowjob with the tongue against the cheek trick, and his booming laughter ricochets off the sick-green, hanging lamps inside the sick-green, empty barroom.

"Oh, please. There's more action to be had watching Hoboken crumble into the Hudson anymore."

"Ain't it, baby?"

"Back in the day, cruising was so much more romantic. Just like Tony and Maria at the dance at the gym."

"Ahhh, the star-crossed lovers. Enamored of each other at first sight. Wandering through the raucous Mambo dancing directly into an orgy on Pier 45."

"You see? Look how those two ended up. Happily ever after."

"Actually, when you think about it, neither one of them really had a happy ending."

"Ain't it, indeed. All I'm saying is Pier 45 is hardly our community center any more. Sadly, there are no longer hummers to be had. Although, today I almost got hit in the head with a size thirteen Needless Markups silk stiletto."

"Wha?"

"Uh-huh. Drag Queens. There were packs of 'em there this afternoon getting ready to rumble. Like The Sharks and The Jets. Only with more sequins and feathers."

"Good one, baby."

"Change is in the air."

"Speaking of Drag Queens, when I was at Tower Records on Fourth and Broadway the other day, I saw Ru Paul."

"He's so tall. Am I right?"

"So tall. Taller than me, I swear it to ya. And definitely a neighborhood celebrity. I'm serious, baby. He couldn't make it half a block without a bunch of gay guys stopping him to shake his hand or courtesy before sharing a conversation. Just like a politician."

"Definitely more outta the closet than Koch. Probably more famous than Giuliani, too. Just more history waiting to happen."

"One day somebody's gotta write it down, huh, baby?"

"Precisely. The way it actually went down, ya know?"

"Think of it. *The Way It Went Down*, a novel by Dominic—"

"I said it. And I really believe it. Make fun should you choose."

"Oh, baby, I'm just ribbing ya."

"Well, you certainly do keep bringing it up."

"I think it's cute, that's all."

"A day will come when our words will be their words, too. It affords credibility to what we're doing here. At least, in my head it does. And it validates the very men who gave their lives for us—so...listen, if you think that's cute—"

"Wha? Oh, baby, I didn't mean cute in a condescending way. You're *cute*. *You're* cute. When you're all impassioned."

"It's exactly neighborhood celebrities like Ru Paul that are gonna represent us, you know? Tell their stories, tell our stories, and make history known. The revolution is upon us."

"Wha? Oh, that's a laugh, baby. Ru Paul? Drag Queens are gonna bring the revolution to life? I have to laugh at that one."

"Well, why not? Somebody's gotta do it."

"Drag Queens educating the masses? Think of it. That's a joke alright. What? Are they gonna book spots on *Sixty Minutes* in between their Time Warner Cable Access do-it-yourself makeup classes?"

"Not just Drag Queens. All of us together."

"I can see it now. Televised beauty pageants. Only all Drag Queens vying to win talent competitions and share their platforms. While wearing their platforms!"

"Each of us will play our part."

"Well, I wanna play a Leather Daddy. And not small time like on Morley Safer. Not me. I wanna march right down to Rockefeller Center and sit on Matt Lauer's lap when I tell my history."

"Now you're blatantly making fun of me."

"Wha? Baby, I'm explaining my story. Just imagine me sitting on ol' Dudley Do-Right Lauer's lap and all the while dishing the dirt with Anne Curry. I hear she's got a mouth like a sailor and a penchant for the homos. Just like a sailor! Talk about making history known."

He's simply being good humored, and again with the rambunctious laughter that bounces from every sick-green rafter in the joint.

"You only get one pass around the circuit party before time expires. You go ahead and party with Anne Curry. Maybe you'll catch her when the fleets are in town. But, I am telling you our time is now."

"Sure, baby."

"Clearly, you find the thought of our living a meaningful existence outside dank bars and dirty bookstores to be some sorta way-off, in-the-distance science fiction fantasy."

"Awww, baby, c'mon. Laugh with me."

"I do not wish to laugh. I don't find your dismissal of a brighter future for us amusing."

"What's eating you today?"

"You don't understand how important this is to me. You know, there is a very good reason to sit in the sunshine on the Christopher Street Pier that has nothing at all to do with securing an anonymous blowjob."

"What? To score a bag of weed?"

He's trying to get me to laugh, to step down from my pointless soapbox argument, but I'm in too deep.

"You don't know me at all."

"Huh? Of course, I know you, baby. "

"Never mind. Let's just keep moving along with this side work."

"The one thing I do know, baby, is that I'd like to get to know you even better."

"You don't know the battles I've fought."

"Oh, yeah? Who are you picking on now, Tough Guy?"

Suddenly, he's the lion from *The Wizard of Oz*: "Put 'em up, put 'em up!"

"When I consider the shit that I've crawled through just to survive. And the way I survive still—"

"We've all seen our share of shit."

"You know, you've made fun of my belief in something better for us since I brought it up at the Stanley Stellar thing at The Gay & Lesbian Community Center."

"No, baby, not at all. I just happen to think there's a lot more shit we gotta crawl through to really see some progress. I do dig your enthusiasm though. And your optimistic outlook."

"So cute when I'm impassioned, eh?"

"Hey, that's my line, baby!"

"How long do we gotta wait? What more do we need to accomplish? Clearly, we can't count on the Federal Government. Somewhere Ronald Reagan is too busy crapping himself and waiting for Mommy to make up his mind for him in between diaper changes. Thank Christ he's no longer in office. Fuck the both of them. Ronald and Nancy. Just say no, alright. Neither one of them can say the word AIDS out loud. Meanwhile, we're *still* dropping like bottles of poppers on the dancefloor at The Monster. What's the point?"

"You're really worked up about this?"

"And you should be as well. History depresses me. It's the future that I'm longing for now."

"Well, here's to a rando hummer in your future, baby. I just might know a guy who's up for the task."

"I'll pass. Something to believe in is all I'm after. Oh, how I laugh when I consider that I thought maybe it was you. Maybe that you and I might—"

"You and I should, sexy fucker. And soon. Listen, it's early and nobody is here yet. We can sneak downstairs in the ice room and mess around if you dig?"

"I don't dig. And I don't care to *mess around* anymore than I want some *rando hummer.* Isn't that the clever turn of phrase you employed?"

"I was just making a joke."

"I'm after things that are way more important than a blowjob."

"Baby, the ice room is way too tight for butt sex."

At this, he laughs so hard that he's forced to steady himself on his knee.

"Wha? Huh? Are you not listening to me? I'm searching for something to get me through the gaddammed hours of the day."

"I'm right here, Dominic. Settle down, baby. I'm your friend."

"What I want is lightyears away from this gaddammed backyard in this lousy city."

"Listen, if it's that important to you—"

"It's important to all of us. Look the fuck around you, man! Don't you see that the time is now? We're standing on the precipice."

"Ahhh. The future."

"We're about to experience the insurgency."

"The insurgency?"

"That's what I said."

Christ, I wish I hadn't. I don't even know what I'm arguing about any longer, all over the place. Clawing at the water around me—desperate to propel myself to the surface, gasping for oxygen, and grabbing at life.

"That's a little extreme, wouldn't you say?"

"Are you gonna make fun of that, too?"

"Actually, I am. Um-hmm. You get back to me when Ru Paul hosts *The Tonight Show*, baby, and then I'll know the revolution is upon us."

He's harmless. He recreates Johnny Carson's infamous golf swing replete with the boop of sinking a hole, and his sweet, benevolent laughter plinks and planks across the barstools turned upside down on the bar tops.

"Will you let the Ru Paul thing go? For fucks'sake, man."

"Sure thing, baby. I was just making a funny. The insurgency, huh?"

"You know, maybe it's me. Maybe it's just me being me. But, I am telling you that I'm convinced that change is imminent. Things could turn around today. I feel the progression of time pulsating inside me with every heartbeat."

"Baby, okay, relax. I'll stop making jokes and you tell me all about it."

"Blood is pounding inside my ears. Lub dub, lub dub, lub dub goes the drumbeat of transformation. You see, the future isn't that far away because the future is here right now. Alive and kicking inside this very moment."

"I'm listening. I get it. I do."

"Do you? I don't believe you. Nah. You're a liar. I'll never believe you again."

"But I didn't—"

"I woke up today feeling changed."

"Changed how?"

"Different. A different man. Ya see, for a very long time I've been afraid. Afraid of everything. Nah, this is wasted on you. It's nonsense."

"Who is frightening you? I'll take them out with one hand tied behind my back. What nonsense?"

"The very thought that you and I might somehow connect on a personal level is —well, there's your nonsense!"

"I don't understand. I was just being silly, that's all. I can be such a dumbbell sometimes. Did I do something to hurt your feelings, baby? Or maybe I accidentally—"

"This just doesn't work. You and me. None of it makes sense. Not in real life, anyway."

"What do you mean?"

"What do I mean? He wants to know what I mean. Look, there's me turning concentric circles afraid of my own fucking shadow. And there's happy-go-lucky, 'Let's go play grab-ass in the ice room' you—walking around with your preposterous promises about what tomorrow holds. None of it works. Foolishness."

"Preposterous? Foolish...wha? I happen to believe in a future for us, Dominic. I have for some time now. What the fuck? I have taken every opportunity available to tell you how eager I am to know you better and explore a little bit of life together."

"Well you, my friend, are misguided."

"If you would fucking stand back for just one moment and look at us—baby, we make perfect sense."

"To who? These dumbfuck drunks that keep coming back for more?"

"Stop making excuses and just be honest about the way you feel."

"You wanna know how I feel? Oh, that's rich. There's the

comedy. Should I tell you what you want to hear? Or are you man enough to take the truth?"

"What are you talking about, Dominic?"

"Which one? Do you wanna know the truth? Or do you want me to say the things you need to hear? Tell me. Which is it? Otherwise, you're a liar. I hate a gaddammed liar."

"Where is all this bubbling up from?"

"Me. This is me. This is the man that you're so eager to know better. Now, do you want to hear about the horrifying visions that haunt me deep in the night? How I'm wide awake until the sunrise sets me free? Because I'm afraid. I'm afraid to close my eyes, ya know? Every gaddammed night. I'm afraid of every gaddammed night."

"Awww, baby. All you gotta do is come to me."

"The shadows on the ceiling play out terrifying premonitions in real time. All alone—that's who I am. Left out in the cold. Like garbage."

"No, Dominic..."

"Night after night. Hallucinations of what tomorrow really holds for me. They play inside my brain like a movie stuck on gaddammed repeat. And for what purpose? What am I to learn from such suffering? Life is you take whatever you can get. Life is you make the most of whatever you can take. Because that's who I am!"

"I dunno how we got here? We were just having a couple laughs."

"Then you haven't been paying attention."

"I am paying attention. I'm here. I'm right here."

"Oh, I see ya standing there. And you shouldn't waste your breath. It ain't nothing that you can fix."

"What did I do?"

"Well, let's take a look-see, shall we? You filled my head full of ridiculous dreams about us. And I let you. There's the kicker. I let you do so. Turns out it's just the same demented beams of moonlight. Different dude, that's all."

"You wait one moment! That's not fair."

"Oh, you wanna fight fair, eh? There's no such game in town, Doorman. You see, I'm standing here telling you that I have changed. I woke up today a different man. That maybe all the sweat-filled, terror-fueled nights have at long last delivered me to the precipice of what I can only pray is some kinda merciful, indelible change. And your response is perhaps I just need a good suck job on Pier 45."

"That isn't what I said."

"Isn't it though? You asked me how I feel. Well, listen up. I'll tell ya again. I feel more certain than I ever have that life is handing me my ticket outta this place. Oh, it's an E Ticket Attraction alright. And I'll be gaddammed if anybody tries to take it away from me."

"If you wanna get outta here then we'll get outta here, baby. Together."

"No way. This is my dream."

"It can be *our* dream."

"Not a soul lays one hand on the future I have fought so fiercely to stand tall at. Anybody that tries to steal away some miniscule hope from inside of me that...that salvation has finally arrived can get fucked. Nope. I won't hear of it. Especially from some gaddammed door guy at some gaddammed fuck bar in this gaddammed backyard in this lousy city."

"I don't understand."

"There is nothing for you to understand, my misguided dumbbell friend."

"Now, you stop right there. I refuse to let you say something you'll regret. You'll feel differently when you're not so heated. And I'll be here to make certain you're good. Because that is who I am. Are you listening, baby? That's who I am. Do you hear the words I'm trying to say to—"

"I've heard enough from you to last me until the end of days. I'm good, Doorman. S'all good. I'm alright for fucks'sake. Let's move on to stocking the shelves, will ya?"

Why do I say no when I want to answer yes? Yes, I hear the words you're saying to me, Doorman. And, no, things are not at all good. I am not alright. Broken is what I am. A deep-rooted sickness that lives inside me. Something I can't tame. Something I can't break. And it's a punishment to me that I should cry myself to sleep every night because I wish that I was never born.

Absolut, Tanqueray, Bacardi, Dewar's, Jack Daniel's, Cuervo, DeKuyper all without a word. He hands me the bottles and I wipe each one down, affix it with a pourer, and situate it in its respective spot on the shelves behind the bar. I catch his eyes in the mirror, hazel in color with flecks of bewilderment, wondering what he possibly could have said to deserve such a berating.

I reach for the pack of Reds that I keep to the right of the cash register. I light a smoke and I look into the enormous gilt mirror behind the shelves of booze, through all of the years, and I search for rescue just in time to observe my mother's eyes—mean, miserable, cold, sealed in a permanent frown, as she draws the lace curtains of our apartment living room abruptly closed. Where I came from, ya know?

No. Not this time. "Listen, Doorman—"

The big, oak door to The Meat Market swings open and its massive hinges erupt with the sorrowful moan of a wounded animal. An angular, lavender-colored slice of dusk perforates the barroom and reveals in its wake the dusty, backlit shadow of a stranger that hobbles inside with the help of a walking stick. A gust of wind off the Hudson pierces the breach and produces tiny tornados of dirt, pebbles, and colorless, falling leaves that fly through the air in cyclone fashion before falling flatly against the floor the moment the unwieldy door slams shut.

"Little Sister? Little Sister? Are you here?"

I recognize his lilting voice immediately, but it is the very picture of him that leaves me without breath. His hair has receded to uneven clumps that form a horseshoe-shaped ring around the sides of his head. His blue eyes are squinty and jaundiced. And his clothes hang off him like an indigent that litters the sidewalks of Times Square, one of those pathetic souls that a person steps over while moving swiftly from the taxi to make a theatre curtain.

"I'm over here, Bruiser. Behind the bar."

"How can you see in all this darkness?"

He supports his frail body with the use of a cane, and his entire frame trembles with every wobbly step. When did that happen? Click clack, thump, clack clack, thump, click clack, thump, click clack, thump.

"Heya...um, do me a favor, huh, Doorman? Can we hit the lights over the bar area, please? It's showtime I guess."

He removes the upturned bar stools from the bar and places them in their right-side position and stares me down with sorrow stuck in his eyes. There is no bridge for me to cross, no way to bring back what is lost, after all the damage I have done. Without words, the doorman crosses the room to flip a switch and light the lights. His motorcycle boots echo in the nearly empty barroom as he brings the joint to life.

"I'll take a Screwdriver, dear. Heavy on the screw."

"I'm on it like Donna Hanover on Gracie Mansion."

I turn around to end my smoke and study his reflection in the elaborate gilt mirror behind the bar. Bruiser is so changed. Little changes one doesn't notice from day to day that accumulate to make a different man. Up close, his close-cropped blond buzzcut, thick red-blond mustache, and tiny round glasses are brittle enough to break off, clearly have in places, and his skin is dry and flaking. Un, Deux, and Trois are swollen and purple, the color of lilacs before they disseminate and die, and Lola is monstrous and screaming obscenities in his ear. He smiles when I offer up his drink and his teeth are rotting and brown. Maybe it's the booze, but more likely it's life.

"How're you feeling, Mr. Man?"

"Eh, I've had better days, Dominic. What do you make of my new walking stick though? Genuine mother of pearl, dontcha know."

"Fancy."

"Bought it on 14th Street. Cost me a whole week's disability check, but I'm worth every penny. Besides, I think it makes me look..."

"Dignified."

"Bite your tongue. Never mind, bring that tongue over here and I'll bite it for you. Jesus, I have to do everything myself."

"Dapper?"

"Hmmm, dapper. Dapper? You know, I've never thought of myself as a dapper man."

"Like Lucille Ball in *Mame*."

"That's right she did play Mame. In the movies. I saw it in the movies at The Adelphi. Or was that The Yorktown? West 88th Street was rife with gay men, all of them dressed up in their pretty Polo Ralph Lauren linen sweaters—pale yellow and pearly lilac and coral pink for chris'sakes, ready to storm the door to the cinema if they had to—so eager were they just to have a few laughs. I remember."

Bruiser's eyes are empty. Already someplace else. And the jokes don't really register. Even as we're trading quips, it's as if he's preoccupied with more important matters, preparing to leave this lifetime for something better. Simply passing the time saddled with his grotesque, decomposing body.

It's unsettling to see. But this is the nineties after all, and I've seen a long line of friends succumb. I worked the shifts of their memorial services from right behind this bar at The Meat Market. I'd make the drinks and light the cigarettes of all the men that would stand on line to enter the big, oak door to pay their respects. And then two days later, just like that, another friend would drop dead. First it was Mark Adam. Or was it David? Randy? West Street was brimming with gay men, all of them dressed up in their finest leather—decorated like Christmas trees with bootstraps jangling like jingle bells for fucks'sake, ready to storm the door to the bar if they had to—so eager were they just to find a few laughs. I remember.

I scan the room for the doorman and he's nowhere to be located, neither sitting tall on his ripped, red leather bar stool manning the big, oak door nor leaning on the cigarette machine, taking his time with a smoke and studying me from across the room. Perhaps he's filling buckets with ice in the sick-green, windowless basement to ready the bar for business. I deliberately gouge my fingernails into my own palms to punish myself because maybe I've stalled for too long this time and maybe I've mistakenly pissed him off forever. For fucks'sake, Dominic, you've really done it this time.

"So, ummm, tell me something new, Bruiser. Whaddya been up to?"

"Oh, you know. Same shit, Sis. Blood transfusions twice a week. Entenmann's Pound Cakes and Ring-Dings for the rest of the days. My nutritionist is about to kill me. That is, if the sugar doesn't do me in first. But, with all the dolls I'm taking, I get so hungry. Honestly, I'm uncertain how it is that Neely O'Hara, born Ethel Agnes O'Neill, ya know, kept her trim figure. Me, I'm absolutely ravenous."

"Ethel Agnes, eh? Who knew? Sweetie, now don't take this wrong—but should you be drinking? I mean, with all the medication and—"

"Oh, puhlease, Florence Nightingale. It's the booze that makes the entire adventure palatable." Shhhhhhlurrrrrrppppppp. "Besides, that topic is decidedly between myself and the nice dyke nutritionist who, at present, is trying to kill me. It's a game we play to see who gets me to the finish line first."

"Okay, okay. You know best."

"I most certainly do not. Nor have I ever pretended to maintain a working knowledge of precisely what it is that keeps things humming along nice and tidy inside me. That I leave to Sara Lee."

"Well, at least you're in good hands."

"I'll have another, dearie. Whaddya say let's line 'em up tonight? I haven't tied one on in forever it seems and...and...listen, are you gonna make me another drink and stop staring? I know exactly what has become of me, er, of...my personal appearance. I didn't step in here for no reminding from you, ya see? Now, make me another drink, would ya?"

"Sure thing, Ethel Agnes."

"Who?"

Highball glass with my left hand, house Vodka from the speed rack, five-count pour, splash of stale OJ diluted with water.

I make the first drinks of the night, flirt with the leathermen as they saunter through the big, oak door, solo and in groups of two and three or more. I laugh at their jokes, light their cigarettes, and find respite in the more mechanical tasks of my job. Every two cocktails or so, I scan the room for the doorman without success. Maybe he's out front keeping the crowd of leathermen neat and orderly, pretending to check identification cards, and all the while shining his flashlight pointedly at their bulbous crotches. And maybe the doorman is loath to ever look at me again.

"Now, let me see. Where was I? Dolls, dolls...oh, ah, ravenous, Sara Lee. Aha! My dress! Eureka, that's it! My dress. My biggest fear is—" Shhhhhhlurrrrrrppppppp. "—that I'll pack on too much weight and they'll be forced to bury me in a Plain Jane house frock. The degradation is neck deep. What if I never fit in that off the shoulder, red-beaded Dolly Levi number again?"

"I suppose you can always wear the opera gloves and the feathered headdress and call it a day. I mean, seated in your casket, nobody is gonna see down below...er, see you down below. Am I right? Dignity and a tasteful hat will always get you through."

"Not at the Harmonia Gardens, Little Sister. I know people there."

"I'd be surprised if you didn't. All those handsome waiters."

"Sweet Mother of Streisand!" Shhhhhhlurrrrrrppppppp. "I didn't tell you!"

"Tell me what?"

"About the Broadway revival. *Hello, Dolly!* Did I tell you about the Broadway revival of *Hello, Dolly!*?"

"You mean the one with Carol—"

"Channing. Yes. The most recent incarnation."

"I read in *The New York Post* that she's been dead for years and just keeps touring with the show. In this production, they manipulate her with puppet strings."

"That's vulgar. Stop it. Carol Channing is Broadway royalty. I won't have a word said against her."

"Unless, of course—"

"—I'm going to say it myself."

"And you are."

"Well, of course, I am."

"I'm all ears."

"What a curious expression. Have you ever considered such an odd turn of phrase? To be *all* ears. That's just dreadful. Now, where was I?"

"Carol—"

"Channing. That's right. Well, according to my sources, Ms. Channing is anything but dead. Word on The Great White Way is that she's alive and dripping. If you get my gist?"

"I'm afraid to ask."

"As you should be. You see, Sis, I have it on pristine authority that the old gal pisses herself so many times during a performance that they've been forced to diaper her up. Those poor, handsome dancers are slip-sliding all over the proscenium during the big cakewalk number!"

"Is this story for real?"

"Cross my heart and hand to Pearl Bailey. Apparently, Actor's

Equity was urged to get involved and sop up the mess. As a result, the show now has a four-hour running time because the stage hands are required to mop the set every time she blows through a Depends."

"Ewww. Who told you that?"

"A chorus boy I know from unemployment. One of the perks of apartment living in supportive housing in the heart of the dance belt. Thank you, Mayoress Edwina Koch, for the nation's first congregate residence for gals like me."

"I always knew you'd make it to Broadway."

Shhhhhhlurrrrrrppppppp. "Housing opportunities for people with AIDS. Can you imagine? And right there on 42nd Street. I couldn't feel more at home."

"You have, as they say, arrived, my dear."

"Honey—I've made it in every porn house in the theatre district. Time was the ticket takers called me by my first name. Ushers bowed down on bended knees. When I finally kick the bucket, they're gonna dim the lights on the marquee at The Adonis. Only then will I have gotten someplace."

"The toast of the town."

"Don't even get me started. Now, where was I..."

"Hold that thought. I'll be right back."

Happy Hour draws to a close and it starts to get busy. I exchange drinks for money, hand over fist, for a good half hour stretch. I wipe the bar and smile handsome for tips and the brisk pace makes the time fly. I empty ashtrays, flirt with the handsome leathermen, and laugh at their jokes as the evening kicks into gear.

When I find a moment to catch my breath, I reach for a Red and light it from a branded The Meat Market book of matches that reads *A Butcher Bar*. I survey my surroundings and my jaw nearly falls to the bar top. I rub my astounded eyes and watch in amazement as the doorman escorts a purple dinosaur through the big, oak door, and she removes her furry head and sits down at my bar.

The dinosaur rifles through her Gucci Marmont Matelassé bag for an ultra-thin cigarette and lights it with a Lady Bic, fits her tortoise Jordache Cat Eye glasses, and applies a thick coat of Cherry Pomegranate Lip Smackers lip gloss all at the same time. Her purple paws travel in several directions simultaneously as her cigarette creates halos around her head, and she wildly punctuates the lavender smoke with exaggerated gesticulation. She looks up and positively beams.

"Claudia! What are you doing here?"

"Jesus Effing Christ! What kinda warm welcome is that? I certainly hope you don't treat all your clientele in such a manner?"

"I'm sorry...hi, hello, hi there, ummm...what the fuck are you doing in here?"

"That's hardly more convivial. Hi, Girl!"

"Shhh! Don't call me that! Especially here."

"Fine, fine. Whatever." She exhales a long stream of lavender smoke into the air and then turns to Bruiser. "I have to presume this isn't the gold star service one receives in an esteemed dive such as this? I mean, is she like this to all the patrons?"

"Only those of us from the Mesozoic Era, Darling. Something about the bumpy skin and knobby scales unnerves him, I presume. It's a prehistoric pub performance."

"Positively Paleozoic deportment."

"You've seen nothing, pretty lady. The ones he's really into he roars at. When he's on the prowl, he picks an argument from right behind the bar. You can hear him yelling all the way outside on the street!"

The doorman decides this is his cue to exit to perform the duties relegated to his professional title, but not before catching my eye sorrowfully, pursing his lips, wrinkling his mustache, and scratching the crown of his silver buzzcut in confusion.

"Claudia, sweetheart, you really shouldn't be here."

"Well, why in the hell not? Jesus Effing Christ. My money is as green as the next guy."

Shhhhhhlurrrrrrpppppp. "Careful now. Deep down beneath this withering exterior, I'm just a shallow girl who can't say no. But, I also happen to be the next guy. And our money is rainbow colored."

"Oh, please, you Handsome Devil, you! I've got all the colors. I may have earned my Equity Card playing Charlene Cha-Cha DiGregorio in a bus-and-truck to Paramus, but I obtained my Silver Elite Gay Card singing at The Blue Whale on Fire Island. Just this side of the Pavillion...or that side of Judy Garland Memorial Park. Depending which way you're going. Or coming."

"Well, Holy Cabooses! I just knew you were an actress. I just knew it! I recognize you even inside all that Mesozoic garb. You're the tap-dancing tampon!"

"Actually, it's a maxi pad. But, who knows from feminine hygiene in a leather bar? Am I right? Yes, guilty as charged. Let me tell you one thing. That costume was a bitch. I'm all but lame from that gig. For that, we can all thank The Brooklyn Academy of Music."

Shhhhhhlurrrrrrpppppp. "Oh, do let me buy you a libation, my dear. I just adore the legitimate theatre. Never let it be said that Bruiser is not a patron of the arts."

"Claudia, this is Bruiser. Bruiser, please meet my girlfriend, Claudia."

"Well, any girlfriend of my girlfriend is a girlfriend to me. Set her up, Little Sister."

"Well, thank you, Bruiser! You know, you look like a Bruiser. I like that in a man. And I shall accept your kind offer. I would like a Gin Martini, Barmaid."

"Claudia!"

"What? You said not to call you a girl..."

Shhhhhhlurrrrrrpppppp.

"This isn't that kinda bar. We don't even have Martini glasses."

"The difference between a Gin Martini in an up glass and a Gin Martini in a rocks glass lies in the eyes of the beholder. Jesus Effing Christ, just pour me the drink, will ya? You've no idea the day I had today, Girl. Er, I mean, Gal. I mean, Tough Guy."

Shhhhhhlurrrrrrppppppp. "Tough Gal."

"What are you even doing here, Claudia?"

"Dominic, are you gonna make me a cocktail or will I be forced to make a scene?"

Rocks glass with my left hand, Tanqueray from the shelf behind me, second up from the counter, without even turning my torso, five-count pour—one one-thousand, two one-thousand, three one-thousand, four one-thousand, five one-thousand.

"I'm afraid you're gonna have to settle for a twist. There's not an olive for miles."

Shhhhhhlurrrrrrpppppp. "Greece's pieces."

"At long last—my Martini! Come to Mama!"

Just then, Bruiser's genuine mother of pearl, 14th Street disability accouterment falls with a pronounced thwack against the sick-green, checkered floor tile. The shock of it ignites in him a squall of sudden, sharp twitches, and a search for breath which crescendos into a prolonged and boisterous coughing spasm. Leather queens are craning their necks and lifting their Muir caps to witness the hullabaloo, Claudia is preciously patting his back with her furry purple paw, and I'm prepared with one combat boot poised on the speed rack ready to jump over the bar top— when, right on cue, the doorman arrives to catch Bruiser in midair.

He cradles the older man's thrashing torso and secures his wildly flailing limbs inside his muscular embrace. He whispers plainly, quietly, soothingly into Bruiser's ear, and instructs him to breathe from his stomach, breath from his stomach, first in and then out, in and then out, in and then out, as he supports the man's frail, faltering body against his own brawn.

Nary a boot-strapped motorcycle boot in the barroom dares to jangle. The DJ turns a knob, and the throbbing music dies a screeching, electronic death. I watch my friend dying by the millimeter from inside the cocoon of his laborious, painful shivering. I hear him gulping for air from across the bar. The doorman's kind eyes meet my own and he mouths the words, "He's okay, he's okay."

He's reassuring me that our friend will be fine at the same time that he's reminding me of all the promises that tomorrow holds for us. We've still got some history to write, the doorman and me. Yes, I see it. Yes, I hear the words.

When at long last his seizure is over, Claudia negotiates a dip at the waist in her purple dinosaur costume to retrieve the fancy walking stick, the doorman plants our friend firmly in a sitting position on his ripped, red leather bar stool, and Bruiser summons a throaty scream from deep, deep within. "What...are they...

looking at, looking...at...looking...why are they staring? Tell them to stop it! Stop staring!"

The music kicks in, something sultry with deep beats by Frankie Goes To Hollywood, and all the performers in this community theatrical reassume their places and pick up their cues. Nothing to look at. Simply a thirty second ad spot and then back to the story at hand.

"Well now...ummm, oh dear! It appears as if I've knocked over my Martini."

"You should never bruise...your Gin...pretty lady. Just look at me. I may be stirred, but I assure you, I am not shaken."

"I'll make you a fresh cocktail, Claudia."

The doorman mouths the words, "Wowzer," and I shake my head affirmatively in his direction. He winks and smiles softly and lights up my world before moving on to bring order to a line of tangled leathermen all attempting to get inside the big, oak door.

Wipe the bar, Meat Market coasters, smile handsome at my friends. "You know, you never did tell me what you're doing here, Claudia?"

"I'll bet she's been auditioning all day. Isn't that right, Broadway Baby? I'll bet you're in high demand when it comes to casting, right?"

"For that, we can all thank The Brooklyn Academy of Music."

"Do you know what I read in *The New York Post*? Reid Miller's column, I believe it was. I read that Madonna is going to be on the boards. In a Mamet play, no less. Madonna! Doing Mamet. Like a prayer indeed."

"I definitely need a new agent."

Rocks glass with my left hand, Tanqueray from the shelf behind me, second up from the counter, without even turning my torso, five-count pour—one one-thousand, two one-thousand, three one-thousand, four one-thousand, five one-thousand.

"And there we have it. A fresh Gin Martini for the lady."

"On me, Little Sister. That one goes on my tab."

"Thank you, Gents. Yes, thank you both. C'mere, you. Ohhh, Dominic, this smells like Christmas! Mmmm. Mmmm-hmmm. That, my handsome friend, is some talented mixology. And Jesus Effing Christ, does Mama need this cocktail after the day she had today."

"Now, you sit right here and tell your Uncle Bruiser all about it."

"You've no idea the injustices involved in pursuing a career as a working actress in this city. Madonna, my ass. She's no actress—that's for certain, but you have to hand it to her for securing a gig."

"She probably blew David Mamet."

"Jesus Effing Christ, the hurdles one must mount...wait, that's not right. One wouldn't mount a hurdle, would one? Scale? How *does* one bypass a hurdle? Leapfrog?"

"Climb over."

Shhhhhhhlurrrrrrppppppp. "Overcome"

"Precisely. The hurdles I have overcome, and, I mean to tell you, in just one afternoon's work. Oh, Dominic, this cocktail is divine. Mmmm-hmmm. Sent down from Jesus Effing Christ himself."

"Here at The Meat Market, we aim to please."

"And you definitely do deliver, darling."

Shhhhhhhlurrrrrrppppppp. "Did I miss the hurdle?"

"Oh, that's right. Where to begin? So, I'm playing Barney at Francine Goldfarb's kid's birthday party on 73rd and Central Park West. She's got a magician. She's got a balloon animal blower.

She's got Barney. She's got a bartender. Live entertainment for the kiddos in the drawing room, party games and canapes for the adults in the parlor. Swanky little soiree for an eight-year-old, right? Well, a three-ring circus is too much for this gal—even when it happens to play out in one of those modernized apartments with sizable bedrooms at The Ansonia. But, that's Francine for you. Francine Goldfarb always goes a little too far with her... oh, let's call it showmanship, shall we? I mean, it's simply *de rigueur* to the nth degree. Who is she trying to impress really? Between the sugar and the Ritalin, the children are all hopped up to begin with—see, there's your million-dollar idea—Martinis for the children. Something to take them down a notch. Nah. The wily little Cretans wouldn't appreciate the downtime. Meanwhile, the adults are all thrilled for the gift of free daycare by the likes of a magician, a balloon animal blower, and Barney. All of 'em clamoring to inch closest to the bartender and eying the bathroom: pretentious as intermission at The Metropolitan Opera, only sans the sparkly ball gowns. And they're all sardined in Francine Goldfarb's elegantly appointed powder room sipping Lilet Blanc and snorting rails of cocaine like it's still the eighties. The parents are all as hopped up as their succubus spawn, you see?"

"Fabulous!"

"You'd think so, Bruiser. You'd really think so. Now, the adults are all chatty-Cathy's and grabbing each other's tails on the sly in the parlor, while their ill-mannered, runny-nosed little jackass children are running circles around the Matisse's and Chagall's and a beleaguered little bitch of a Lhasa Apso, who's actual given name *is* Matisse, and they're taking turns grabbing Barney's tail in the drawing room. Isn't it funny that they call it a drawing room? You wanna know why? Because the writing's on the wall. I'm telling you this is a three-ring circus that only the Ringling brothers could call home. So, I decide that maybe I need some fresh air because, Jesus Effing Christ, it's hot inside this rented purple head of mine."

"This can't end well, Claudia."

"Hardly that, Dominic. You know me, Dominic. The epitome of a consummate professional. Also, all that other crap to boot, because the theatre *is* my life. My name is my reputation. For that, we can all thank The Brooklyn Academy of Music."

"Noted."

"Well, I make my way through the ill-mannered drawing room and past the runny-nosed parlor games, and into the solitude of Francine Goldfarb's Bradbury & Bradbury retro wallpapered bedroom. And just beyond a California king size bed layered to the coffered ceiling with autumn faux fur capes, I discover a fire escape toward freedom. The perfect spot for an overworked gal to take in the view and grab a breath or two of fresh air."

"Strange, but you'd think this Francine of Central Park West would rent a coat rack or hire a coat check?"

"You know, I never thought about that, Bruiser. Precisely on target. But, it's so difficult to know what to expect this time of year. And it's sooo hot...so warm for this late in September. Am I right? Anywhooo, I climb out onto the iron balcony for a breather when I remember that underneath my slip and tucked into my girdle is a doobie I twisted up for the cab ride home. And I'm taking in the view of Central Park from Francine's makeshift boudoir veranda, unzipping my centrosaurus couture, and wriggling my hands inside my girlie girdle to free me some sinsemilla salvation, when I realize I'm gonna have to remove my furry purple head in order to smoke. Well, when I do so—Jesus Effing Christ, the breeze on my sweat-soaked brow is unadulterated heaven. And I'm literally on my second hit of this sweet sinsemilla when I hear the sudden rustling of six little nitwits who thought maybe hiding under a dusty pile of autumn faux fur capes might somehow be more titillating than the live entertainment of a magician and a balloon animal blower in the drawing room! And now they're shrieking and crying, and all fucked up for life because they witnessed Barney remove his head to blow a joint while overlooking West 73rd Street."

Shhhhhhlurrrrrrpppppp. "Yuck! Children are so fragile."

"Right? Grow a pair, will ya? Wait until you're twenty-eight—I'll show ya something to cry about. Well anyway, needless to say my employer was none too pleased with my professional work performance. And now I'm frantically attempting to snap up my girdle, and the spawn are shrieking so violently they're practically turning blue from lack of oxygen, and at this point, Francine Goldfarb is already on the horn with my agent, or the building's security officer, or Effing Reid Miller at *The* Effing *New York Post*. All the while Matisse is barking to beat the band, and I just know it's mere moments before the coked-up, choked-up party parents arrive on the scene to find me in my slip and girdle with my furry, purple head on a stairstep next to me. So, you know what I do?"

"Ooohhh, tell it! Tell it!" Shhhhhhlurrrrrrpppppp.

"I sit right down, and I finish that marijuana cigarette. All of 'em are staring at me with their jaws fallen to the high-pile, hand-knotted silk rug: Francine, the snot-nosed little brats, their coke-head parents, the magician, the balloon animal blower, even Matisse the Lhasa Apso. I can feel the eyes of the passers-by on 73rd Street wincing up at the crazy lady dressed in her girlie girdle and smoking a spliff on the fire escape of The Ansonia and it doesn't bother me a bit. Because what can I do, right? Where am I gonna go? So, I sit there. And I smoke. And I get so baked that when the building's security officer arrives to escort me from The Ansonia, all I can do is laugh like a crazed Linnet Bird getting evicted from her gilded, iron cage."

"Sweetie, you need a new agent."

"Tell me about it. And somewhere Madonna is gonna win a Tony Award for blowing David Mamet, Girl!"

"Yeah, Girl! You tell her, Claudia. She's nothin' but a big ol' girl!"

"Jerome?"

"Jerome!"

Shhhhhhhlurrrrrrppppppp. "Jerrrooommme!"

"Jerome! What are you doing here?"

"Jesus Effing Christ—we really gotta work on that warm welcome of yours, hon. I mean, leather bar or not, it is the service industry."

"This is New York City, after all. The customers deserve punishment." Shhhhhhhlurrrrrrpppppp.

"I'm sorry...hi, hello, hi there, ummm...what the fuck are you doing in here, Jerome?"

"Stromboli."

"I'll take two. Extra sauce!" Shhhhhhhlurrrrrrppppppp.

"Huh?"

"I had stromboli and a tossed salad with creamy garlic dressing. Now, I've got agita. And I really gotta walk that shit off. Not to mention all those calories. Christ, what was I thinking scarfing all those carbs?"

"If memory serves, you'd worked up quite an...appetite."

"I most certainly did. Ya peeping pervert! Ya big ol' peeping pervert, you! I also ate like a Gavoon. Or did you miss that part?"

"There's no possible way I can catch every single episode, Jerome. So much exposition. Some weeks it drags on and on and on, and I can forgo several episodes without missing one bit of storyline."

"C'mon, Gay Boy. You're addicted and you know it."

"Wait one minute. I'm not the one showing up at your place of employment, now am I?"

"Oh, that. Well, there is that. You see, I had a huge meal, and a constitution was in order. A couple blocks along the river and ba-di-bing, there I was standing in front of Meaties."

"Uh-huh. A straight shot twenty-two blocks up Eleventh Avenue and ba-di-bing there you are standing on the doorstep of everybody's favorite, neighborhood leather bar. And it's called The Meat Market, Straight Boy."

From across the bar, the doorman mouths the words, "Are you okay?" and I shake my head affirmatively in his direction. I'm actually enjoying myself. For the first time ever, some of my favorite people are sitting at my bar.

"Ahem. Hellooo. Hellooo, I'll take a Screw—"

"Now, where are my manners? Let me see. Jerome, you already know Claudia by way of our party line telephone conversations. And Claudia, this is Jerome of elusive courtyard communications."

"Jesus Effing Christ, Dominic! I know who he is. I know him, I know him. Hi there, Jerome."

Fat, black curls fall against his thick eyebrows, which he pushes out of his silver-blue eyes as he offers up a dazzling smile.

"Heya, Dollface. You're more lovely in person than I could ever imagine."

"Wow. Likewise, I'm certain, Jerome. Ya see, Dominic? That's how a person greets a person."

"Or, in this instance, how a person greets a person in...now, how did you put it? Centrosaurus couture?"

"Oh, this old thing. You see, I was—"

"I think purple compliments your eyes." Oh brother, this guy is as suavecito as they come.

"Hellooo out there! My turn. It's my turn now. I wanna meet the stromboli!"

"Jerome, this is my pal, Bruiser. Bruiser, this is my cuddle buddy, Jerome."

Jerome extends his arm to offer up a handshake and the dance of muscles plays out with the grace of a ballet. One sinewy pectoral *tour jetés* effortlessly into a *glissade* of rippling bicep, and an *arabesque* into muscular, veiny forearm and an outstretched, manicured hand. All the while he's grinning from one ear to the next with perfect, polished soap opera teeth. "How's it hanging, friend?"

"Ooo, he's a charmer, this Jerome. Can I keep him? Can I keep him? I like this one."

"And I like this Meaties Factory place of yours. There's a very congenial feel to this bar."

"Uh-huh. Well, it is filled to the brim with your particular demographic. Dinosaurs and Joy Boys. Wasn't that the way you so eloquently put it?"

"Something like that. Who knows from demographics, eh? Whaddya got for beer, ya big ol' girl?"

"Don't call her a girl. She'll have a hissy."

"I'd play nice if I were you, Jerome. You're on my turf now. These people would knock over a bodega in Mott Haven if I asked them to do so."

"I don't doubt it for a moment, Dominic. I'd lead the charge myself."

Shhhhhhlurrrrrrpppppp. "And I'll bring up the rear."

"So, let me see now. I got Bud Lite, Coors Lite, Keystone Lite, Miller Lite, Michelob Ultra, Amstel Light, Corona Light Mexican Lager, and Wachusett Light IPA."

"I shall partake in a Wachusett Light, if you please."

Grab the flashlight, Wachusett Light IPA from the cooler on the left.

"On the house, Romeo. Always happy to welcome a new Mouseketeer. Okay, Screwdriver, Martooni, Wachusett. Is everybody set for a moment? I gotta go flirt with some strangers to pay my rent. I'm only stepping two feet away, and I'll be right back. I'm leaving the three of you to your own devices, and I expect nothing but exemplary behavior."

Wipe the bar, Meat Market coaster, smile handsome for tips toward a decent share on Fire Island this year.

"What can I get...'Sparre! Well, doesn't that just make sense."

"Listen, Brudduh, I doan know what it is I just uttered, but I cannot tell yas how happy I am tuh be unnerstood fawh a change. Yuh with me? Ya' dig?"

"I most certainly do dig. What's your pleasure, pal?"

"One Drambuie wit' a long pour of house Scotch of de rocks, please. Right, or what? Do yuh got any Angostura Bitters fawh dat, or what? Only if it ain't no kinda problem, *paisano* of mine. Yuh got me so fahr?"

"So far I got ya, man."

Rocks glass with my left hand, Drambuie from the shelf behind me, third up from the counter, without even turning my torso, cheap-ass house Scotch from the speed rack, two-count pour of both—one one-thousand, two one-thousand, skip the Angostura Bitters altogether.

"You guys, this is my friend Guasparre. Guasparre Gagliardi. Now, I know you've met Claudia, and everybody knows Bruiser. And this is my neighbor, Jerome. Or Jeromeo, if you're nasty."

"Such a freakin pleasure tuh make all of your acquaintances. Okay? Of cawhse, I already know de pretty lady, okay, or what? And Boosuh and I go way back tuh a long time ago. So nice tuh see yuh all. Ya' dig? So far at dis particular moment I must say dat dis has been a very pleasant evenin' fawh me."

"Hold that thought, will ya, 'Sparre?"

How rare it is that I get to visit with so many of my favorite people all at the same time. It's like a party given in my honor— except there's one person missing. I wave my arm across the bar to the Doorman and motion for him to join us. He points at his own chest, all mock surprise, "Who me?" and separates a sea of leathermen to stand by my side.

"Heya."

"Hi there. Whassup?"

"Listen, Doorman. I owe you an apology. I know this. The way I behaved before—that's just me being...I dunno, nervous, afraid, and I realize it's no excuse, but—"

"Look, I got a line forming out the door. Maybe we can discuss this a little bit later."

"Sure. Sure thing. But, just gimme two shakes of your time, eh?"

"Okay. So, what can I do for ya?"

"You see, it's not that far off from what I was trying to explain to you earlier. About the future. This thing has happened. Well, this thing is happening. All of us are here together. Each of us playing our part."

"If you wouldn't mind, it's not the best time for a history lesson."

"Yeah, I know that. It's just...well, the moment is here. Or, it is beginning anyway."

"What? What's beginning, baby?"

"Baby. You called me baby. Good. Okay, that's good. Listen I know I sound like a madman, but all I want is for you to be here with me. By my side, okay? Just for this moment, okay? We'll start slow. If you still want me. I mean, you still want me, right?"

"Wha? Oh yeah, I still want you. But you gotta do something for me."

"Name it."

"Can I walk you home after work tonight, baby?"

"I can't think of anything I'd dig more, Doorman."

"That's great, baby! Now, I should really get back to the door."

"Oh, fuck the door. Well, just for a second anyway. Shots. We need shots, okay? All of us together. Bruiser, and Claudia, and Jeromeo...oh, and Guasparre, and Doorman. Now, just gimme one second."

"Wha? Oh yeah."

"Jesus Effing Christ!"

"Ya girl! Ya big ol' girl!"

"Yuh Manhattanite homosexual types are so freakin' funny, Brudduh!"

Shhhhhhhlurrrrrrrppppppp.

Wipe the bar, screw the Meat Market coasters, rocks glasses, one, two, three, four, five, six, Jack Daniel's from the shelf behind me, second up from the counter, because it's the first bottle I grab, smile handsome at my family.

"A toast, my friends. Life always offers you a second chance. It's called the future. And the future is dependent on this precise moment with all of us gathered. Our history brought us here together."

And we lift our glasses to what's past, and to what's around the corner.

I perform the mechanical duties of my job and catch myself grinning large for the remainder of the evening. I start my closing side work, unstack the cardboard Meat Market coasters and return them to the cabinet, fresh batteries for the flashlight, and inventory the beers I'll need for tomorrow's restock of the cooler. I make the final drinks of the night, flirt with the leathermen and the hardcore party boys, pour a long slug from the Twenty Year Scotch, and pray for the night to end.

Bruiser and Claudia excuse themselves to catch the last half hour at a Midtown piano bar where she promises to sing the Sondheim classic, I'm Still Here. The picture of the two of them walking toward the exit arm in arm tickles me, him hobbling with the aid of his mother of pearl, 14th Street special, and her with her Gucci Marmont Matelassé bag, tortoise Jordache Cat Eye glasses, and furry, purple rental head intact.

Guasparre Gagliardi disappears into the dark shadows of the backroom, and I swear I can hear strangers choking on his foreskin from across the room. Jerome plants a kiss on my cheek citing an early call to set day and wobbles toward the door, but not before sharing a gregarious goodnight handshake with his new buddy, the doorman.

"Almost ready to call it a night, baby?" He saunters up to the bar and massages the back of my neck with his lion's paw, and I smile and give last call.

"Last call! Last call for alcohol, gentlemen! You ain't gotta go home, but you can't stay here!"

And with a single index finger, the doorman flips a switch that transforms all the starlight into soot gray skyline, bare bulbs illuminating painted black plywood walls, the backside of Guasparre Gagliardi scurrying toward the sidewalk, and smoldering cigarette butts in ashtrays across the barroom.

I collect my cash register drawer and hop over the bar toward the sick-green, fluorescent lighting of the sick-green, windowless basement office. I take no time to face and stack piles of fifties, twenties, tens, fives, and singles. I'll catch hell from the owner for the oversight tomorrow, but my priority just now is getting out of this joint with the doorman and finding the future. I stuff a generous wad of cash tips into the front pocket of my jeans as I collect my leather jacket and smokes, and close and padlock the sick-green, office door on a spectacular evening at The Meat Market.

The doorman is waiting for me as I round the sick-green basement stairs. He kisses me on the cheek, slaps me on the ass, and just like that we step out the big, oak door and directly into the purple morning.

"Whaddya say let's walk along the water, huh baby?"

"Sounds like a plan."

We cross West Side Highway and bide our time until we find a broken stretch of chain link fence, and duck beneath it to follow the riverside walkway downtown. I slip my hand inside his and wrestle with his enormous fingers until the fit feels perfect, and we walk for a time in silence with the Hudson River splashing against the pavement and depositing tiny droplets of moonlight on our smiles, and boots, and jeans.

"You certainly are in a good mood tonight, baby. Are ya rich? Did you make a fortune in tips or something?"

"Nah. It's about so much more than money."

"Tell me. What it's about then?"

"I don't know what's been going on with me lately. Oh, this afternoon. Fuck, I am so remorseful about the way I treated you, the hurtful things I said to you."

"How about we call it history, huh? Growing pains. Concentrate on the future. Maybe bringing our dreams to life."

"You're a good man. You listen to me. Nobody ever listened to me before. Man, these last few weeks. The nightmares that have been circling inside my brain. Even during the daylight. These... these terrifying visions play out right in front of my eyes. Oh, I'm remiss to even share. You'd think me certifiable. And yet somehow with the good fortune of—I dunno even know which stars to thank...suddenly I am certain that this place, right here, is exactly where I need to be."

"I like it with you next to me. That's what I've been trying to say to you all along."

"I hear you now. Oh, I heard you before, too. But, I didn't believe it. It's like I couldn't let myself believe it. And today, I woke up changed somehow—a different man. Standing on the precipice of some momentous, existence-altering reality. For so long, I've been afraid to live my life because I'm petrified. Absolutely frozen with the fear that I'm destined to expire before I see all of life. I've been afraid of dying. Physically suffering heart failure. With all of the symptoms, too. A constricted chest, the tingling extremities, gasping for breath, so real I actually experience the dying part... instead of participate in the living part. Oh, it's crazy. I must sound fucking crazy."

"No, baby. You can trust yourself. Trust your body to do the breathing for you. Let go and let life wash over you. The symptoms will soon become memories of terrifying sensations, and nothing more."

"Well, that's just it. Doorman, today I woke up and realized that when the choice is either to change for good or stay the same forever, there really is no option. Who's got the time for a heart attack? Certainly not me. And I'll be damned if I'm afraid to live my life, and...and any heart attack that's gonna happen will find me fighting my way to securing a fully realized future."

"With a man right beside you who happens to be crazy about you."

"Wonderful. We're both bonkers. Maybe we can get a sweet deal on a Junior One Bedroom at Bellevue. How do ya feel about First Avenue?"

"I've never been a fan of the Upper East Side."

"Thank, Christ. Me, too."

The Blue Harvest Moon is overflowing. Its silver rays tango on everything in its path; the crumbling riverwalk, the brownstones built in the mid-19th century beside twisting Gingko tree-lined streets, and two men walking arm and arm along West Street. I let my head fall into the crook of his shoulder, find rest for a tiny moment, and for the first time in months, I close my eyes without the fear of darkness.

There is comfort in the stillness as we walk past Charles Street, West 10th Street, Christopher Street. The tiniest refraction of lilac, blue, orange sky discovers the horizon as our boots click clack in unison beyond Pier 45. We follow the river to Barrow Street, my street, and then we trace the cobblestone to the luminescent aggregate stairsteps of my apartment building.

"This is me. Eighty-Five Barrow. You wanna come upstairs and do dirty things?"

"I was hoping you'd make your move. If we do this, there will be rules. Do you think you can play by the rules, sexy fucker?"

A tiny growl grows in the back of my throat, and he kisses me deeply. His tongue is salty and invasive inside my mouth, and secured within his muscled arms I notice his unyielding hardness pressing against my own. My head reels backward and I let go until I am completely supported inside his embrace. *You can trust yourself. Trust your body to do the breathing for you.* Let go and let life wash over you.

And in an instant without notice, a cordovan maroon Pontiac Bonneville Firebird Trans Am careens up onto the sidewalk and immobilizes our bodies against the mid-19th century brownstone bricks. I feel its hot engine breathing against my torso and groin, and it is nearly on top of us. Seconds drip like lifetimes. And my brain trembles in repetition with the perilous heaving of the car engine, *vrrrooommm, vrrrooommm, vrrrooommm.*

In cat and mouse fashion, the driver inches the vehicle closer and closer, pressing us tightly into one another. An uncomely laughter rises from the open windows and perforates the late September evening. I can feel the breathing of the Firebird Trans Am's exhaust against my groin, *vrrrooommm, vrrrooommm, vrrrooommm.*

"Well, well, well. Ju fuckeen' *maripositas.* Look at this, *hermanos mío,* the fuckeen' butterflies. They are sooo pretty. I find it good enough to eeeat. *Hermanos mío*, I am suddenly very hungry." Instantly, he is menacing.

Of course, it's the same cordovan maroon Pontiac Bonneville Firebird Trans Am and the same thugs that assaulted me earlier in the week. This time they are out for blood, to not wound a thing but to put it to death. Two men catapult from the front doors, and three more—intoxicated and howling viciously, fall out of the back seat. Malevolently, they approach from all directions and rip us from our embrace. The driver shoves me against the bricks and the others circle unflinchingly around the doorman.

"Why don' ju waaahhhtch wheeere ju'are walkin', *putas*?"

"We were just—"

"She doesn't want to pay attention. She doesn't want to play nice. Thought ju mighddda learrrnt jourrr laaayssson, *mariposa*."

"Fuck you."

"Ayyy! What a beautiful mouth this bitch has."

His eyes are aflame. He spits at the sidewalk, and his nostrils flare, as he sucks his teeth and snarls beneath his breath. His mouth grotesquely contorts up in such a way that I think he might laugh. A fist against my jaw and I falter for balance as he grabs me by the back belt loop and pulls my body into him hard, one hand suffocating my windpipe and the second pinning my hands into my shoulders, with his crotch pressed into my ass.

My heart is turning flip-flops. "Just get lost and leave us alone. We won't say a word to anybody."

"Ju fuckeen' *maripositas*. Maybe we want eberrrybody to know. To learrrnt a laaaysssson."

They're prodding the doorman with a baseball bat, poking at his massive biceps and taking pot shots at his balls. When they corner him, one of them spits in his face, and when he throws a punch four men are immediately on top of him. I lose track of him in the jumble of blurred body parts, primal grunts, and the sickening thud of fists against flesh.

I examine the sooty clouds above me as they eclipse the Blue Harvest Moon, and I study the demented beams of light from beneath the surface of unsullied dread. I realize I have to take action. I elbow my captor in the ribs to free myself, and he tightens his grasp until I hear my shoulders crack and feel the cold metal barrel of a pistol against my neck. I struggle no longer. He releases me from his grip completely and I dare not move one step.

"Go ahead, efaggot. Ju try to help jourrr boyfriend and I'll whack ju before ju make a second fuckeen' estep."

They're kicking the doorman in the ribs and making him squirm across the sidewalk by playing the baseball bat in repeated slaps against his crotch. He's a formidable man, but not a match for four with a club. Lace curtains in city apartment living rooms abruptly draw closed.

The driver traces indecipherable words on the nape of my neck with the muzzle of the pistol, and whispers methodically, hypnotically, melodically into my ear. His breath stinks with anger for the world that bore him into this mean, miserable, cold lifetime.

"First we are going to beat de sheeet out of jourrr boyfriend and den we will habe our fun with ju."

"Fuck yourself."

He licks my ear and slaps my crotch, and when I bend over from the pain, he trails the gun from the crack of my ass to the top of my spine, until he rests it at the back of my head. He snorts like a bull, fetid breath, furious and filled with bravado.

"Did you eberrr get fuckcd with a big Puerrrto Rrrican *pinga*?

Answer to me, ju fuckeen' efaggot. Do ju want it inside of ju? Tell me how bad ju want dis inside of ju."

The doorman is swinging his fists randomly in the air, fighting to find his balance, solely for some semblance of a foothold. Time is running out for me. And you wanna know what life is...ya wanna know?

The driver of the cordovan maroon Pontiac Bonneville Firebird Trans Am is so close behind me I feel his ribcage inhale and expel all the hate from inside him. *Trust your body to do the breathing for you. Let go and let life wash over you.* His hand quivers and the gun barrel shakes unsteadily against the back of my head, as he thrusts his throbbing cock in repeated measure against me. This motherfucking bull is hard like a brick.

"Fuck yourself. Get offa me!"

He guides me into position by clutching the hair on top of my head, then forces my jeans down from around my waist with his free hand. He pushes the crotch of them to the pavement with his sneakered foot as he unzips his fly. He pulls me onto his hardness and rapes me savagely, pushing into me like a brazen animal, ever deeper and more furiously, ravenous for his turn to curse and convulse and spill his seed. With my right arm, I elbow his ribs for a second time, and I note the echo of gunshots and feel the fire from the bullets that split the purple morning into shards. Whack goes the rake! Whack goes the rake! Whack goes the rake!

I do not realize I've been shot until I feel the burning on my close-cropped, blue-black buzzcut. I pull my hand from my head and gaze in disbelief at the blood dripping from my fingertips and seeping into the cracks of the blue, harvest moonlit cobblestone of Barrow Street.

Blood clouds my peripheral vision. It pools inside of my

mouth. *Vrrrooommm, vrrrooommm* as the cordovan maroon Trans Am squeals backward and peels off into the soot gray horizon, leaving behind it a noxious cloud of exhaust and the fumes of uncomely laughter that perforates the late September evening. The sound of it echoes in my brain.

Colorless, falling leaves rain from twisted arthritic branches, whipping up tiny chaotic cyclones, as I struggle to pull my shaking limbs beneath me. I gather my trembling body in a pile of dead, brown leaves to protect myself from further harm. With a tremendous clap of thunder the skies open wide, and sheets of rain pelt the battleground and its whimpering, beaten-down infantry.

I hear his laborious breathing, pained and unsteady, as he crawls on skinned, bloody knuckles to sit at my side. He turns his face to spit blood and his cacophonous hacking sends an electric jolt through my aching, broken frame.

I scream in agony, but no voice comes out of me, solely murderous music that covers my face and takes away the light. I linger in the aftermath of this pummeling and shiver with fear.

"Baby—you talk to me! You talk to me right now!"

The doorman lifts his torso to a sitting position beside me. His face is swollen beyond recognition and his t-shirt is wet with blood. He cradles my thrashing torso and secures my wildly flailing limbs inside his muscular embrace. And he whispers plainly, quietly, soothingly into my ear.

"Don't you fucking leave me here alone, baby. Do you hear me, Dominic? Don't you goddamn dare try and pull a stunt like that."

It is all I can do to find breath inside me. If I can just continue to...breathe from my stomach, breathe from my stomach, first in and then out, in and then out, in and then out, as he supports my faltering, failing body with his own brawn. There is no longer light. I'm desperately clawing at the air to pull oxygen into my lungs and grasping at life.

"Dominic!!   Dominic!!   DAAHHHHHMMIIIIIN-NAAAAAHHHHHCCKK!!"

I search for strength in empty pockets inside my body. My head is cracking open, and my brain is spilling out and staining the city sidewalk squares of the West Village. In and then out, I tell myself. First in then out. In and then out. For it's all that there is. In and then out. In and then out. In and then out. In and...one breath for life and the next for...

HEXADECIMAL #FFFFFF

T HERE IS white and there is colorless. White absorbs every wavelength and colorless transmits every wavelength. White is the blending of all colors. The sum of all the colors of light add up to white.

Light appears colorless or white. Sunlight is white light that is composed of all the colors of the spectrum. A rainbow is proof. One can't see the colors of sunlight except when atmospheric conditions bend the wavelength and create a rainbow.

The hexadecimal color #FFFFFF has RGB values of Red: 255, Green: 255, and Blue: 255. Each of the color values cancels the other color values out and together they compose a hue of 0°, and a saturation of 0.00%.

In a CMYK color space white is made up of 0% cyan, 0% magenta, 0% yellow and 0% black. White has a saturation of 0% and a lightness of 100%. CMYK is a subtractive color model, which means all color is subtracted from it to make white.

The New York City White Party is a legendary, fundraising

event. It began as an effort to raise money when gay men were being subtracted from the community. The dress requirement at The White Party is always all white. Held at The Saint during the snow-white month of February, the festivities coincide with the Full Moon.

Even though the Full Moon is 400,000 times less bright than the Sun, it is at once white and devoid of color. During the day, the Moon competes with sunlight that is scattered by the atmosphere, so it appears even whiter.

The surface of the Moon is perfectly white. In fact, one of the most reflective objects in the Solar System is the Moon.

Tighty-whities are snug white underwear. The term followed the launch of the very first men's briefs in 1935. White briefs were the first alternative to male undershorts, and constantly sold out, because the shape fitted close around the crotch and thigh and appealed to men so much.

In many societies the color white has long been associated with purity and virtue, and is the classic color of wedding dresses. In the 1700s and 1800s, however, white was associated with mourning and death and brides chose to avoid such colorless grief on their wedding day.

In the song White Wedding, Billy Idol addresses the person he is singing to as Little Sister. This is the title he has given to his companion and not a reference to an actual sibling, although he did get the original idea for the song at his real life little sister's funeral.

When someone is very shocked at something that they see, or that has happened, they appear as white as a ghost. The idiom means extremely and unnaturally pale, most often due to illness or death.

The white light of death is a perfectly natural and explainable phenomenon. The incurring of significant damage to the brain's occipital cortex—the area known for visual processing, results in visions and the seeing of intense lights.

White light represents a metaphorical rebirth, and it offers up feelings of satisfaction immediately prior to death. When the brain is dying, it creates this feeling as a defense mechanism. While the white light may inspire hope for heaven or a completely new life, it is simply one's vision shutting down—one's brain going haywire in its final moments.

SEVEN

HIGH QUALITY surgical lighting is critical to perform sophisticated procedures. Simply stated, the measurement of surgical lighting is the relation to how it reflects the appearance of color. Surgeons depend on white light to minimize as much shadow as possible. If you want to perform surgery well, he reminds himself, you have to see what you are doing.

A Neurosurgeon saunters confidently into the stillness of an Operating Theatre. The clack of his white boots reverberates against the colorless, homogenous poured flooring and shatters the sterile, silent environment. Just another early morning call to set, he considers, as he pedantically readies a steel tray with clamps, curettes, dissectors and drill bits, forceps, and impactors. Well, at least the commute wasn't unbearable this early in the morning— just a straight shot twenty-two blocks up Eleventh Avenue, even though the physician's answering service did interrupt what was looking to be a stellar dumbbell bench press day.

He smiles from one ear to the next as he tells himself there will be plenty of Chest Days squandered in his expansive home gym once he pursues a fellowship at Columbia or Cornell and retires at age forty, set for life. After all, he didn't pursue four years of pre-medical education, four years of medical school, a year of internship, and these last five years of residency at New York University's Department of Neurological Surgery so that he could waste the days sculpted and shirtless and lifting weights. And he chuckles aloud at the great fortune of how his life turned out. Not in it for the love, he tells himself. He's in it for the loads of cash money.

So much time spent diagnosing common cerebrovascular disorders, tumors, and strokes. It is a rare occasion these days when he finds the opportunity to get his hands dirty with emergency trauma involving the brain, and to actually make a difference. He'd never been content to simply lift his barbells and water his window boxes. And he may have developed a physique Michelangelo would have paid to immortalize, with its sinewy biceps, and powerful pectorals, but he wasn't put on this planet to celebrate his dazzling smile.

In addition to exacting intricate surgeries, he'd been afforded the gift to change lives with a God-given talent and the ability to care for his fallen brothers. Especially when it came to performing complex surgical procedures on patients not much older than himself, like a thirty-something year old man they discovered left for dead in the West Village that was being prepped for emergency treatment just now.

The Neurosurgeon employs a systematic approach to scrubbing in at a sterile sink inside the surgical suite. He initiates a numbered stroke method, one one-thousand, two one-thousand, three one-thousand, practicing a predefined number of brush strokes designated for each finger: thumb, index, middle, ring, pinky, palm, back of hand, and arm, keeping the hand higher than the arm at all times. This, he knew, prevents bacteria-laden soap and water from contaminating the hand.

He repeats the process on the other hand and arm, again keeping hands above elbows at all times, and maintaining imperious count, one one-thousand, two one-thousand, three one-thousand. He dries himself with a sterile towel using an aseptic technique and prepares to don a gown and sterile gloves until he notices an Operating Room Nurse enter the great, white room and guide the gurney which transports this morning's patient to center stage.

The Neurosurgeon nods his head to his team member and extends an elbow to offer up a greeting, and the dance of muscles plays out with the grace of a ballet. All the while he's grinning from one ear to the next. "How's it hanging, friend?"

The Operating Room Nurse acknowledges his superior for a brief moment as he puffs out his enormous chest and exaggerated cleft chin and positively preens, all bravado and charisma like Marky Mark. He gowns the Neurosurgeon by holding a surgical smock at the shoulders and allowing it to unfurl gently, making certain there's enough room to prevent contamination by accidentally touching the white poured flooring. The Operating Room Nurse shuffles and poses beneath the white surgical lighting, offers up the armholes and guides each of the arms through the sleeves, first the left, then the right, and assists by pulling the gown up over the Neurosurgeon's shoulders and tying it off.

The Operating Room Nurse picks up the left glove, and

places the palm facing away from himself. He slides his fingers under the cuff and spreads them so that a wide enough opening is created, and the Neurosurgeon thrusts his hands into the glove. The Operating Room Nurse gently releases the glove, never once allowing it to snap sharply, and unrolls it over the wrist. He performs the same dance with the right glove, and then the Operating Room Nurse steps aside and moves on to matters more pressing.

I hope this doesn't take all morning, he says to himself. I'd like to be at South Ferry and make it home to St. George and Staten Island before dawn explodes. During rush hour the boats are packed with commuters going to or returning home from work, and it's not an opportune time for a relaxing ride on the ferry after working a hectic graveyard shift at the hospital. If the Operating Room Nurse had his way, he'd duck out right now. Anymore, his favorite time of day was grabbing a beer, a Meatball Submarine, and nabbing a bench seat on the ferry ride to the Staten Island side —taking the larger, less choppy boats, just relaxing and experiencing the scenery of life.

And who would believe me if I told them there was life in the other boroughs? The part of Staten Island north of I-278 looks more like New York City than New York City itself, he tells himself, which could easily be mistaken for New Jersey these days if you don't know better. Nah. Staten Island is a pretty decent place to live, he concedes, when you can afford a house and only need to visit Manhattan for competitive work wages. He surveys and smooths his uniform from its brilliant white, squeak-free hospital-grade sneakers to his industrial surgical gloved fingers, and his crisp, colorless KN95 mask.

He glances at the Neurosurgeon and laughs beneath his protective face covering. Brother, those hoity-toity Manhattanite types are so freaking funny! These are the same men who show up at the most extravagant shares on Fire Island every summer and somehow can't afford a lite beer.

The only time he ever visited Fire Island—or the entire southern shore of Long Island, for that matter, he wandered the boardwalk from Cherry Grove to The Pines wondering precisely what was the big deal about the place. *Maddon' mi!* Now he really wanted a cigarette. Standing here daydreaming was a complete waste of his time.

Hopefully this procedure begins soon and concludes mercifully he thinks, as he recites a quick Italian litany for the dead, and genuflects, because right now stalled in this bleak, colorless operating room waiting for life to transpire is more painful than getting your foreskin tangled up in your zipper.

The room quickly fills with colleagues and friends and relations. There are familiar faces and spiritual acquaintances who have shared procedures just like this for many lifetimes. These are the courageous souls that find the fearlessness inside themselves. This tiresome team huddles over a thirty-something year old man this morning, all of them gathered in a colorless surgical suite to bear witness and stand tall at the precipice of something larger than any of them can comprehend.

The theatre doors swing open, and their massive hinges erupt with the sorrowful moan of a wounded animal. An angular, slice of dawn perforates the Operating Room and reveals in its wake the backlit shadow of a Nurse Anesthetist that travels inside with the help of a dual cylinder, portable intravenous pole-mount that provides anesthesia. A medical wagon trails behind him that bears several baskets filled with procedural equipment to administer medication, keep a patient asleep and pain-free, and constantly monitor every biological function of a patient's body.

He's an attractive man with a close-cropped blond buzzcut, a thick red-blond mustache, and tiny round glasses that exploit his intellect. Today, his hair stands on end in uneven clumps that form a horseshoe-shaped ring around the sides of his head. His blue eyes are squinty and exhausted behind his spectacles. These early morning cakewalks are bullshit, he mutters to himself, and he supports his tired body with the use of the IV pole. Its overburdened frame trembles with every wobbly step. Click clack, thump, clack clack, thump, click clack, thump, click clack, thump.

The Nurse Anesthetist delivers the anesthesia medications through an intravenous line. As he prepares the cocktail, he blows kisses to the team of technicians and grumbles a grouchy, "Good Morning," and stumbles over the connective lines and electric cords. He knows general anesthesia is more than just being asleep, it ensures that the anesthetized brain doesn't respond to pain signals or reflexes. He attaches a mask to the patient that delivers gas, and examines the motionless body and takes uninterested, obligatory inventory from brow to balls. Handsome enough, reasonably endowed. Honestly, tomorrow the Nurse Anesthetist won't even remember.

Once the patient is soused but good, the Nurse Anesthetist inserts a tube into the mouth and down the windpipe with the sound of a shhhhhhhlurrrrrrrpppppp that ensures the patient gets enough oxygen. From that point forward, it is the Nurse Anesthetist's job to monitor and adjust medications, breathing, temperature, fluids, and blood pressure as needed. Any issues that occur during the surgery are corrected with additional medications, fluids and, sometimes, blood transfusions. Same shit as any other day.

His stomach growls obtrusively. *Well, Holy Cabooses! Now I'm absolutely ravenous,* he thinks. It's gotta be time for my breakfast soon. Maybe just this once they'll have something decadent to eat in the cafeteria—Entenmann's Pound Cakes or Ring-Dings. Nah. My nutritionist is about to kill me. That is, if the sugar doesn't do me in first.

Well, what the fuck do they expect waking up a man of my stature so early? And to perform such delicate procedures on top of all things. Time was the surgeons called me by my first name, he recalls. Ordinary surgical nurses bowed down on bended knees. When I finally kick the bucket, they're gonna dim the lights on the marquee at Saint Vincent's Hospital. Only then will I have gotten someplace.

Vincent's was ground zero of the AIDS epidemic in New York City and housed the first and largest AIDS ward on the East Coast. The patients were ravaged with lesions and having three-ways and, every now and again, you'd turn around and there stood the good lady herself, the Mayoress Edwina Koch, directly in the center of the mix. I practically ran that hospital single handedly he boasts, very nearly out loud.

During the height of the epidemic, the flood of patients was so intense, every available bed was taken. The diseased spilled out into the hallways, then throughout the surrounding corridors, where we used masking tape to mark off makeshift rooms. Sure, there were other AIDS wards and treatment centers in New York City, but none of them treated patients with the human compassion that Saint Vincent's did. I fought ceaselessly that we should give kind care to those poor, lonely dying men.

Oh, there were funerals every week, the Nurse Anesthetist recalls. We got used to going to funerals. I had four roommates and we all lived in a huge loft on Perry Street and all of them died. We lost our own doctors and nurses. Somehow, I survived, he reminds himself. I watched the rest of them die by the millimeter. The kiss of death was scant to touch me. Oh, for fucks'sake! When is this thing gonna start already? Lola's thirsty! Lola's thirsty!

A follow spot projects a white-hot beam of light onto a songbird perched high on an iron balcony at the top of the coffered ceiling. It's the perfect platform for an artist of such magnanimous stature to take in the view, and maybe grab a breath or two of fresh air.

The Chanteuse's most striking feature is her glamorous mane of sultry, soap opera hair. Big, bouncy curls that she flips back and fluffs when she's making polite cabaret patter between songs, or flicks over her shoulder when she's performing for the room and all the heavens above. Oh, how she adores her audiences. And how her audiences love her right back. One really must catch her act for themselves—a standing gig, but anymore it feels more like a Revival Meeting.

The Chanteuse possesses the unique talent to gather her fans close and help them to feel better. She is a healer of sorrow-filled souls. She sings 'em all and they stay all night. And then they roll out feeling somehow lighter, happier. For a short while at least. For that, she repeats, we can all thank The Brooklyn Academy of Music.

For a long moment, the songbird occupies the white iron balcony and takes her time enjoying a sinsemilla marijuana cigarette. She circles her pouty lips around its fraying end, engorging the glow of its white-hot ember, and releases silky streams of white smoke high into the Operating Theatre. She sits and smokes. The Chanteuse is fully aware that she can stall as long as she wishes, and her fanatical fans will rest complacently in her tender palm. She caresses them. She coos to them until they're unable to hush their unbridled, contagious passion for her. And then she bursts forth like a crazed Linnet Bird at long last set free from her gilded cage.

Dressed in a figure-hugging, elegant white slip style evening gown with a slit that travels from her delicate diamond ankle bracelet to the top of her thigh, she is scintillating. The silhouette of her figure causes near pandemonium. Her nipples protrude playfully, and her hips are soft and round and lovely. A shiver of ecstasy washes over the crowd as she teases her descent down the rungs of the fire escape, and the spotlight follows her every move —as if even one soul would be foolish enough to turn an eye away.

"Uh-uh. Drinks first, Dolls. Now, I'll have a frosty cold Gin Martini, if you please. Extra, extra dirty. No olives, thank you very much. I've got a figure to look out for."

The Chanteuse can feel the eyes of the surgical team wincing up at her—adorned in her almost see-through slip. Her gorgeous, pouty lips curl upward into a salacious, smoldering smile and then she purses them and lights them ablaze with her matte white Lip Smackers lip gloss.

"Well now...ummm, oh dear! It appears as if I've knocked over my Gin Martini. Oopsie."

Barefoot and with a perfect pedicure painted white she slinks rung by rung by rung, only stooping to coo here, and to wiggle there, as she takes the stage of the colorless, homogenous poured flooring. The very breath of her audience has grown labored with anticipation and she hasn't even uttered a note. Oh, Audra Ann somebody has nothing on this Chanteuse. She should win a Tony Award for her entrance alone.

"This smells like Christmas! Mmmm. Mmmm-hmmm. That is some talented mixology. And, Jesus, Fucking, Christ, does Mama need this cocktail."

They're eating from her hand at this point. And she knows that the time has come to set them free, to deliver them at long last, to help them to feel somehow lighter, happier. To heal their sorrow-filled souls. With poised sophistication and pointed glamour she turns to her accompanist, who waits at the ready with hands positioned on the keys of a white baby grand piano, and coos "Oh, Randy, darling, I think...let's do I'm Still Here."

"Ladies and Gentlemen, the time has arrived. We're here to do a job. I'll lead the charge myself," announces the handsome Neurosurgeon.

He removes his surgical cap and fat, curls fall against his eyebrows, which he's forever pushing out of his silver eyes. He disrobes without modesty or inhibition until he's wearing only a stethoscope and scrub bottoms as the bright, white lights caress his exaggerated cheekbones, and his tiny nipples.

He sniffs his armpits, first the left, next the right, and fingers the fluff of palindromic curls. He plants his feet, and he bucks his hips, as tiny beads of sweat collect in the center of his chest and make a slow, methodical descent down his torso.

The Neurosurgeon climbs on top of the gurney and he spits on his index and middle finger and uses them to methodically drag a trail of saliva from the base of his throat to the elastic band of his antiseptic white scrubs. He brings his perfect lips close to the thirty-something year old man they discovered left for dead in the West Village and whispers, "Are ya ready, ya girl? Ya big ol' girl!"

There is depersonalization and there is dissociation. Both refer to a dreamlike state when a person feels disconnected from their surroundings. The exact cause of such conditions is unclear, but it often affects persons who have experienced a life-threatening or traumatic event, such as extreme violence. In these cases, it is a natural reaction to feelings about experiences that the individual cannot control. It is a way of detaching from the horror of living.

The word dissociation itself means to be suddenly disconnected from others, from the world, or from oneself. This can involve out-of-body experiences or a feeling of being unreal. There may also be changes in bodily sensation and the reduced ability to act on an emotional level.

The term dissociative disorder describes a persistent mental state marked by feelings of being detached from reality and stepping outside of one's own body. Dissociative disorder is a coping mechanism that helps one escape.

The process of dissociation usually occurs outside one's own awareness. The experience involves a disconnection between memory, consciousness, identity, and thoughts; these parts splinter, leaving the subject with a feeling of disconnection. Dissociation is a general term that refers to a detachment from many things, even life itself.

The Neurosurgeon, the Operating Room Nurse, the Nurse Anesthetist, the Chanteuse—there's only one person missing from this esteemed collection of exquisite souls. He stares down the operating room from outside the windows with sorrow stuck in his eyes—hazel in color with flecks of bewilderment, wondering what he possibly could have done to deserve such a thing.

There is no bridge for him to cross, no way to bring back what is lost, with all the damage that's been done. Without words, the doorman steps into the operating room, his motorcycle boots echo against the colorless, homogenous poured flooring for lifetimes, and he falls to his battered and war-torn hands and knees and sobs.

EIGHT

The first time I wake up, I'm surrounded with milky white phosphorescent beams of light. Thick ribbons of illuminated pathways ricochet from billowy and blurred, unfamiliar surroundings. Light refracts as it travels through the vacuum of space in this new atmosphere. From here, I see the Sun in the sky on the very plane where I reside. From where I exist, when I see the Sun touching the horizon at sundown, and when I watch a sunrise, the light never departs the horizon. I bask in the incandescent dusk and dawn, and the perpetual daylight emanates from inside me.

I float on the warmth of an autumn breeze. I leave my damaged body behind alongside the cessation of physical pain and all the anxieties are swept away forever. My bodily senses are deadened, but not so my mind, for its pleasure is invigorated at a ratio which defies all description. The psychological suppression that for so long tormented me with existential nightmares melts away, and a calm feeling of the most perfect tranquility succeeds it.

When the entire brain has shut down because of power loss, there is no longer a need for consciousness of pain, nor fear, and the brain's operation grows forever blissful rather than panic-inducing.

I am built from the white light created of harmony and beauty of the highest degree—overflowing with unbounded joy and rapture. Oh, that I would give my entire earthly existence for this one instant, this realm beyond every day, unconstrained by the infinite boundaries of space and time. A variety of higher human consciousness survives the physical limitations of life, and I soar like an eagle within its limitless boundaries drawing fat, lazy circles in the sky.

That's the first time I wake up.

"Ummm, wait one moment...I believe I've dialed the wrong number—" as the Nurse Anesthetist blows kisses to the team of technicians, stumbles over the connective lines and electric cords, and delivers more anesthesia medications through an intravenous line. I emit small bubbles of breath until my lungs are on fire, overcome and about to burst—one one-thousand, two one-thousand, three one-thousand...

"Dominic! Dominic! Did you wake up, you hungover whorebag? You gonna answer that call, sweetheart, or do I need to interrupt my workout and act as your personal answering service?" admonishes the handsome Neurosurgeon, echoing across the courtyard, down Barrow Street, throughout the West Village, and further onward toward the heavens.

Whack goes the rake as a tube is inserted into my mouth and down the windpipe with the sound of a shhhhhhhlurrrrrrppppppp. The Nurse Anesthetist attaches a mask that delivers gas as a gust of wind off the Hudson pierces the breach and produces tiny tornados of dirt, pebbles, and colorless, falling leaves that fly through the air in cyclone fashion before falling flatly against the floor for the moment. "You better make it a stiff one, Dominic! You look a little wobbly."

The Chanteuse peppers her big, show-stopping number with dialogue derived from a personal realization. She sings about the adventures she's witnessed in her young life, and explains that even at such a tender age she's outlived it all.

"I went to the White Party once."

Good times and bum times, I've seen them all and, my dear, I'm still here.

"It was one night after my Revival Meeting at The Carlyle Room. Somehow, I lost my very anesthetized friend, and someone told me they saw him at the White Party. So, I marched right in and found him wandering the hollows. And we clung to each other for dear life—one tentative step at a time for what seemed like an eternity, ultimately feeling our way back to Second Avenue."

I've been through Reno, I've been through Beverly Hills, and I'm here. Reefers and vino, rest cures, religion and pills, and I'm here.

"I realized something that night. There's a lesson to be learned. Experiencing the White Party is a lot like living in an alternative reality. No one can hear you scream, it's difficult to breathe, and you step into a world of spiritual acquaintances only to end up desperate to be home and safe."

The Chanteuse understands first-hand that the good and the bad in life are bound to come, alternately or sometimes simultaneously, and she arrives at the realization that, with the sacrifice of her youthful tenderness, she's managed to trample through life and that she is a survivor. She's the greatest star. She is by far.

Plush velvet sometimes, sometimes just pretzels and beer, but I'm here.

The Operating Room Nurse spews a hot stream of Italian curses guaranteed to wake up his dead mother: *"Va fongool! Vai a fare in culo! Facia-brota skifosa. Mi Meengya, Stonato!"*

The others in the Operating Theatre simply stare at him with upturned noses, keeping their hands above their elbows at all times, a huddle of overworked medical professionals sporting over-sized gowns and modeling for each other at the biers. They know that lessons are rarely learned when the situation is solely viewed in black-and-white, and that an enlightened understanding of the technicolor picture depends on travel to foreign countrysides, and an innate ability to swallow other folk's peculiarities.

They've all arrived to see me off. Somebody has gotta write it down...record all the intimate observations—before they're gone, and nobody remembers it right. The way it actually went down, ya know?

"I apologize fawh such verbal ejaculashun. It's just that I'm very late. Tuh meet my boyfriend. De love of my life. On de Staten Island of New Yawhk City. Ya' dig, or what? Yuh got me so fahr? Yuh wit' me, or what?"

One moment I'm listening to Guasparre Gagliardi *"va fongool-ing"* in his Staten Island Italian accent, and the next I am a tiny, red-yellow spark that flies fearlessly and higher into the smoggy yellow New York City skyline toward freedom, a leaf that evades the colorless firmament and dances in the breeze—sometimes soaring, sometimes dipping, tripping over itself and landing in a seventies-style blue and cream checkered, hospital-issued antimicrobial tiny, private hospital room in an emergency medical care facility in Greenwich Village.

Echoes of taxi horns, the city's submarines, bellow through the window. Red is stop and green's for going. If you travel with your eyes to the ground, counting sidewalk squares and listening to the glass crunch beneath your combat boots, you can easily miss daybreak. Walking the West Village is always an adventure. There is no other plane of existence with so many spiritual acquaintances asking for directions to return from the white light. The first words that I hear drift up from the city sidewalk.

"How do I get to West 5th?"

"Dere is no West 5th."

West 4th Street tangles up and crosses West 10th in a way that confuses all souls. I can picture the corner in my head. The Riviera Cafe—best joint in town for Bloody Marys and man watching.

"How do I get to West 11th?"

You simply follow West 4th, which is the third street after West 10th. Slice joints selling pepperoni pie so oil-slicked it renders its paper-plate delivery vehicle translucent in three seconds, always dribbling down my chin, and the constant parade of handsome strangers wearing tight-fitting white t-shirts and worn-through 501s. I know this place.

The amber-colored, late autumn is escorted through an open hospital room window with the breath of the pleasant breeze...so warm for this late in September. The salt sea air off the Hudson River invades my nostrils. With the flipping and clopping and flapping of seventies-style blue and cream checkered hospital-issued antimicrobial curtains against the whitewashed cinder block walls, I open my eyes and am awake.

My dream has come to its conclusion. The movie has ended,

and the credits have rolled. Now it is time to engage in the real world once more, and the milky white sunlight of the day ricochets from billowy and blurred impressionist pastels to brilliant pop art.

I bring my fingers to my face and explore the gauze bandages wrapped circumferentially around my head. Medical dressing covers the entire right side from the crown down to the chin, some kind of post-surgical compression wrap, and my body throbs with pain from brow to balls. I let my hand fall to the clean, stiff cotton sheets. This is a place to lie and not a bed, a temporary trundle with wheels and collapsible sides. Though the room is unfamiliar, I recognize it as a unit in an emergency medical care facility. A bed number where problems are fixed.

Beside the bed rests a rickety tray table on wheels that holds a melted ice pack stained pink, a styrofoam cup overflowing with fresh chips of ice, and a hermetically sealed gallon plastic bag that displays a wad of cash, my wallet, and the keys to my apartment. My unlaced combat boots stand tall on the floor. My neatly folded, worn-through 501s rest on a blue hospital chair, and my leather motorcycle jacket is draped over its furthest corner. A smallish, hermetically sealed plastic lined trash can on the seventies-style blue and cream checkered, hospital-issued antimicrobial tile floor contains my crumpled and lifeless blood soaked sleeveless, blue flannel shirt.

Blue light projects from a mounted television that plays an afternoon soap opera. The sound is turned down and nobody pays attention as Jerome Cameron is shirtless and covered in television blood in an episode of *Another Tomorrow*. The camera pans over his exaggerated cheekbones, and his tiny brown nipples, his dazzling smile and his perfect, polished soap opera teeth.

The cramped room houses a tiny toilet and a miniature steam radiator covered in years and years of toxic lead, cheerful blue paint. It hisses and my head goes chooga chooga chooga, as a locomotive pulls into the station. I notice him for the first time. In a second blue hospital attendant chair, he sleeps at long last—for so long impoverished of rest.

His gray buzzcut glints with matted sweat. His left eye is swollen closed. He won't see a thing out of that for some time. His face is graffiti-covered with the stains of congealed blood, and even in repose, he exudes masculinity with his thick, graying mustache dripping over the corners of his seductive, sleepy grin. I digest him with my eyes, knowing nothing more than to breathe this man deep inside me, until I feel ribbons of him expanding in my chest and intoxicating my brain. So mesmerized am I by him that I barely notice the freight train running through my head, and the tiny hairs at the scruff of my neck standing tall with adoration.

His lumbering lion's paws are reduced to raw meat covered with great purple welts for knuckles, flesh and bones pulled away from tendons. His fingernails are caked with dried blood and blooming purple patches on his arms reveal the story of how long his battle lasted, until the final kick transpired, and he collapsed to the concrete. He will pull through, but there are scars that will last forever. A stranger who didn't understand the fortitude, the valiant bravery, of this muscle-ripped man would consider him lucky to even remember his own name.

"Ju arrre awake. *Hola, Papi! Como tu ta?*"

A handsome, Puerto Rican emergency medical care facility nurse enters the room dressed in hospital-issued blue and cream checkered scrubs adorned with a Diamanté brooch. He peers in my eyes with a penlight, thumps the bubbles in an IV drip with the flick of his antimicrobial painted blue fingernails, and addresses me with a kind, familiar cadence. My gaze doesn't leave my savagely ravaged roommate, until the nurse addresses me directly.

"Jayyys. Jour husbant. He nayyyberrr left jour side, ju know? Carriet ju in herrre in heees arrrms. Caaaberrrt in jour bloot. Thayyy practically steeeched heees foreheat in the hallways becaaas he woult not leaf jour side. Heee is alwaysss watcheeen. He waaantet to be herrre when ju woke up. *Dios te salve, Maria*, heee wasss beeeten weeeth a bayyyseball baaat."

"How is he?"

"Nayyyberrr miiint heeem. *Como tu ta?* Ju waaant shotsss? Or do ju theeen ju can swallow peeels, *mijo*?"

"Yes, please. Water with pills."

Flowered Dixie Cup with his left hand, water from a blue antimicrobial pitcher, three-count pour—one one-thousand, two one-thousand, three one-thousand, and two pills designed for a horse to swallow.

"Leeesssin! Theees will make ju dance like Cheeeta RRRiberrra ant fuck like RRReeecky Marrrteeen."

"Wha? Huh? That's pretty ambitious in my condition, I think."

"Dunt yoke. I neeet ju to gayyyt some rrrest. *No hay día como hoy.*" He dances off.

Beaten with a baseball bat. Why would someone do that to him? My eyes travel through the network of his abrasions and contusions. His swollen face and scuffed limbs and blood caked motorcycle boots hold the answers, I presume.

I drift off for a small time. My mind travels the backroads of adolescence once more. A frigid Chicago morning. Winter's icy tears pelt the windows of the home where I grew up. Seated face to face with my father, a Cornflower Blue Corning Ware bowl filled with warm water and a washcloth rests in my lap, as I work with a disposable razor to shave his face. His eyes are empty. Already someplace else, preparing to leave this lifetime for something better.

"You will soon be the man of the house, my son."

"Oh, Papa, don't talk that way."

"Well, it must be said. How childlike you are. Immature and unprepared. Filled with dreams that only a young man dares to chase after, eh? In the small time ahead, your childhood will be stolen from you. Overnight, you will grow to become a man."

"You're not going anywhere."

"Who knows of the mysteries the future holds? Do we live in the stars? The days grow short and soon I shall know. Now, first some advice. Listen with your heart, and reason with your head. When you feel frightened or uncertain, remember that without a connection this world is miserable and cruel. You must find inside yourself the ability to understand other folk's peculiarities. Open yourself up to welcome the gift of love from others, my son."

"Ok. I will, Papa."

"Ah, but this you already know, eh, my boy?"

"What are you talking about?"

"I apologize for leaving you at such a tender age. The things you will witness in the days ahead will circle in your brain for a lifetime, but you will survive them. The injuries will soon become memories and nothing more."

"Am I hurting you?"

"I'm fine. Now, the time has arrived for me to thank you."

"Thank me? It's only a shave, Papa. I do it myself each day."

"You do, huh? So impatient to grow up. Now, no more interruptions. Listen closely."

"Okay, okay."

"I learned a lesson from you, Dominic."

"From me?"

"Are you paying attention?"

"I am, Papa."

"You taught me that it doesn't matter who you love so long as you love. If your heart sings it makes no difference—a woman, a man. As long as your love is honorable and true, let it bloom in your heart for as long as you can hold it close. This, my son, you so graciously shared with me. Heed your own young wisdom. Do not give it breath as a mere secret. May it ring in your ears for each of your days, and I promise to carry it through all of the ages. I will be here to remind you. Love if you can, my son. Love, if you're able."

"I will, Papa. I will."

The click clack, slap, clack clack, slap, click clack, slap of a Nubian princess dressed in hospital-issued blue and cream checkered scrubs entering my cramped emergency medical facility room wakes me. The slap of her heels against the blue and cream checkered floor tiles startles me, and I let out a tiny yelp. She carries with her an antimicrobial blue bowl of warm water and a washcloth.

"Honey, stop yo tryin' to run away from me. Lorell ain't gonna hurt you! Girl, what dey got you on dat you so spooked and scared as a rabbit? I just came fo to wash the sleep out yo eyes. Take away some of this dried blood on yo forehead."

"I'm sorry...hi, hello, hi there, ummm—"

"What an unfortunate thing to happen to a leatheh man like you. Whateveh you boys be callin' you damned-fool selves this week." She giggles to herself and gently dabs at the dried blood on my head and takes away the nightmares.

"I ummm—"

Lorell gently clears her throat and removes a Canal Street-Special Golden Yellow and Opalescent Blue Hermès Silk Head-scarf from her pocket to carefully dry my scalp and wipe away the tears.

"Thank you."

"Girl, next time you best be sharin' what they got you on. You got sumthang fly, Boo? Don't you even bother to answerin'. Well, shiiit. I gon' go out de way I came in. Looks like you go yoself a visitah."

Just then, the handsome man who transported me to rescue mindlessly swats at a streaming amber angle of afternoon sunlight with the preposterous fortitude to perforate his time of rest. He scratches gingerly at his brow, grunts sorrowfully and with pained breath, and opens his hazel eyes.

From three feet across the medical facility room, he mouths in an over-exaggerated manner, "Are you okay?", not a sound from his lips, and I shake my head affirmatively in his direction. His smile could light up fucking Times Square. Immediately, he fosters a desire in me to find rest, and seek shelter, in his benevolent arms. I'd do so but I'm too tethered to machines to transport myself to his side, and my muscles are exhausted and immobilized with pain.

"Hey, baby."

"Heya."

"You're awake. How are you? How do you feel, baby?"

"I'm good. I'm pretty good."

"You gave me such a scare. I haven't left this chair for hours."

"That's what I hear."

"We should probably call the nurse."

"He was just here. Gave me Percocet to take the edge off. Christ, the pounding in my head."

"My poor baby."

"My head is playing something tribal by Frankie Goes To Hollywood. You'll forgive me if I can't call forth the name just now. It's right on the tip of my tongue, though."

"That's okay. You can tell me the name of the song later, baby. I'm not leaving your side."

"And you—oh, my goodness. Look at the bruises. Head to toe. Your eye is swollen closed. Are those stitches above your eyebrow? Those are stitches. How are you?"

"Nine stitches. It's nothing. You know me, baby. Sore muscles are a part of my routine. I've had harder workouts at The Chelsea Gym. And that's including a trip to the steam room. Man, am I happy to see your handsome mug."

"I'm just thrilled it's still attached. It is, right? Still attached? Christ, this headache."

"We should probably—"

"The kind of a headache that stops all the other traffic in the brain. Suddenly all the lights are red." Red is stop and green's for going.

"Let's call for the doctor. I promised I'd let her know the moment you woke up. She's on shift right now. Laura. Dr. Laura is her name. Oh boy, are you gonna dig her, baby."

"Does she got any more of those horse pills? The more Percocet she doles out, the more I'll dig her."

"I told her I wasn't gonna leave until you came around, regained consciousness, ya know, and maybe never ever leave again after that. She's the one, baby—Dr. Laura, who arranged for this extra chair so I could sleep right here by your side."

"Good, good. She sounds kind, this doctor. And it's so nice of you to wait for me—so sweet..."

His quiet laughter ricochets around the seventies-style blue and cream checkered, hospital-issued antimicrobial room. From his reclined position, he pantomimes a slug to my chin and winces with pain. "Yes, that's okay, baby."

It takes him a good three minutes to sit up straight in the blue hospital attendant chair. Each muscle flares red like a siren as he puts it to use, the massive veins dance on his forearms, and he cradles his rib cage with a swollen, tattered palm as he winces and sighs.

"Oh, that looks painful."

"Let go and let life wash over you. *The injuries will soon become memories and nothing more.*"

"What did you just say?"

"I said you'll feel better in no time. *The days ahead will circle in your brain for a lifetime, but you will survive them.*"

"I hope that's the case. I need to shake the anesthesia and this Frankie Goes To Hollywood headache altogether."

"Yes, Dr. Laura said you'd have a headache. Something about the anesthesia. Just let me rest here for one moment, and then I'll go find the good doctor."

"I'd appreciate that. I'm due at The Meat Market by six o'clock this evening. That's the leather bar where I work in the Meat-packing District."

"Wha? Oh, good one, baby. Looks like you've still got your sense of humor."

"They're lucky it's not a Thursday night. They'd be in a jam without me behind the bar at a Blackout Party."

"Who else could they get to keep their eyes on Gagliardi, eh?"

"You said a mouthful."

I watch him scrunch up his face painfully as he shifts to gain balance and to ultimately stand. He negotiates using his muscles with the kind of movement that is precise and well-thought through, like the calculation of a competitive chess player.

"See that, baby? It's nothing. I'll go locate Dr. Laura."

"Doesn't look like nothing to me. Are you certain you're alright? It's just as easy for me to pick up the telephone. I can dial someone from my bedside."

"Don't you be silly, baby. The aches and pains I've earned are the ones I grow strong from. Anymore sitting around for me and we'll end up with that Junior One Bedroom at Bellevue. And we all know how I feel about the Upper East Side."

"Thank Christ. Me, too."

He shuffles to my bedside. He caresses my brow tenderly with his swollen digits and trails his forefinger lightly from my cheek to my lips. His smile is warm and familiar and feels like home. Home is a place of safety above all. Home is a place where you feel loved and appreciated. I remember.

"Don't go anywhere, baby," he mouths in an over-exaggerated manner, and gently presses his lips against my left temple. Then, he turns and steps outside the seventies-style blue and cream checkered emergency medical facility room.

I listen for long minutes as he shuffles along the corridor, which I presume leads to a blue and cream checkered nurse's station, Dr. Laura, and getting me released from this joint. Man, these last few weeks. Such a good man. He listens to me. Nobody ever listened to me before. How remarkable that he should tell this Dr. Laura that he wasn't gonna leave until I came around, regained consciousness, ya know, and maybe never ever leave again after that. I mean, who says something like that? Such good fortune, Dominic. I dunno even know which stars to thank. I'm hardly accustomed to such attention. Especially from a man I've never met before in my life.

NINE

"ALRIGHT, Claudia. Start from the beginning...but go slowly. I'm still a little wobbly from the anesthesia."

"Jesus Effing Christ, Dominic. How many times do I have to retell the same story?"

"Until I'm able to take it all in and process it. Digest and understand it, ya know? Now, don't leave anything out—not one piece of information."

Claudia is seated at my bedside at the emergency medical care facility in Greenwich Village, sipping hot tea from a blue, white and gold Greek cardboard coffee cup that reads WE ARE HAPPY TO SERVE YOU. She's all energy this afternoon, wearing too much make-up, smoking ultra-thin cigarettes and wildly punctuating the lavender smoke with her exaggerated gesticulation, and almost spilling out of the blue hospital attendant chair—not to mention the plunging neckline of her best, little black audition dress.

"Okay, okay, okay. And please don't get yourself so roused. I cannot go through your brain on the blink again, Girl. I'm simply loath to bear such a situation. There's too much on the line right now. So, as soon I got the word, I hopped a taxi—"

"Nope. Even further back in the saga than that. Start from the beginning, Claudia. I need to take in every detail so I can put the pieces together for myself and comprehend the magnitude of the circumstances."

"Fine. Here we go again. Please pay attention, Dominic, because the entire account unnerves me so I can hardly tell and retell it one more time. It's like I can't relive it again. And, Jesus Effing Christ, I don't even wish to let my mind explore any alternative outcome. I can't do that. I cannot allow that my thoughts should go in that direction and dwell in that space for then I will let it touch me emotionally...because was it to somehow turn out differently...well, I'd be crushed, ya know? You know that, Girl, right? I'd be devastated. I know you know."

"I get that. But in order for me to gain any perspective, I need to gather all the facts, no matter how minute. Just take your time and recount the tale from start to finish. I promise I won't ask this of you again."

"Fair enough. And away we go. So, I get this telephone call from my agent—and this is going back several weeks now, four, maybe five weeks, who remembers? You know I go to these auditions, and then I forget about them completely because, honestly, what would be the point of getting my hopes up? There's thirty other girls standing on the line in character shoes right beside me. All of them with perfect, curled soap opera hair and a nice, bouncy rack wearing their best, little black audition dresses just like me. But this one audition—feels somehow different, ya know? Like the casting people saw what I was actually doing up there. Looked up and noticed me—*recognized* me for my talent, and my ability to help people feel better, even just for a little time. And I walked out of the room feeling good about my performance that day. Jesus Effing Christ, the process is positively harrowing if you dare even let it touch you emotionally."

"Oh, I'll bet, sweetie. Putting yourself out there like that in the face of so much rejection—"

"Oh, it's not just the rejection. There's so much talent all around me. And believe me it takes a lot more than perfect, curled soap opera hair and a nice, bouncy rack to get them to even look up from your resume let alone book you for a callback. And I get the callbacks. You know that I get the callbacks. And I go. You know that I go. And afterwards, it's radio silence. No nada. Not a peep. I know from rejection."

"A lot of it is luck."

"And timing. Timing is everything. I mean, you could sit in those audition rooms for six hours or more until you're finally on deck, and you're fluffing your hair and shuffling your sheet music, and the chick before you sings the same exact song that you've prepared and knocks it outta the park. Jesus Effing—whaddya supposed to do then? How does one recover? That's why it's always best to go through these things and not think too much. Do your absolute best and leave the entire experience in the gutter on 43rd Street. Unanalyzed like a visit to an unfamiliar plane or, or...Girl, do you need your ice pack? Is it time to swallow your horse pills? You look a little flush."

"That's because I'm chomping at the bit. I'm fine. Now, please keep on with the story."

"Do not get yourself overexcited, Dominic. I will march right up to that nurse's station and go all Shirley MacLaine if you force me to do so, Girl."

"Why do I always gotta be Debra Winger?"

"Because somebody has to be, I suppose."

"Always the bridesmaid."

"Now, where was I? Oh, that's right, busy getting noticed. So, a week or two after attending the audition where I felt...I dunno, recognized or whatever, the same creative team wants to see me again. Could I please prepare a song that particularly showcases my musical belt? Now A, that's hardly a problem because my set list at The Carlyle Room has basically turned into fifteen Eleven o'clock Numbers back-to-back, and...Jesus Effing Christ, I can't remember the last time I saw you there! I know, I know—that would entail getting you into a shirt with a collar. And two, it isn't that unusual that directors and musical directors ask to see me a second time because that's what comes from attending auditions for years and getting your name out there. For that, we can all thank The Brooklyn Academy of Music."

"What did you sing for them?"

"Oh my gosh, who knows, Girl? Like I said, that's going a couple weeks back. You know me—some mornings I barely remember to feed the dog and remove my Coke can curlers before hopping on the subway. But I do recall it was something that must have really hit the spot, because they sent two other girls home on a dime. Ya know, come to think of it, they asked me to sing something belty and I hit them with my Merman note and then we just stood around chatting for a bit. Isn't that peculiar? The musical director asked me what I knew from playing dramatic scenes and I told her I was a regular Camille. We all laughed, and then I took the subway to meet you downtown at Dirty Dicks where we had those fancy Martinis with the pickled string beans. Jesus Effing Christ, those things are potent. Do you remember that afternoon, Girl?"

"Vaguely. Dr. Laura tells me each day more little memories will resurface until I feel myself again. Whatever that means. She also hooked me up with a shrink...a therapist. We're gonna discuss my panic disorder. Whatever *that* means. Now, what I do recall is that we were talking about you. Well, you were talking about you. And you were just arriving at the good part."

"Indeed. So, last night I get this late-night phone call. I swear to you, I almost didn't answer. I mean, any time a single gal gets a telephone call after ten in the evening it's never good news. Who could be calling that late? It's either a horned-up ex-boyfriend or Mama calling from Indianapolis to inform me some distant relative kicked the bucket. Usually, I don't even answer because they can keep all of it on ice overnight, the horny suitors and the forgotten relations."

"Even the forgotten relations with the horny suitors."

"Precisely. But this time...this time I sat straight up in bed and thought perhaps it was a good idea to take the call. And, of course, it's my agent. And, of course, he's wondering if I could meet Bobby at the theatre first thing in the morning to run a few scenes for the casting people. And I'm thinking to myself what theatre and Bobby who? So, I say to my agent...I say to him it's kinda late to be calling and with such short notice to show up for a random audition. Nervy, you know?"

"Absolutely."

"And he's gobsmacked. Well, I ask him exactly what theatre and Bobby who is so important that he should wake me up at ten in the evening?"

"You didn't!"

"Well, Jesus Effing Christ, of course I did."

"Girl!"

"Right, Girl? I know, right?"

"Aaand—"

"And it turns out he's calling on behalf of The Winter Garden. It's The Winter Garden Theatre calling. And Cannavale. Bobby Cannavale. Bobby Effing Cannavale!"

"No!"

"Yes! Yes, Girl! And the director wants to see me read sides at the Winter Garden Theatre with Bobby Cannavale for a revival of *Funny Girl* they're planning for the springtime!"

"Claudia! You're making shit up again—"

"That's what I thought. Claudia, I said to myself, this can't be for real. Talk about gobsmacked. But my agent assured me the whole thing was above board and, I swear to you, I peed a little puddle right there on my knockoff Peking Chinese Rug after I hung up the telephone. I barely slept a wink all night through on account of the Coke cans in my hair and the nerves in my stomach dancing the jitterbug."

"Well, of course. Who could sleep after such news?"

"I woke up frenzied this morning. I practically ran uptown with Coke cans still in my hair. Thankfully, I shuffled my hair and fluffed my sheet music first. And then I hopped a taxi to the Winter Garden Theatre and read scenes with Bobby Effing Cannavale. And not just one scene, Girl. Scenes! Like plural. Like, I was there for an hour. Maybe more. Who knows? Time existed on a completely different plane. And, Jesus Effing Christ, is he handsome—and charming, and talented. Come to think of it, everybody in the room was so kind to me."

"Aaanddd—"

"Aaanddd what?"

"Do not play coy with me. Now what? What now?"

"Well, that's it. Now, we wait. We sit and we wait."

"Well, seeing as my skull was lodged with a bullet only two days ago, it doesn't appear I'll be rushing off anytime soon."

"Oh, my Sweet Angel. Here you are stuck in a medical center, and here I am going on about me. Me playing Fanny Brice. Girl! Can you imagine?"

"Claudia, I have all the time in this world to discuss my best friend starring in a major musical revival playing Fanny Brice. That's why enterprising homosexuals invented the Broadway theatre. You know, so we'd have something other than bullets lodged in our skulls to occupy our minds."

"I need to come back to earth. It was just another callback."

Beneath the bandages, the bullet hole is a cold and grim reminder of the life and death the last two days have fostered. Rough at the edges and scorched. When they first discovered my lifeless body, the Angel of Death was already tasked with lighting the way for me to a different dimension. All times are nothing but a vast puzzle to the living. All of them are important and none of them are sequential in the way we experience them.

For a human soul there are infinite paths. The Angel of Death can cocoon a soul until its heavenly metamorphosis is complete, and she alone can choose to hand over a charge that is not yet bound to the next existence. Still, the man carried me in his muscle-ripped arms all the way from Barrow Street.

When I arrived, the Neurosurgeon discovered a bullet graze wound that was the result of the early morning shooting, but exploratory tests showed something completely different. The bullet was lodged in my skull. A computerized tomography scan, a medical procedure that uses specialized x-ray equipment to produce cross-sectional images of the head, confirmed that the bullet entered from the right side, went through my brain, and was stopped by the back side of my skull. Talk about hard-headedness.

Less than an hour after my admittance to New York University's Department of Neurological Surgery, they were performing brain surgery on me. For six arduous hours, a team of surgeons trod through gray matter to locate the bullet where it appeared on the CT, and to their surprise, it could not be located. Due to reflection off the projectile intruder itself, the x-ray image was blurred and presented inconclusive details.

With my head cracked open, having previously stained the city sidewalk squares of the West Village, the team employed high-tech tools to explore where the bullet disappeared to. It was discovered lying with its tip directed to the back side of my brain, touching the surface of my skull, and pulsating along with every pump of blood—thump, splash, trump, sploosh, thump, splosh.

Evidently, because the direction of its tip was pointing outwards it was surrounded by multiple air pockets, and the bullet was easy to remove. The Neurosurgeon said that careful work by the Nurse Anesthesiologist prevented the brain from any swelling. The bullet was held with forceps and pulled free. Post-surgery, I was given supportive treatment by a team of emergency medical care facility nurses dressed in hospital-issued blue and cream checkered scrubs, and regained consciousness the next morning.

"Girl, what panic disorder?"

"Wha? Huh?"

"You said Dr. Laura diagnosed you with some sort of panic disorder? Is that right?"

"Episodic paroxysmal anxiety."

"I was a Theatre Major, hon..."

"Panic attacks. Sudden, unreasonable feelings of fear and anxiety that cause physical symptoms such as a racing heart, fast breathing and sweating. Fly with them frequently enough, and they promote you to an elite group of those suffering with panic disorder."

"Sounds fancy."

"It does have its privileges. It comes with a shrink—a therapist. A therapist. I'm still trying to get the lingo straight...er, down."

"Poor Boo. Tell me what I can do to help?"

"You can please stop with all the smothering. You know I detest that shit. And that baby talk, for fucks'sake. I have never once answered to, nor do I ever intend to stand up and proclaim to be, somebody's Boo. Which reminds me, there is one thing you can help with..."

"Anything, but—"

"How do I know a man named—"

"—we gotta make it quick."

"Where are you off to? Another audition?"

"Romeo."

"Huh? Wha?"

"Romeo. Jeromeo. The nickname stuck. The name you called him the other evening at The Meat Market. You do remember Jerome, right?"

"Well, of course I remember Jerome."

"Thank goodness, Girl."

"One can't live across the courtyard from all that beefcake

without the image of his sinewy biceps, and powerful pectorals, and his dazzling smile seared into one's brain. And I'm not a girl."

"Of course, you're not, dear. Seems like it's all coming back. Anyway, I'm late to meet him."

"You can't leave now. How do I know—wait one moment! Why would you be meeting Jerome? You don't mean...the two of you? Are the two of you..."

"Oh, I said nothing of the sort. I'm simply late for our book date. We're reading Nietzsche together."

"Which Nietzsche?"

"How the hell do I know which Nietzsche? Do I look like a Philosophy Major to you?"

"A Boadway show *and* a boyfriend? Man, you do move quickly!"

"Well, I haven't signed on the dotted line for either one yet. But things do look promising, don't they, Dominic? It's just like you toasted...what was it? Oh, that's right. About second chances and the future. Wow, what a day! Now, what was it you mentioned you needed my assistance with? Can I sneak you in a pack of Reds? Do you want one of those sweet little personal cheesecakes from Bleecker Street? You just name it, dear."

"I need your help putting a name to—"

"Jesus Effing Christ, look at the time! I'll be positively delinquent. Listen, I'll be back to visit this evening. We can discuss whatever is on your mind. How's that sound, Girl?"

"Yes. I'd like that. And don't bother coming empty handed. Either bring along the shirtless soap opera lothario or one of those Bleecker Street cheesecakes."

"Sounds like a plan." She collects her Gucci Marmont Matelassé bag, fits her pink Christian Dior Cat Eye Sunglasses, and smiles so wide she can barely contain herself.

"Go on, now! You better hurry, Miss Brice. You're gonna miss your tugboat."

With a kiss that leaves a perfect, pink imprint on my forehead and a wave of her manicured French tips, she takes her exit, giggling to herself, and humming something by Jule Styne.

TEN

THE SUNLIGHT PAINTS SATURATED SHADOWS, golden and azure and violet across the courtyard apartments, as if a street artist had at first plotted and then brought artistry to life with deliberate brushstrokes on the brick walls and glass windows of Barrow Street. The colors shimmer, trade off, and reflect like a kaleidoscope put to action. From my perspective, enveloped inside the late morning October illuminations, only the brightest celestial objects stand out against the parade of vibrant hues.

This is precisely when I spot Jerome, dressed only in Calvin Klein tighty-whities. He feeds his Basset Hound, Frank. He waters his window boxes, and plates Pop-Tarts alongside one freshly plucked, window box Gerbera Daisy plopped into a tiny, jade glass vase on a breakfast tray. I set aside an *Interview Magazine* featuring a spread with Marky Mark grabbing his crotch photographed by Bruce Weber, and send salutations to my sculpted and shirtless neighbor through the windows. Jerome immediately places his activities on hold, and rests his elbows on the screenless windowpane, as we share our recently established ritual of morning check-ins.

"Cowabunga, Duuude!" as he offers up the Shaka sign, curling his three middle fingers and extending his thumb and pinky, posing with his tongue out, and then falls into a silly fit of laughter.

"Likewise, I'm decidedly certain. And you're hardly fooling anybody—you've never surfed a day in your life, Jerome."

"I grew up on Long Island Sound."

"So did Patti LuPone and you don't see her hanging ten."

"The chick from Lady Marmalade?"

"No, that's LaBelle."

"Huh? So, guess what? I've got news. I booked a guest spot on *Baywatch*, brother! I'm working on my character as we speak."

"Well, how cool is that? What's the role?"

"I play a washed-up cadaver on the beach. In the script they call him Washed-Up Cadaver on the Beach, but I've named him Marlin. You know, just so I can explore a backstory for my character. It's my debut on Prime Time television, and I gotta get this perfect. Even if he already happens to be deceased and doesn't have any lines in the script, Marlin has an entire history that needs investigation in order to bring him to life for the savvy Prime Time television viewer."

"The underlying message that is not explicitly apparent. I get it. Sometimes you have to pay close attention to the rumblings *beneath* the surface to figure out what's actually going down."

"Whoa. That's epic, Dudette. Ya big, ol' Dudette."

At this, we both laugh uncontrollably. Claudia steps into the room across the courtyard, jammied-up in pink plaid boxer shorts and an oversized Nickelodeon muscle t-shirt that belong to

Jerome, to join our party line conversation. Her Clairol Nice'n Easy No. 6R Light Copper soap opera curls reside in Coke cans. She cuddles her petite frame against her lover and leans out the same screenless window to bid her morning tidings. Instantly, her nipples come alive in the cool October morning, which she covers in modesty with one palm over each.

"Jesus Effing Christ. What are the two of you going on about? I heard you giggling like schoolgirls all the way from the bedroom. Sheesh, it's chilly outside. You can almost see your breath this morning."

"Well, natch, Dollface. That's how the seasons happen."

"Thank you for the lesson in meteorology, you sexy thang. If *Baywatch* doesn't pick you up—and how could they not after witnessing first hand your sculpted torso and those ripped abdominals, grrripple, ripple, ripple—you could always do some time as a weatherman. That's acting, too. And Sam Champion has nothing on you, Romeo." She tickles him unmercifully and he laughs uncontrollably. "Dominic—how are you feeling this morning? Did you take your medication?"

"Supplements, dear. They're called—"

"Suppositories? Suppositories, ya big ol' girl?"

"Romeo, you stop that right now or there'll be no post Pop-Tart nookie for you. I promised to keep watch of our own little leatherman and I have every intention of fulfilling that agreement. It's barely been days that he's home from the hospital—and a girl's gotta keep a close eye on such a specimen."

"Specimen? Now, I'm a specimen? Like a Holstein?"

"Holsteins are girls, Dominic. You're not a girl, remember?"

"She's a stool specimen! A big ol'—"

"Very clever. Grow up, will ya, Romeo? I'm fine, Claudia. I'm more relaxed these days than I've felt in ages. Calm as a clam. And lookie! Lookie here! My buzzcut is growing back where I was shorn."

"Shorn or shaven. Shaved or shorn? Which is it, Girl?"

"Whichever the word. My hair is growing back with vigor. I'm finally starting to put this entire nightmare behind me. Man, these last few weeks. Addison says I'm making tremendous progress learning to let go. Relinquishing with aplomb. Releasing the past with proverbial leaps and bounds says he. I'll tell you the truth: had I realized the healing that talk therapy can encourage, I'd have installed a shrink...a therapist, a therapist...they like to be called therapists—I'm still trying to get the lingo down—anyway, I'd have had my head shrunk a long time ago."

"Speaking of shrunken heads, that is one rad scar, bro."

"Yes, Straight Boy, there is that. Eight inches of scar tissue I did nothing to earn. Evidently, the outside takes longer to heal than the inside. You'd think it would be the other way around, right? I'm continually gritting my teeth and bearing down hard to kick-start the hair follicles to completely cover up that beast of a barren patch. All in good time, I suppose."

"I find it very sexy, Girl. Straight outta *Pirates of Penzance*."

"There is nothing straight about *Pirates of Penzance*."

"You know what I mean. A disfigurement such as that reads very butch."

"Thanks for playing along, Claudia. I can assure you that procuring such a sexy stigmata wasn't worth all the deaths I had to die. I just hope that my hypermasculine scar tissue doesn't steal the spotlight from my resplendent return to the Harmonia Gardens this evening."

"Harmonious wha? I thought the thing was at Meaties tonight."

"The Meat Market. He means The Meat Market, Marlin. Dominic, did he tell you he insists that I call him Marlin now?"

"It's just until we wrap Episode 73 of *Baywatch*, Dollface."

"Isn't a marlin some type of fish?"

"It's a gnarly name, ya big ol' girl."

"It's a type of tuna, I believe."

"Nuh-uh. It's method just like Brando. Brando was no chicken of the sea."

"Not right now, Romeo. Mommy is talking to the lady across the courtyard, okay?"

"It's Marlin, if you please. Yeah, yeah, okay."

"You're certain you're up to this evening, right, Dominic? I mean, well you know, returning to work...and all things."

"It's time now, Claudia. Growth only happens when what was once an open wound becomes an almost invisible scar. Facts must be faced. In order for me to realize even the tiniest modicum of progress, I must once again enter the world of the living."

"Well, I'll be right there beside you, Girl."

"We'll both be there. I'm coming, too. Right there at your side —that's where we'll be. It's gonna be a righteous affair."

"I may even sing something."

"Thank you both. A guy couldn't ask for better friends."

"You got it, Girl. Can we hang up now? Jesus Effing Christ, I'm practically freezing my *tetas* off hanging out this window."

"The radiators are already hissing over on this side! It's only October. Okay, Goodbye, Claudia. Bye, Marlin."

"Aloha, bro!"

"See you tonight, baby...er, I mean, Dominic. I mean Dominic."

"Yes. See you tonight then."

The yellowed, paper window shades draw to a close, as do the performances of the windowsill songbird and her brawny, brainiac boyfriend. I close the window and still hear them frolicking in the apartment across the courtyard. She tickles him unmercifully, as he chases her into the bedroom, trips over his Basset Hound, Frank, and stubs his big toe on his Bowflex Xtreme Body Tower SE2000.

"Ouch! Wipeout! That's a fresh pedicure. And I gotta be on set in a matter of days."

"Here, now. Lemme see that big toe, Marlin. Uh-oh! Looks like somebody's hanging ten."

"Patti LuPone?"

"Huh?"

"Riptide!"

There are days when I wonder if there'll forever be a Molière sex farce playing in the apartment across the concrete courtyard that's littered with glue traps. *Le freak, c'est chic, freak out!*

I laugh to myself as I reach for a Red and light it from a branded The Meat Market book of matches that reads *A Butcher Bar*. I exhale a long stream of billowy, blue smoke into the air, unfurl a yoga mat, and sit to practice the mindful respiration that Dr. Addison is teaching me.

Addison called it intensive training in Buddhist meditation without all the Buddhism attached. Basically, the idea is to focus attention on your breathing—learn to heed its natural rhythm, the ebb and flow, first in and then out, in and then out, in and then out, and to consciously experience the relaxation of each inhale and every exhale.

People with a panic disorder breathe with judgment. If you listen too closely, you add a personal narrative of questions like, "Why is this breath shorter?", "Why can't I get enough air?" or "Why does my chest feel tight?" and spin into an overreaction. A person won't suffocate, stop breathing, or die from an anxiety attack. A panic attack won't turn into a heart attack either. The objective of mindful breathing is to learn self-awareness and the ability to differentiate between a frightening negative commentary and what's actually happening. Heady stuff, this therapy.

When I feel more relaxed, I move into a shower that knows no temperature more than lukewarm. The water spray is pins and needles and massages my muscles. I menace a cockroach in the bathtub with my big toe, and watch it and the last few weeks circle the drain and disappear. If you hold every bad memory in your left hand, and every good memory in your right hand, it's astonishing to realize how much we invent that blurs the lines. Christ, how talented we are at creating our own fictions in an effort to navigate our emotions and quell our nightmares.

The water trickle tickles my flat tummy and the hairs around my treasure trail as steam rises around me in fat, drippy clouds. It reminds me of the scene when Dorothy liquidates her evil, green nemesis and watches her woes dissipate before her eyes.

Long drips of steam anchor me to the ground and transform my environment into a quiet, defined space. In front of the mirror, I towel myself and trace a path of fading yellow bruises.

I swipe away water droplets and inside the mirrored glass I recognize an attractive man, and a smile that forms easily with a space between my two front teeth big enough to pass a dime. I inspect the thick mustache that extends well beyond the corners of my mouth and trails smile lines to touch my chin. I actually catch myself grinning at my reflection. I search my brown eyes for answers, and the possibilities from which my future grows rains to my feet. It's right here in my brain: the power to transform myself. "Okay, this is who I am now."

The yawn and stretch of a jungle animal trumpets in the bedroom, followed by a tiny fart. He enters my world and mouths the words, "Who me?" in an over-exaggerated manner. He laughs intimately and wraps himself around me as his massive biceps dance and the veins on his muscled forearms swell. I rest quietly in the doorman's embrace and tell him he's the only person I know that gives indefinite hugs.

"Well, baby, where else would I rather be?" he replies. "This is life, real life."

The doorman kisses me roughly. His stubbled jaw against the nape of my neck arouses in me a lustful desire. He tugs at the towel secured around my waist, and it falls with a disinterested thud to the subway tile bathroom floor.

"Take my hand and follow me, baby. No more words. It is time."

"I'm ready."

"If we do this, there will be rules. Do you think you can play by the rules, sexy fucker?"

"Whatever you want to do is what we'll do. There isn't a thing I can do to stop you. Not that I'd want to."

The doorman and I fit together as if we were made just for this. The proximity of him alone sends me into a trance—rapture that isn't complete until our bodies are huddled as one, breathing labored breaths in unison, falling into each other for the rest of our days.

With an unstifled growl, he lifts me off my feet and carries me to the bed and lays me down on the mattress with a soft bounce. We lock eyes just long enough to feel safe with one another. Then, he's all business.

I breathe him inside of me, ravenous to take him deeper and starving for the pungent sweat-soaked musk of our lovemaking, the beauty, the fear, the very real sense of brotherhood, the history, our history, inside my airway, in and out, in and out, in and out, until I require it for sustenance, to survive.

With his teeth against my neck, I squirm. He delivers a litany of foul words inside my ear, rhythmically, hypnotically, grinding his manhood against me as he traces his rough beard against my collarbone. He snarls and chews on my lips, spits hard in my mouth, and his own saliva drips from the corners of my breathless jaws as I instinctually, helplessly, purposefully buck my dick against his dick.

I feel my back arch in anticipation, knowing where his fingers will soon arrive. My head rocks back against the pillows as an instinctual moan escapes my lips.

He licks his fingers and watches my reaction, takes notice as my body writhes. I feel his touch on my nipples, our tongues tangled in a kiss, and then he's inside me and changing my breathing with every thrust. He tells me he's going to make me beg for it. I grunt, unable to articulate any response. Moments later, he's intoxicating my mind and delivering me spiraling in his embrace for thousands of lightyears.

He can do whatever he wants, and he does. Over and over, I beg for mercy that never comes. It's hard to hold back. Difficult to make the moment last. Always caught between the thrill of climax and extending the pleasure we never want to end. With labored and heavy breaths, we close our eyes and say goodbye to personal narrative and self-awareness. We let our bodies crash and retreat, crash and retreat, until we collapse, supine beside each other and gasping to fill our lungs with oxygen. We fall into an embrace and laugh until our stomach muscles ache.

For what remains of the afternoon, we lounge in bed with our limbs wrapped around each other—trading confidences and sharing cigarettes, kissing passionately and wrestling to perfect a perfect fit, fingering deep-veined muscles and tracing tattoos, and sleeping away the hours without worry. It's after four when I prop my head on his chest, and study the afternoon drawing long shadows. Stairstep by stairstep on the fire escape outside my bedroom window, the light follows a path toward the sidewalk and into early evening. I kiss his lips softly and he smiles, still lost in slumber, and I pad barefoot across the rooms to the kitchen.

Using ingredients that Claudia and Jerome bought at Balducci's to stock the cupboards, I prepare a banquet: scrambled eggs and peppered bacon, strong black coffee, cantaloupe cut fresh, and raisin toast with fig jam. I didn't even know I owned a toaster. When I was still in the emergency medical care facility, and the doorman purple with bruises and broken ribs, my thoughtful neighbors across the courtyard filled the cabinets with food, organized the apartment, and ensured that the gas bill had been satisfied.

I balance two plates on my forearm like a waitress at The Empire Diner and, as I walk through the bedroom door frame, he is propped up against the headboard, awake and thumbing through the pages of a Paul Monette novel. The kindness of his smile lights up the entire room.

"Okay, mister, make way. I arrive bearing a feast of foodstuffs courtesy of our friends across the courtyard, Fred and Ethel Mertz."

"Yes, but which one is Fred and which one is Ethel, baby?"

"It's just like us, Doorman. They wrestle to see who's gonna be on top."

Instantly, he's playfully puffed up like Stanley Kowalski. "That ain't the way it works around this household."

"Great. It's only been a short time and the honeymoon is officially over. Already you've got me barefoot and chained to the kitchen."

"Just in the nick, too. I'm as ravenous as an ape. I nearly scarfed a pillow!" He pantomimes scratching his armpits simian style, discovering and investigating a feather pillow with his sniffer, and swallowing it whole. Stanley Kowalski fills his cheeks with air and bulges his eyes until he falls into playful laughter. "Yummo. This looks terrific."

"Remind me to thank the Mertzes the next time we meet, will ya?"

"I'll thank them for us. I've got a workout planned with Jerome before you and I are due at The Meat Market later tonight."

"I'll use the time to dress for this evening."

"Who is this Paul Monette person? Looks like you could build a library from all of his books around your place."

"Paul Monette is only the greatest writer to ever come out of Yale University. Also, a personal hero to me. He won the National Book Award. He's an author, a poet, and an activist best known for his essays about gay relationships. A gay historian, if there is such a thing."

"He tells stories about us?"

"Exactly. One day somebody has gotta write it down."

Together, we clean up the breakfast dishes and decide to not make the bed. The doorman excuses himself to go lift dumbbells with his buddy, Jerome, and for a long moment I allow myself the luxury to lie in the sheets that smell of our lovemaking.

I smoke half a joint that I excavate from the ashtray, and my mind drifts off as I consider how change becomes us. At one time my emotions were moody and extreme and now they are as variable as the rest of the family. Where my face was creased with worry, it is now soft with the beginnings of laughter lines. There is such freedom in growth—yet also a powerful sense of arriving home, of belonging, and of wishing to stay forever.

At one time, standalone mode was triggered by the universe because I dwelled in so much fear. Now, I have someone with me when the Sun gives way to the stars and when it returns to ignite again the colors of the daytime. *What love gives you is the courage to face the secrets you've kept from yourself, a reason to open the rest of the doors,*" writes Paul Monette.

I lay out my uniform for the evening's events: engineer boots, chaps, harness, vest, motorcycle jacket, and Muir cap. Moving forward, dressing is as much ritual as it is rite. I drop to my knees, as the heady, hypermasculine scent of leather overtakes my nostrils and arouses in me the nature of who I am. I work to a sweat as I polish my engineers and oil my chaps with concentrated, trance-like effort.

I step inside my engineer boots and the weight of their wooden heels falls hard against the seventies-style parquet floor in a series of solid, pronounced clomps. I walk taller. I swell and swagger. I don my chaps next, my favorite part. They're purposefully built one half size too small—rendering the leather taut and slick against my body. I slide the chaps over my thighs, wind the zippers from ankle to crotch, breathe in my own aroma, and the power slowly overtakes me.

Certainly, there is fetish to the rugged masculinity of wearing leather, a material with an allure that speaks to men who love men. It is a political statement. It is a tradition. It is wearing the uniform of the courageous souls who came before me. Where we came from, ya know? When I wear my leather, I feel pride. I feel power. I feel the security of belonging to someplace. Above all else, I feel as if I've finally arrived home.

ELEVEN

THE SIGHT of the doorman and I swaggering through the West Village dressed in full leather before sundown must really be something. We gather the attention of more than a few of our flannel shirted, button-flied brothers craning their necks and lowering their mirrored sunglasses to have a closer inspection. He smiles at me swollen with pride. He pulls a pretend punch on me that lands as softly as the hazy yellow, late autumn sunlight on my kisser. He curls his bicep and mouths the words, "Hi Baby," as he grasps my hand firmly and pulls me close beside him. "He's with me," he announces to the neighborhood as we promenade down Hudson Street.

I nab a peach from an outdoor bodega just because I can, and hand it off to a homeless man who's realized temporary digs outside the Garden of St. Luke in the Fields, a West Village oasis filled with leafy trees, wildflowers, blooming bushes, and carefully manicured gardens. He accepts the offering and gazes at us admiringly prior to breaking into a goofy, toothless grin and taking a juicy bite of the pilfered, streetcorner fruit. Maybe it's the booze, but more likely it's life. Honestly, tomorrow he won't even remember.

There's a serenity between us as we walk past Christopher Street, West 10th Street, Charles Street, and the tiniest refraction of orange, lilac, blue sunset dips into the Hudson River as our boots click clack in perfect unison. We travel in a world beneath storefront awning signs for The Cowgirl Hall of Fame, A Different Light Bookstore, and Corner Bistro, beside Post No Bills signs covered over with advertisements boasting performances by Marky Mark and The Funky Bunch on dingy, basement stages, broken umbrella branches and all but barren Ginkgo trees, and on top of Silence=Death stenciled sidewalks, steam clouds emanating from manhole covers in the street, and leaves hidden in mine bomb fashion that crunch beneath our polished blue-black boots as we step outside of the drawing amber shadows.

The avenues grow larger and more crowded with traffic as we progress further West, a sea of yellow taxi cabs. Commuters scurry home from another day at the office and enterprising homosexuals hurry closer toward happy hour at any number of West Village destinations. I reach into the pocket of my leather jacket for a Red and the doorman lights it with a brass, flip top pocket lighter, and I exhale a cloud of smoke into the burgeoning night, the soft white streetlights, and this evening's primal rites.

"Now don't laugh at me, Doorman, and isn't it curious but I'm nervous—even after all these years. I'm apprehensive about taking my place behind the bar tonight...let alone everything else that this evening holds."

"It's gonna be fine. Just another night, baby. We'll get through it together. How about that? You and me."

"Yeah, I'd dig that. But it isn't just another night—and you know precisely why and what I mean. Christ, it's so much more than going back to work for the first time. We walk these streets and now we're the men who found the fearlessness inside themselves to document their surroundings, to tell the history. All the things this evening means. We're lightyears removed from where we stood a couple of weeks ago."

"I've been thinking about that, too. How much time do we spend ruminating about the past? Worrying about the future? How much of life do we miss by getting tangled up in our own thoughts? So, whaddya say we concentrate on just this moment? We'll tackle this one first, and the next one, and then the one after that."

"Doorman, you're beginning to sound just like my therapist, Dr. Addison. Now, don't be jealous. Every gay man develops a crush on his therapist. With you, it's different. You're a good man. Well, not that Addison isn't a good man. But, you're sexier. You also listen to me free of charge."

"So, that's the attraction. I'm your sexier, low-cost alternative to therapy."

"This is all new territory. Nobody in my life ever listened to me before."

"I will always listen."

"It's more than that too, ya know. You challenge me with questions no one ever thought to ask before. The answers reveal surprises from inside of me that lift me up to be a better man. That's the reason I love you the most."

"Wha? Oh, yeah?"

"Yeah. I'll be the first to say it and I don't care. I love you.

Consider it said. I profess to stop making excuses and just be honest about the way I feel. I love you, Doorman."

"Man, these past few weeks. Am I right, baby?"

"Yes, you're right, baby."

"Do you wanna know what the kicker is? I mean...what it is that I've actually learned?"

"Whassat?"

"I've watched you from afar for...well, for forever. I fantasized about holding you, and kissing you deeply, and knowing you more intimately. And all of that—oh, man, it's so good, much better than I ever imagined. But, there's more than that to spending your time with somebody. Something I mistakenly supposed I was destined to never have a shot at: a reliable, safe place for me. A place where I feel appreciated and nurtured—and needed. Somebody needs me. Nobody in my life ever needed me before. And it just so happens to be a man who takes my breath away. The same man I choose to hold my heart chooses me back. Suddenly, the world is overflowing with immeasurable possibilities."

"When did you become such a poet, eh?"

"Well, we haven't been apart for weeks now and—"

"So, say it. Say it already or I'm gonna explode."

"If you stand back for just a moment, and look at us, baby, we make perfect sense."

"Aaand..."

"I love you right back, Dominic."

He pulls me into him and kisses me. His breath is sweet and as his strapping arms pull me into his torso, his massive biceps dance and the veins on his muscled forearms swell. My dick jumps to attention beneath my chaps, inside my jeans.

"Don't let's start with that again, will ya? I'm sore from this afternoon's workout. Three times? I haven't gone three rounds since I was a kid in the stuffy, city garage in the alley."

"It was three times and a shortie for good measure. Honestly, who's keeping track, baby, eh?"

"I am, that's who. I'm counting my blessings every moment anymore. You say why don't we concentrate on the here and now for a little while. Well, I say let's build a lifetime together of moments made of blessings."

"Now who's the poet, huh?"

We continue strolling as the stink of the pungent Hudson River drifts across the avenues to take over the West Side of Manhattan. The October dusk teases the red brick low-income housing as the Sun wanes and draws elongated shadows on the empty basketball courts and cordoned-off city parks.

"I can't help myself, Doorman. I've spent forever pushing people away. Like I didn't deserve to be loved. You know, I really believed that. For my entire life, I shut the door on everything I cared about. You're the only one that never gave up on me. For that I am so grateful."

"It would appear that we're stuck with each other, baby."

"Oh, I wouldn't have it another way. How foolish I've been, eh? This is life, real life."

"Just you and me, baby."

"And our beautiful family. Don't forget them. There's Claudia and Jerome, too. Man, they never once swayed an inch. Right beside us through this whole *mishigas*."

"They're good friends to both of us. That Claudia...oh, how she makes me laugh. We've gotta go see her show. We owe so much to her for looking after you all those days in the hospital. And Jerome—helping me to get set up in your apartment when I had busted ribs and broken knuckles, swollen from brow to balls."

"Did I tell you they're stopping in for tonight? Claudia said she might sing something."

"He'd love that."

"Which reminds me, we should probably shake a leg and do this thing, eh?"

"Yep. It's time we got there, baby."

The Sun has yet to fully disappear into the ravenous Hudson River, and we pick up our pace as the very first stars of evening find their place. A left and then a right, and we're standing in front of The Meat Market. The scene unfolding catches us completely off guard. We stop cold in our tracks and rub our astounded eyes, stand for a time in amazement as we digest the happening in front of us.

The line to step into the big, oak door to The Meat Market trails to the corner and surrounds an entire city block. The stampede of mustached men in plaid lumberjack shirts and tight-fitting jeans, some of them shirtless in the cool Northeastern evening, circles in serpentine style. The bar isn't scheduled to open for an hour or more and hundreds of leathermen stand on line, smoke cigarettes and flirt with each other, hold one another close and kibitz, and gobble Black Beauties and boogie to cassette performances of The Ritchie Family and Vickie Sue Robinson as they bide their time to enter the bar—all of them waiting for who knows how long to celebrate something momentous. They've all arrived to see him off.

The two of us part the crowd with welcome slaps on the back and hugs from friends and strangers alike, and the doorman's hands are nervous as he fumbles with the keys to unlock the door.

These men, they're the proof in the pudding. These courageous souls document the surroundings so that one day we can better learn more about ourselves. Where we came from, ya know? This is the genesis of us. Our history, brotherhood and all.

The first thing I do is hop over the bar top to set up my station. Doorman swiftly fills bins with buckets of ice as I wipe down the bottles, affix them each with a pourer, and situate them in their respective spots in the speed rack; Vodka, Gin, Rum, Scotch, Whiskey, Tequila, Triple Sec, within fingertip reach, so I can access the ingredients to mix drinks without having to turn my back to customers. I affix bottles of Absolut, Tanqueray, Bacardi, Dewar's, Jack Daniel's, Cuervo, DeKuyper all with pourers, and sit them in their spots on the shelves behind the bar.

The music kicks in, something sultry with deep beats by Bronski Beat, and beneath that the resonance of shuffling of familiar faces and spiritual acquaintances with whom I've shared agreement for many lifetimes as the bar permeates to its limits. I light a smoke with a branded The Meat Market book of matches that reads *A Butcher Bar*. I exhale a cloud of smoke into the night, the blue-black lights, the throbbing primal rites, and turn to face a community of leathermen, and off we go.

Wipe the bar, Meat Market coaster, smile handsome for tips to pay my electric bill.

"Heya. What can I get ya?"

"I'd like a Highball."

"Could you be a little more specific, please?"

"Clearly, you didn't graduate from the New York Academy of Professional Bartending."

Indecisive. Toys with the notion of Bisexuality. Likes his men how he likes his women.

"A Highball is any drink that contains one or more types of alcohol and some sort of mixer like—"

"Exactly. I'll have that."

"Wha? Huh? A Bay Breeze, a Rum and Coke, a Cape Cod—they're all examples of Highballs."

"Goodness, you're pushy. What do you get a commission with every upcharge? Fine, fine. I'll take...that last one."

"One Cape Cod coming right up."

Highball glass with my left hand, house Vodka from the speed rack, three-count pour—one one-thousand, two one-thousand, three one-thousand, splash of stale Cranberry diluted with water.

"Hey! Why is my Highball red?"

"Three fifty, please. That's the cranberry juice."

"Sheesh! And there goes my share on Fire Island. All because I was forced to pay extra for cranberry juice."

Wipe the bar, Meat Market coaster, smile handsome for tips to pay my gas bill.

"*Hola, Papi! Como tu ta?*"

"*Hermosa! Hola!* What can I get ya?"

"The cheeep sheeet, pleeessse. I won't be rrrich until I meeet my husbant, ju know."

We've danced this dance before. Hospital-issues blue and cream checkered scrubs. Diamanté brooch.

"Don't I know it. Coming right up."

Rocks glass with my left hand, house Tequila from the speed rack, three-count pour—one one-thousand, two one-thousand, three one-thousand.

"*Juan dólares,* two *dólares, tRRRes dólares, quatro dólares.*"

"This one's on me. The least that I can do. We all take care of each other, eh?"

"*Weeeeeeeepaaaaaaaaa!*"

Wipe the bar, Meat Market coaster, smile handsome for tips to pay my rent which is due in a week.

"Look who's here!"

"Who might dat be, my good man?"

"You. I was speaking about you."

"You're a very comical person, *Googootz*! Everybody stabs deir meatball de same way. Wit' a fawhk, yuh fuwhk. Yuh got me so fahr?"

"What can I get ya, 'Sparre?"

"One Drambuie wit' a long pour of house Scotch of de rocks, please. Ya' dig? Right, or what? Do yuh got any Angostura Bitters fawh dat, or what? Only if it ain't no kinda problem, *paisano* of mine. Yuh got me so fahr? Yuh got me so fahr, or what?"

"So far I got ya, man."

Rocks glass with my left hand, Drambuie from the shelf behind me, third up from the counter, without even turning my torso, cheap-ass house Scotch from the speed rack, two-count pour of both—one one-thousand, two one-thousand, skip the Angostura Bitters altogether.

"And how's your night going?"

"I'm celebratin' two tings dis evenin', my friend. Yuh with me? Well, de one tin', of cawhse, yuh know. Ya' dig? Poawh Boozuh. It breaks my heart in pieces. Yuh got me so fahr? On de soul of my mudduh—may she rest in peace, of cawhse, I am brokenhearted."

"We all are, sweetie."

"But de othuh tin', Brudduh, should come tuh yuh as a wonduh and astoundment on dis day of doom. I've been accepted tuh a college! I am attendin' de CUNY College of Staten Island. I'm studyin' medicine tuh learn how tuh be an Operatin' Room

Nurse. Ya' dig? Okay, or what? I've always had a need in me tuh give back tuh de community. Yuh know dat I am a community givuh. Practically everybody in dis place knows what it is that I have tuh give dem."

"This is wonderful news, Guasparre! Your drink is on me. I'm proud of you."

"I thank yuh fawh de congratulashuns and de drink. And de pride in me."

"Never forget one of your first medical procedures was performed right here in the bathroom at this bar. Always remember, it's all fun and games until somebody gets their foreskin tangled up into a knot."

"Of cawhse. *Mi Meengya, Stonato!* Hey, d'ja do somethin' different wit' your hair, or what? You're lookin' extra special handsome tonight and all dat business."

"It's a new pomade I'm trying out, 'Sparre."

"Yuh Manhattanite homosexual types are so freakin' funny, Brudduh!" as he disappears into the darkest corners of the already populated backroom, and I swear I can hear strangers choking on his foreskin from across the room.

"What was that? 'Sparre? For some odd reason I thought that fellow's name was Spumoni. Spumoni? No, Sambuca. That's it. Sambuca. Hello, Girl! And how are we holding up?"

"Claudia! You came! Everything is good."

"Well, of course, I'm here. Where else would I be?"

Her perfect, Clairol Nice'n Easy No. 6R Light Copper soap opera hair is piled on top of her head, secured with glamorous rhinestone barrettes. She's scintillating in a figure-hugging, elegant cobalt blue slip style evening gown with a slit that travels from her delicate diamond ankle bracelet to the top of her thigh. She's a star in every aspect.

"That handsome doorman escorted us to the front of the line the moment he saw us step out of a taxi. I'm hardly accustomed to all the attention. Who am I kidding, Girl? Jesus Effing Christ, I'm loving every minute of it."

"That's my girl!"

"And where's my Romeo? Hey, Jerome! Where the eff fore art thou? Listen, I mean no offense, Girl, but handsome as he is...well, you gotta keep your eye on him in a joint like this."

Jerome, the soap opera stud from *Another Tomorrow*, is only steps behind her. Where else would he be? He's attired in ass-hugging, pinstripe pants and a matching vest with no shirt that showcases his muscular shoulders and well-defined torso. A puka shell necklace completes the look. Leather queens are craning their necks and lifting their Muir caps to witness the arrival of the soon-to-be Broadway star and the *Baywatch* babe with the dazzling smile and the perfect, polished soap-opera teeth.

"Duuude! This is some shindig. We almost had to stand on line to get in the door, but then my buddy, Doorman, saw us and bumped us up to the head of the line on account of Claudia becoming a big Broadway star and all."

Her performance at her initial auditions was so spot-on, that without additional callbacks, Claudia was offered the role of Fanny Brice in a much-celebrated revival of *Funny Girl* to open at The Winter Garden Theatre on Broadway. The production—the first revival to play The Great White Way since the original show catapulted Barbra Streisand to stardom—is, as phraseology would have it, the talk of the town. With rehearsals in progress and a premiere date scheduled in the springtime, within the last few weeks Claudia has literally burst forth onto the theatre community and the borough of Manhattan at large. Herb Ritts himself was commissioned to photograph her and posters and other promotional material featuring the chanteuse now conspicuously appear across the island on crosstown buses, taxi cabs, and even on one celebrated and oversized tribute billboard in Times Square.

It takes a lot more than perfect, curled soap opera hair and a nice, bouncy rack to get them to even look up from your resume let alone book you for a callback in this town. Fame couldn't have recognized a more deserving, talented gal. For that, we can all thank The Brooklyn Academy of Music.

While Jerome's dubiously researched, multi-layered performance of Washed-Up Cadaver on the Beach on Episode 73 of *Baywatch* has yet to be Emmy nominated, it afforded him his first Prime Time television exposure alongside a hefty salary increase and additional scenes playing a consummately shirtless Neurosurgeon on daytime television. He'd never been content to simply lift his barbells and water his window boxes. And he may have developed a physique Michelangelo would have paid to immortalize, with its sinewy biceps, and powerful pectorals, but he was put on this planet to celebrate more than his dazzling smile.

It's only a matter of minutes before the doorman stands between them, kissing Claudia on the cheek and affectionately pulling fake punches on Jerome and laughing boisterously. I think to myself that this is a picture for the ages. Our history. It fascinates me. And being a part of history as it happens affords me a place to belong. The proof in the pudding. Mark my words—one day they'll teach these lessons in schools.

I break for a smoke and catch myself in the enormous gilt mirror behind the shelves of booze. I am a handsome, fortuitous man. So many of our unexpected predilections reveal something deeper about us when we stare down our own reflection and challenge ourselves with questions no one ever thought to ask before. Man, these past few weeks. Suddenly, the world is overflowing with immeasurable possibilities. I exhale a cloud of smoke into the night, the blue-black lights, the throbbing primal rites, and turn to face my beautiful family.

"Shots. Okay, we need shots. All of us together—sweet Claudia, stromboli-scarfing Jerome...oh, and my handsome Doorman, who lifts me up to love and fosters the need inside of me to be a better man. Now, nobody moves. Just gimme one second."

Wipe the bar, screw the Meat Market coasters, rocks glasses—one, two, three, four, Jack Daniel's from the shelf behind me because it's the first bottle I grab.

"To what should we toast? Think, Dominic, think. Of course, I know. To Bruiser."

"I shall never scarf stromboli and not think of the man."

"I'll bet they're flying the flags at half-mast on Fire Island right now, Girl."

"Wha? Oh yeah. Man, he'd love that."

We lift our glasses and bid our friend a safe passage. He's everywhere around us. I feel him near. I mean, it is New York City, after all. The customers deserve punishment.

"Wait. I'm not yet through—"

"Oh, no. Here she goes—the big ol' girl. Ya big ol' girl!"

"Jesus Effing Christ, Dominic."

"Wha? Oh yeah, baby."

"Now, raise your glasses with me. Just once more and then we'll be done. I promise. Recently, I met a poet. I'd known the man for ten years, maybe more—and then I allowed myself to look into his eyes. And do you wanna know what I saw? The reflection of me. Man, these past few weeks. Christ, these past few hours, eh? So, I studied my reflection, and I learned a life lesson. I bid you to take tight hold of your dreams, dear friends. How much time do we spend ruminating about the past? Worrying about the future? How much of life do we miss by getting tangled up in our own thoughts? Nobody has to write the history down because it lives inside us. The way it actually went down, ya know? The universal gemstone discoveries that exist between the lines—the subtext. The subtext is the meaning of life, both hidden and heart-touching. So, whaddya say we concentrate on just this moment? We'll celebrate this moment first. And the next one, and then the one after that. Oh, our history may have brought us together, my beloved family—but it is our future which belongs to bringing our dreams to life."

ACKNOWLEDGMENTS

This book would not exist without the inspiration and guidance of Ethan Mordden, Paul Monette, and David Wojnarowicz whose preeminent literary contributions taught me to be a man. Peter Hujar and Stanley Stellar engraved hieroglyphics and painted pictures that brought the words to life. To each of them, and so many men like them who discovered the fortitude and grace inside themselves to capture history in motion, I am profoundly grateful.

Special thanks to my editor, Riley Lewis, who graciously accepted the challenge to learn the language of my community, familiarize herself with its characters, and investigate the breadth of time in which our history revolves.

My family of friends have performed the tasks associated with comrades, confidantes, and cheerleaders through the years, and any likeness on these pages illuminating their radiant features and my ceaseless adoration of them is entirely intentional.

Finally, if you or somebody that you love is struggling with panic disorder and anxiety attacks, I urge you to seek supportive counseling with a mental health professional. Talk to a friend, a pastor or minister, or a trusted general practitioner. While frequently recognized as a more manageable mental health challenge, living with panic disorder can be a terrifying and sometimes debilitating experience. Take time to breathe, close your eyes and practice mindfulness, meditation, yoga, or self-hypnotism—whichever panacea you can grasp hold of that works the best for you. If you encounter difficulty finding someone who understands, reach out to me at subtextnovel@gmail.com. I will always listen.

It is with great admiration and sincere appreciation that excerpts from the following appear in this work of fiction:

"How Glory Goes" from *Floyd Collins*, copyright ©1997 by Adam Guettel.

"Marcie" by Joni Mitchell copyright ©1967 Reprise Records.

"Le Freak" by Bernard Edwards and Nile Rogers copyright ©1978 Atlantic Records.

"Love Train" by Kenny Gamble and Leon Huff copyright ©1978 Philadelphia International Records.

"That's The Way Love Goes" by Janet Jackson, James Harris lll and Terry Lewis copyright ©1993 Virgin Records.

"I'm Still Here" from *Follies*, copyright ©1971 by Stephen Sondheim.

Becoming A Man: Half a Life Story ©1997 by Paul Monette.

ABOUT THE AUTHOR

FRANK ANGELETTI was born in Madagascar and reared in Rangoon. No, that's not right. Frank was raised in the jungle with the help of Baloo the Bear and Bagheera the Panther. No, that's just a lie. Frank was born in Chicago and attended public school. After graduating from Loyola University, he relocated to New York City, where his creative prowess ignited. Says Angeletti, "I kissed the folks goodbye, got on a Trailways Bus and headed for the Big Apple because I wanted to be a Rockette. I had 87 dollars in my pocket and seven years of tap lessons.".

He honed his writing skills at The Village Voice and short stories and essays penned by Frank appeared in The James White Review, Christopher Street Magazine, Utne Reader and Next Magazine. He designed non-profit advertising initiatives for Gay Men's Health Crisis (GMHC), and financed his tenure in NYC with a series of odd jobs including Front Waiter at Gotham, Maitre'd at Cafe Un Deux Trois (entertaining Liza Minnelli, Meryl Streep, and Sting on a nightly basis) and Bartender at NYC's notorious leather bar, The Eagle.

At the advertising agencies Leo Burnett, Digitas and Element 79, Frank brought to fruition some of the most memorable and wildly successful Print Ads and Television Commercials for several high-end, luxury clients including Celebrity Cruises, W Hotels, Nestle Purina and Jaguar USA. Frank is a two-time CLIO Award nominee for his digital efforts on behalf of KitchenAid.

In 2007, Time Out NY Magazine hailed HOMOVIZION, his digital magazine, as "Eye-blazing, ear-popping, crotch-pounding design" and listed Angeletti among 20 NYC Digital Artists to Keep Your Eyes On.

In 2016, his charity-based art installment, A BROADWAY PRIMER, featured 22 reimagined visual conceptions of Broadway Posters and played an open-end run in Chicago. The artwork raised more than 5K dollars to benefit some of the nation's leading AIDS organizations.

Frank is a graduate of the New York Institute of Photography, and a member in good standing of Certified Professional Photographers (CPP). Presently, he works as an Editorial, Commercial and Lifestyle Photographer, and his efforts have graced the pages of The New York Times, The Advocate, Out Magazine, Bon Appétit and Food Network Magazine, among others.

His book SUBTEXT, A Nervous Novel is a love letter to 1990s NYC and the irrepressible gay community of a former time. The story's ultimate message delivers a riveting, personal narrative of hopes and dreams, and the disappointments that must be overcome if one is to perceive all the beauty that life has to offer.

In his free time, Frank enjoys growing facial hair, playing the piano, and long walks with his Welsh Terrier, Helvetica ("Vettie").